LITTLE
RAW
SOULS

LITTLE RAW SOULS

stories

Steven Schwartz

Autumn House Press

pittsburgh

Autumn House Press Staff

Editor-in-Chief and Founder: Michael Simms
Managing Editors: Adrienne Block, Caroline Tanski
Co-Founder: Eva-Maria Simms
Community Outreach Director: Michael Wurster
Fiction Editors: Sharon Dilworth, John Fried
Assistant Editor: Alecia Dean
Associate Editor: Giuliana Certo
Media Consultant: Jan Beatty
Publishing Consultant: Peter Oresick
Tech Crew Chief: Michael Milberger
Intern: Christine Stroud

Autumn House Press receives state arts funding support through
a grant from the Pennsylvania Council on the Arts, a state
agency funded by the Commonwealth of Pennsylvania, and the
National Endowment for the Arts, a federal agency.

ISBN: 978-1-932870-65-7

Library of Congress Control Number: 2012938060

for Liza

a space where the little raw soul

slips through.
It goes skimming the deep keel like a storm petrel,
out of sight.

The little raw soul was caught by no one.

—"The Glass Essay," Anne Carson

contents

LITTLE
RAW
SOULS

BLESS EVERYBODY

THEY'D been led to our land. The woman, Meredith, was far along in her pregnancy, and the coincidence of her name being close to "Mary" struck me, no place to lay their heads as they awaited the birth of their child. We—I—owned two hundred acres, cut out of the red rock along the Wyoming-Colorado border. Indians had long ago run stolen horses into the box canyon at the end of our property, and after them, rustlers had done the same thing with cattle. I'd poked around in the red dirt and once dug out the shoulder bone of a bison as big as my thigh. Arrowheads, spear points, and shards of clay pottery I'd turned over to the local museum; rumor had it that this was as sacred ground as any that ran along the Front Range from Colorado to Wyoming.

Peck Foster, my neighbor of the adjacent two hundred acres to mine, had given the couple my name and number and told them to call me about the one-room cabin on our property. The young couple had parked outside the gate and took it upon themselves to walk the land and see if they could find the person who presided over this "magical" place. It seemed like a good story, this being led to the land. I didn't believe in providence, but I was retired and had time on my hands to be amused by such notions and told them I'd meet up at the gate to our property.

That "our" is misspoken. I'm divorced and Rosalyn took her share of the property in a cash settlement. I used a chunk of my retirement money to buy her out—I'm sixty-eight years old, and I'd worked as an inspector for the highway department thirty-nine of those years. I'd always wanted a piece of property as fiercely beautiful as this one. Every time I passed it on the road at sunset the red rock glowed like hot coals in an evening fire—a view of the openhearted earth. When it went up for sale, I talked Rosalyn into putting our money down. I was land proud, no doubt about it. A little stream called Watson Creek ran through the valley and turned the cottonwoods leafy with shade in the spring, as they were now.

They were waiting for me by the gate. When I'd spoken to the husband on the phone, he described their lifestyle as "migratory," but he certainly didn't sound like a dangerous drifter. I'd have put the man in his mid-twenties and the woman a few years younger and their Volkswagen bus older than the both of them combined, rusted on its fenders and painted a robin's-egg blue with a bumper sticker on the back that said BLESS EVERY-BODY. NO EXCEPTIONS. The van's tires were bald and its grill had picked up a couple of tumbleweeds and was chewing on them like too much spaghetti in a child's mouth.

"Thank you, sir, for meeting us," Calvert said, sticking out his hand. He was a thin man with a big toothy grin, and blond hair down to his collar, his eyes all afire at hello. He tipped his hat to me, a brown felt fedora with a white feather tucked in the band.

They showed me their wares: ceramic leaf earrings and beaded hemp necklaces; tiny "sweetheart" notebooks no bigger than the palm of my hand with paper that still looked like the wood it came from; sassafras and strawberry scented drip candles in day-glo colors. They went to craft fairs and sold what they could, and took temporary jobs. "We're realistic people," Calvert said. "You can't live off today what you did in the sixties."

2

Sixties or not, they didn't look like they had a practical bone in their bodies, not with that baby in their future.

"Sir, we'd just like to stay here a few nights," Calvert said. "We want our child to absorb some of this"—he spread his skinny arms in a panorama over the expanse of my land—"*holiness*, before we move on." I thought: people really talk like this?

He patted Meredith's swollen stomach. She looked as if she were due any day.

"Where you going to have the baby?"

Calvert clasped his hands together. "Wherever we may be."

I looked at Meredith, hoping I wasn't hearing what I just did. But she had that dreamy come-what-may look. "There's a good hospital in town," I said. "You should check in with them."

"No need," Calvert said. "We'll be taken care of."

"Uh-huh."

"We just followed our hearts here. We came over the pass and looked down and just knew. Isn't that right, Mer?"

Meredith nodded, still that dreamy look.

"I'd feel much better if you saw a doctor or midwife while you were here. We got a clinic in town that helps those in need."

"You *are* a kind man," Calvert said, as if my reputation preceded me. "Your hospitality will not go unnoticed."

Meredith's stomach made a shelf of the long dress she was wearing, a thin faded shift of yellow daisies, not made for pregnancy, just oversized. Her ankles and toes had a film of dirt, and I wondered how long it had been since they'd had hot showers.

BEFORE she retired a year after me, Rosalyn had worked in the public school system, first as a teacher, then a district administrator. She appreciated the threat of liability. I did too, working as an inspector for the highway department. She'd moved out to Eagle Estates (I still had our old place in town) and her backyard sloped down thirty yards to an artificial lake with her own dock.

"You haven't heard the best part," I said.

"I can't wait."

"The wife is pregnant." I suddenly realized I'd been calling her "the wife" with no good reason. They'd never said they were married. "I tried pushing them to see a doctor while they're here."

"Wait . . . did you say '*pregnant*'? As in living-out-of-a-van *pregnant*? How many months?"

"I'd say seven. Not being the best judge of such matters. She's pretty ripe, though."

"Oh, Charlie, what have you gotten yourself into."

"Maybe nothing. They just want a couple days to rest their bones. I'd be more worried if there was anything there to *get* into. It's still the same empty one room place with a bed and stove and a hard tile floor. Nothing to lose, nothing to break, and nothing to disturb. They want to walk the land, that's fine with me. Soak up the vibes or whatever they believe. Anybody breaks a leg, blame it on nature. I'm not running an amusement park up there."

"Anything happens they could sue you."

"I'll take my chances."

I'd come over to take Martin. Rosalyn was going to Atlanta for a week. We shared custody of Martin, our golden retriever, going on twelve years now. Before that we'd had Betsy, a springer spaniel, and when we first married, Noah and Victoria, a couple of dachshunds who fought like the brother and sister they were. It wasn't lost on us that we always gave our dogs dignified people names, no Bandit, Snuggles, or Doodles for us. These were our children with hopes for their futures, limited as they might be. Rosalyn traveled every month or two working part time now as an educational consultant. Last month she'd gone to Hawaii. She didn't travel alone either; she had met a man when she was in Cleveland. He was a VP at a large educational testing company, and all I knew about him was that he was divorced with three grown children. She had put up a picture of him on her dresser. I suppose it was her way of introducing him to me since she knew I'd be over to take care of her plants while she was away. Her new man was a square-faced gent with blue eyes, a tennis tan, and hair graying around his temples—mine had gone almost all white. He was closer in age to Rosalyn, who was thirteen years younger than me at fifty-five, the new thirty I was hearing. Nobody said that about sixty-eight, not yet anyway.

Rosalyn put down her iced tea on the marble patio table. She'd fixed up the place with abstract paintings that reminded me of geometry problems (we'd had pictures of those grinning dogs of ours hanging in the old place—I still did), plush white sofas (she was always chasing Martin off of them), and long drapes.

"I'd better be going. I got some painting to do on the basement."

"Almost finished?"

"I'm getting there." Rosalyn hadn't been inside our old house for months. I was fixing it up to sell. We still owned it together, free and clear, our one common possession if you didn't count Martin. Just to keep it fair, I paid her a little rent every month until I could get it sold and move out. I was going to live up on the land. I'd priced running electricity from the utility poles at the road, and it would cost me three thousand dollars. Right now all I had was a well that pumped out rusty water. I'd warned the couple not to drink from it. Nothing would happen to them, just the poorest tasting water around from all the iron in it. They said that wouldn't bother them, the water was still purer than any that came from a faucet.

Rosalyn had spit out that water when we first went to look at the land. "Ugh," she'd said. She'd spoken with such vehemence that we got into an argument.

"Well, you don't have to make such a sour face," I said.

"It's terrible. It tastes terrible."

"You coming or not?" I had asked her.

"I'll wait here," she said, standing by the locked cabin. She had looked in the windows and shaken her head. It was clear she didn't appreciate the place. She wanted some mark of human existence up there, or maybe she just couldn't imagine endless days with me and my thoughts and nothing between us but open space and sky above. And those thirteen years that separated us in age.

When I got back from walking the property, I asked her, "Are you going to complain every time we come up here if we buy the place?"

"Maybe," she said.

"Then maybe you shouldn't come up here," I told her.

"Maybe I won't," she said.

I looked at her. "What's that mean?"

"It means I'm not going to sit around and warm my feet by the fire and watch golden eagles nest and pretend to be happy." A dust devil had come up and was spitting dirt in our faces. Rosalyn shouted through it. "I'm going to continue working part time, I'm going to volunteer more, I'm going to the health club, the malls, the museums, I'm seeing friends, eating out, traveling. I want a life, not an *afterlife*. I don't want to close up shop. It's all right if you want privacy, Charlie, but that's not what I want. This fucking dirt!" she said and swatted at the dust, then ran for the car. I got in after her, walking slowly.

"And does this busy life of yours have any room for me?" I asked.

"We should get back," she said. Which was answer enough.

It's a terrible thing to get to the end of a marriage and run out of good will about the future. Once you stop talking about what's ahead—or start talking about it separately as we had done —it makes you feel as if you're on a train platform waving goodbye to the departing life you used to have. I always wondered if she agreed to sign the papers for the land just to have a reason to divorce me—two years ago now—and if I'd made her sign them because I honestly believed the place would bring us closer, like people do in a last ditch try to stay happy by having a child.

6

"I'd be a little more concerned about letting those people stay up there if I were you," Rosalyn said now. We were sitting on her dock. She didn't own a boat and didn't want one. But she liked to come down here and read a good mystery and have me come over and join her for a drink. "It's your pride and joy," she told me. "I'm surprised you don't make them produce a passport to step on it." We could joke about what it meant to me now. And she was right, I could have planted my own flag up there. She wore white slacks and a low-cut pink sweater that I wanted to believe she'd put on for me. She'd never looked better. It all agreed with her, retirement, this big house, the traveling, the new man, the freedom—even me being here to always depend on. I would come over as long as she needed me, and not a moment longer than she wanted me to. That she knew this should have made me an object of concern if not outright pity in her eyes, but all I saw was gratitude when she put her hand on my stubbled cheek and said, "I don't know what I'd do without you, Charlie."

OVER the next few days, I finished painting the house, replaced a couple leaky windows, and pulled up some soiled carpet beyond cleaning in the dining room where we never could get Victoria's and Noah's markings out—always fighting for dominance, those two. Martin followed me around, seeming to enjoy the liberty of jumping up on the old familiar couch without getting shooed off, and made a few half-hearted attempts to chase rabbits around our backyard. He was good company, and I would have liked more of it, but we were pretty fair about sharing him, and Rosalyn said he still liked to stretch out his front paws for a dive into the lake when she threw a stick, like the excitable puppy he used to be. So it was good to shuttle him between us. Just like a kid, he had his own bag packed and ready to go with his special food, blanket, and medicine for his arthritis.

I was pulling some unidentified boxes from the crawlspace in the basement when the phone rang. I ignored it at first, let the voice mail pick it up. But it rang insistently again, and I went up-stairs and answered.

"Charlie?" It was Peck, my neighbor up at the land. "You better get up here," he said without any preliminaries.

"What's going on, Peck?"

"Those people, the ones you let stay . . ." Peck was slow to rile, but he sounded mad as I'd ever heard him. "That fella shot a deer. With a *pistol!*"

"I'm coming." I got my rifle and was in the truck in seconds. Martin jumped in the back. I still had paint on my hands.

You would have thought a wounded mule deer shot in the leg couldn't get far. That would be a misconception. A deer on three legs can outrun any man on two. This wasn't the point, of course. The point was that this crazy fool had tried to shoot one out of season with a pistol and without a hunting license and with No Hunting signs posted on both our properties. That made him a poacher in the eyes of the law, even if I lied and said I'd given him permission. His van could be impounded, his gun taken away (a good thing, in my view), and the both of them fined more than they were worth.

"What the hell got into you?" I said when I drove up. I was jumping out of the truck before the engine had stopped cough-ing. "Are you nuts?"

"Sir," said Calvert, "I . . . we needed food." Where was Mere-dith? Down by the creek I suspected, maybe washing clothes in the stream.

"Food?" Peck was standing there red faced. His family had owned a thousand acres of this land going back a hundred years until they divided it up. Peck and I had worked out a lease to let his horses graze on my property, and between our parcels the animals found plenty of room to roam. I'd gotten a better offer for cattle from the sprawling McDonald ranch to the east, but cattle tore up the place worse than horses, and frankly horses were just prettier. I'm sure Peck was thinking the same thing as me: this fool could have shot one of his horses. "What gave you the idea you could hunt up here?"

Calvert, all twenty something years of him, let out an exasperated sigh. "I was just trying to feed my family."

"You ever heard of a grocery store?"

"I thanked the land for its bountiful offering," said Calvert. I looked at Peck, who screwed up his face in disgust. "I thought you'd understand."

"Here's what I understand. You leave that deer out there to die and it's wanton waste, not to mention cruelty. I'm obligated to report this to Wildlife, and if I don't, I'm up my own damn creek. Any way you look at it, you've done something mighty illegal."

Calvert mumbled something. He had the fedora pushed down over his forehead, his eyes darting around under the brim. I asked him what he said.

"Nobody has to know."

"I know."

"We're wasting time," Peck said. "Let's go. We'll argue about what to do later."

WE went in three different directions. I told Calvert that if he found the deer first to stay with it and we'd be by eventually. I mapped it out so we'd circle the perimeter and move toward the center, gradually tightening our radius. We'd meet in the upper canyon where I suspected the deer had gone to bed down, if it were still alive. The shot could have hit more bone than blood depending on where it went in the leg. I won't lie and say I didn't enjoy getting off a double lung shot. You could drop a bull moose in its tracks with a clean shot like that and I'd always been taught that was the fair shot you took—and you didn't take it until you were sure. I'd been hunting in Wyoming with an old friend and the wind had been blowing—though I won't blame it on that—and I got an elk in my sights. I squeezed the trigger and watched the animal crawl fifty yards with his legs splayed out before I could get there and put a bullet through his head. I'd hit him in the spinal column and paralyzed his backside. He'd been moaning when I got to him, and then a strangulated, gurgling sound came from deep in his throat. Todd, my hunting partner, didn't say anything more than "Damn wind," and there had been a terrible crosswind, but I had no business taking that shot and couldn't get the picture out of my mind of that creature dragging his hind legs like a busted wagon and trying to reach some kind of finish line that he thought would save him. I hadn't hunted since and that was six years ago.

Martin started barking when we came to a pile of brush with some wooden boards from a collapsed outbuilding. The deer, a big one close to three hundred pounds I figured, had its black-tipped tail drooped between its legs and had risen up from the thicket. His antlers were budding out and his coat had started to turn reddish brown from its winter gray; those big ears were twitching independently of each other just like a mule's, trying to hear our movements upwind from him. He was considering whether it was worth bounding out of there, his flanks moving in and out like a bellows, exhausted, pained, and I saw too when he did bound up that his back leg was still barely attached to the bone. Calvert had shot him in the hip and about severed the leg. It was a horrible sight, worse than when I watched that bull elk crawl ahead like an amputee. This leg was swinging around as if it were a piece of the poor creature's intestine hanging out.

I squared my shoulders, calmed my shaking hands and squeezed my left eye shut to line up a shot I prayed would go straight into its heart. It did, or close enough to drop him after a good two hundred feet before he flopped over. Martin ran up, sniffed warily and then backed off and lay down with his face on his front haunches whining and waiting for me. The buck's eyes bulged with hard pain in them. A mule deer ran different than a white tail, starting up from go and bounding eight feet and then coming down on all four feet at once like a landing craft, and I thought it was terrible to lose one of your legs when you got around like that, and that this buck had died without his due dignity.

I blew my whistle in short bursts. Before long Peck showed up. He'd already heard the shot and we stood there silently looking over this big fellow and trying to decide what to do with him now. We could try to get one of our trucks up here and move him back to Peck's place and gut him there, but I didn't think that would be easy given the steep incline and loose shale down to this spot. If we were going to eat this meat, and I sure as hell wasn't going to let it go to waste, we needed to cut him up now and let him cool and then pack him out. The worst thing was to let him stay warm. He'd spoil for sure.

"Where's the kid?" Peck said to me.

"I don't know. Did you see him shoot it?"

Peck shook his head. "All I know is he's carrying around a pistol and shooting up things like he's in a saloon. I gave them your number, Charlie. I should have checked with you first. We got no business letting strangers stay up here. This ain't no Woodstock."

"Can I have your knife?" I said.

Peck's knife was good and sharp and I cut around the diaphragm and reached all the way up and felt for the trachea. If you did it right, cut from stem to stern, and you had the strength and a steady hand, you could pull the whole business down from the windpipe and avoid the mess of cutting out the gut sack by itself. I sliced the trachea across its diameter and started pulling. We each had a foot braced on one side of the buck and were yanking. I told Peck to hold up a moment while I sawed more through the center of the pelvis channel and then we started pulling again. It was the easiest way. I didn't want to cut out the organs one by one and risk piercing the gut sack and transferring the digestive juices to the meat and spoiling it. Somebody was going to eat this creature and do him the honor of a good death. It was ugly to think of his last hour or two with his leg twirling around like that. I stuck my hand back up past the lungs and grabbed inside the throat and Peck pulled with me and we gave it one good heave and tore everything out. It was about then, just when I'd started to skin it and fold back the cape, that Calvert came up, panting. He took a good look at the buck's insides and bloody cavity and fainted.

PECK said, "This fella's one lame excuse for a human being." We stared at his sprawled out body and shook our heads. "If he don't come to in five, you'd better take him over to the hospital." I said I would and asked him what he thought I should do about the deer.

"Might as well enjoy it," he said.

"But should I report it?" Peck gave me a puzzled look. He'd bred horses all his life and he knew them as well as anybody, but an animal was still an animal to him. "Nobody's going to know any different if you don't."

"I'm not worried about somebody finding out. I just want to do what's right."

Peck opened his hands; he'd lost two of his left fingers in Vietnam. He was quiet about it except once to tell me he woke up every day and looked straight through that hole and saw the war. "If it was me? I'd get those people on their way and fill up your freezer with that meat. Case closed."

This made sense to me. You could say that an ignorant individual had made the mistake of thinking he could shoot his dinner and that it was more an accident than a crime. You could say, too, that they were young and naive. But what you couldn't say is that any of it was right, the way a crooked line down a highway wasn't right, and you had to fix it. I'd had a perfect record over the years of inspecting roads. I saw plenty of bulges and rough spots in the concrete and places where the excavation had cut corners, and I had offers, some lucrative, if never put in so many words, to look the other way. Rosalyn once told me that cheating was so pervasive in the schools these days it was almost an anachronism to be honest, maybe even quaint. But I'd never been tempted.

When we got back to the cabin, Meredith was there staring dumbfounded at her groggy man coming through the door. She'd set up a little housekeeping in the cabin, a box of teabags and some water boiling in a pot on the stove, a couple tooth-brushes and toothpaste on the one windowsill, and two sleeping bags rolled out on the bed next to a flashlight. This was no kind of place to be expecting a baby. I'd always planned to build on and shore up the foundation to get the drainage working right so there wasn't mold growing up the walls. The last owner had used the place for storage and that was about all it was good for now.

"What happened?" she asked, her eyes wide.

"I'll see you," Peck said—wisely making his exit. Up to our elbows in blood, we'd washed our hands and arms in the stream, but you really never got out the stains unless you scrubbed at them with a brush. We had the deer and all its dismembered parts in the back of my truck after dragging up the whole mess —and Calvert too—on a tarp.

"He just needs to sit down," I said. "He fainted." I helped Calvert over to the bed and he lay down and held his head and moaned. He put his arms across his eyes and stayed that way. Meredith sat down next to him. "You have one?" she said to him. He made a clenching sound with his teeth and nodded. She turned to me. "He gets these terrible migraines. They make him vomit and faint." She got up and went over to a plastic jug of water. A towel and washcloth were laid out neatly on a corner of the bed and she picked up the washcloth and got it damp and then came back and folded it over Calvert's forehead. He was still gritting his teeth and his toes were pointed out the door, his fingers clenching the bare mattress.

"I'm going to report this in the morning."

Meredith turned her head toward me. "Report what?"

"The deer. You can't shoot a deer without a license. Even on private property." I repeated what I'd told Calvert, it was illegal and despite having the animal all carved up in the back of my truck and my burying the carcass tomorrow, we'd broken the law of the land.

"I'm sorry," Meredith said. "We should have asked permission first." She had changed from this morning and put on some stretchy sweat pants and washed her feet and combed her brown hair, her eyes a soft shade of jade. "Calvert didn't want to. He said we'd sell some of our stuff in town. But I can't wait. I need some meat now. My baby needs it. Calvert doesn't think so, but I know different. I'm hungry all the time."

"Where'd you shoot him?" She pointed down by the stream.

"I was *hungry*," she said again.

"You should have just asked. I could have brought you something."

"We're not beggars," she said.

Calvert moaned, "Your voices!"

"He can't stand noise when he gets like this," Meredith said. "Let's go outside and talk."

WE stood there in the dark with the stars pulsing above and not an artificial light in sight. I had mixed feelings about running electricity over here and plundering the darkness. Peck's house was on the other side of the ridge and hidden from view. You could hear coyotes howling, and I'd seen the remnants of a mountain lion's kill, and what did it matter if another deer died on the property one way or another? I could hide the evidence, ignore the deed, and the taint to the land—the purest thing I had in my life at the moment—would disappear. But there's a thinner line between rigidity and tolerance than most people think. I'd always tried to stay on the latter side of that line, but I knew my position as of late had been corrupted by a foolish kind of anger that wanted everyone held accountable.

I went to my truck and got out my jacket and put it around her shoulders. She was standing there with her thin arms shivering and nowhere to go but back into that dark cabin with her partner sprawled out and his head exploding.

"I think about getting away." She looked back at the cabin.

"Are you afraid of him?"

"No." She pulled her arms tight around her chest. "Sometimes."

I wasn't surprised that Calvert who snapped his "Sir!" out at me might be the same fellow who could slap around this young woman not long out of her girlhood with her pretty pale face. For all that traveling she didn't have much color to her. She was more pallid than Rosalyn ever looked when she was pregnant and had three miscarriages, before we stopped trying. We had that river of disappointment under our feet, too.

"Come with me now," I said, and Martin trotted up behind me, as if to make his appeal too. He'd been guarding the tailgate of my pickup with its deer payload.

She shook her head. "He'll find me. He'll—"

"You need to see a doctor. You need care. Nobody's going to harm you. I'll see to that. I know a lot of people here in town, folks who can help you legally." She winced at "legally."

"I don't want anything to happen to him," she said.

I had the idea that Calvert was no stranger to outstanding warrants, and that this had made my place more attractive to him than any so-called holiness of my land. "I'll take you somewhere safe," I promised. I had in mind the extra bedroom of my house, and if she wasn't comfortable with that—I had no untoward motives—I'd put her up in a motel and talk to the safe house people in Fort Collins where Rosalyn volunteered.

"I've got to go back in," she said.

"You need to eat," I said. "You need to take care of your baby."

"When he gets a migraine, he'll sleep forever afterward. I can meet you at the gate in the morning. I have to get my things out of the van and I want to make sure he's asleep because he has the keys in his pocket."

"I'll be here at dawn. Bring whatever you can carry and don't worry about the rest. We can fix you up later." The sleeves of my coat hung over her hands like sleepy puppets. I had all these thoughts I shouldn't have had, not the obvious ones that pertained to the wants of an older man in the presence of a young, comely woman and how she might save his flesh and soul and that he might be so delirious he wouldn't know the difference between the two, but ideas about how the unexpected descended and snapped its fingers in your face and said, "Awake!"

"You'll really come?"

I said I would. I'd be there at 5:45 when the sun cast its first light over the place.

I told her she could keep my coat, but she was already stripping it off saying no, Calvert would get suspicious. Before she ducked inside, she called back to me, "Bless you."

I WOKE with a start. I had left my wallet in my jacket pocket when I gave the coat to Meredith to put around her. I'd slept fitfully, if I did at all, on the surface of a plan that was simple in its execution and complicated in its reasons. Why was I getting involved? Peck had advised I chase them out of there as soon as I could. Rosalyn would have seconded that or told me to call social services and get the police involved if I suspected abuse. She would have told me I had some kind of hero complex to want to do this all myself, and maybe she'd be right.

I got up to check my jacket that I'd hung over the chair. My wallet was still there, all the money and credit cards inside, and I felt ashamed of myself for suspecting that Meredith had filched it while she was wearing the coat. I sat there a moment on the edge of the bed, flipping the wallet open and closed in my hands like a jackknife. I lay back down and must have fallen asleep because when the phone rang I jumped up again and didn't know where I was for a moment. The numbers on the clock said 4:50 a.m. and my first thought was that it was either Meredith or Calvert.

But it was Rosalyn. "I'm sorry," she said. "I . . . I feel terrible calling you."

"What's wrong?" I could hear her sniffling, then blowing her nose. "Where are you?"

"Home."

"From Atlanta?"

"I came home early."

I looked at the clock; it would take me twenty minutes to get from town to my land. Rosalyn never called at this hour. She was nothing if not independent and whatever motivated her to phone me up at five in the morning must have come at a price. "Speak to me, Rosalyn."

"I didn't know who else to call."

"Uh-huh," I said.

"I'm sitting here on the floor, it's dark, the house is cold, and I've got mascara running down my face. I didn't sleep on the plane—I took the red-eye back."

"What do you need, Roz?"

"Would you . . . would you bring Martin back today? I know it's earlier than I said, but I could really use his company. Is that all right, Charlie? Would you be okay with his coming here early?"

"I'll bring him over," I said. "I got to do something first, but I'll bring him back after."

"Thank you, I really appreciate it. I'm so sorry I woke you up. I didn't know who else to call."

"You said that."

"You're mad at me."

"I'm not mad." I glanced at the clock again. Ten minutes had gone by, and I still had to throw on my clothes and scrub my face and teeth. I thought about that old saying, why buy the cow when you can get the milk for free? As far as I went with Rosalyn, she got the cow free and to hell with the milk.

"Why do men lie, Charlie?" She was slurring her words and I could picture the bottle next to her; Rosalyn always held the neck of a wine bottle like she was shaking your hand with a firm grip. "You never lied to me."

"I never lied to you," I agreed. I felt pain compress across my chest, as if someone were cinching a leather strap as hard as he could; if I hadn't been talking to Rosalyn, if I hadn't been witnessing her anguish over this man she loved the way she used to me, if I hadn't been thinking I could make it all better if she'd just give me another chance, I would have thought I was having a heart attack.

"Forgive me for waking you?"

"I was getting up anyway. I have an appointment." I heard her take a long gulp of whatever she was drinking.

"An appointment?"

"Somewhere I have to be."

"Oh," she said quietly.

"I'll bring Martin by afterward. Later this morning. I promise."

I went out the door, leaving Martin snoozing on the rug with his blanket smelling of me and Rosalyn both and drove up with one thought in mind, to get Meredith out of there. I should have had the sheriff come with me. I knew him a bit, and he was a calm, reasonable fellow, but I knew too Meredith would change her story out of guilt or fear if we both showed up.

She was waiting for me, just like she said, and she had a backpack with her when I pulled up outside the gate. She looked just as forlorn as she had last night, but I shouldn't have been surprised when I got out of the truck and she gave me that wan, helpless smile, like she had no choice in the matter. Calvert stepped out from the clump of scrub oak where he'd been crouched down and pointed his pistol at my heart. The only thing I didn't know was whether or not they'd planned it from the beginning, whether Meredith had had any hesitation at all or just thought me another sad fool.

"You promised her money—if she'd fuck you." He jabbed the pistol toward me. "Right?" I looked at Meredith, her slack mouth and pale hungered face and tried to find the truth in it.

"You told him that?"

"Shut up," said Calvert.

"What happened to 'sir'?"

"Fuck you. You were going to turn us in for shooting that deer."

"I still can."

He grinned at me, waving the gun around like he intended to lasso me with it. His fedora, with its dirty white feather, was pushed back on his head, and I saw he had a pretty good receding hairline. I should have been more afraid than I was; I don't know why I wasn't.

"You're a stupid old man, just like I thought."

"You going along with this?" I asked Meredith, who had her lips pressed tightly together.

"Hey, you," said Calvert. "Don't talk to her."

"You're not going to shoot me."

The dust splattered up at my feet. Nobody had ever shot at me before, and I stared at my feet. "Maybe I won't miss next time, old man. Maybe I'll get my deer."

"Let's just go," said Meredith. "Please."

"Throw your wallet over here!" Calvert commanded. "Get it," he told Meredith. And even this, the tone, I wondered if it was for my benefit alone. Would they have a good laugh down the road? Would she cry over what she'd done? Would they count my money and go for . . . whatever made them happy? Did he treat her so badly he owned her soul?

Calvert took out the cash and threw the wallet back at my feet. "Give me your keys," he said. I threw them to him. "Turn around and put your hands on that gate." He told Meredith to come over and tie my hands to the gate. She wouldn't look at me while she did. She smelled of wood smoke and oranges, and I told her so, and then I felt a whack on my head that turned my land dark.

"What happened to those people?" Rosalyn asked me later that day when I brought Martin over and she kneeled down for him to come running into her arms.

"They just left."

"Just like that?"

I snapped my fingers. "Just like it." She'd taken a shower and put on a black slip dress that had a scoop neck that showed off her freckled chest. Black for mourning or black for seduction; both were probably true. She wanted to see my eyes light up, to be appreciated by a man, even one cuckolded by thieves, a man who had decided he would stop punishing himself in all the obvious ways.

"Charlie," she said, "you look so tired. That's my fault." She seemed to have come out of her sorrow. I had a mean bump on my head and my vision wasn't back to normal, but I could see well enough to drive. The one thing Meredith had done for me was tie a slipknot making it easy to get out.

"I've got to leave," I said.

"Another appointment?" Rosalyn said this teasingly. Then her face went soft as a bruised peach. "You want to come back tonight?" She never asked me over at night.

"I think I can do that," I told her.

Maybe fortune came with getting your head clonked.

She walked with me outside. "Whose is that?" she said when she saw the couple's blue van parked in the driveway.

"I'm borrowing it for a few days. From some acquaintances."

She stared at the bus with its bald tires and cracked windshield. "What's wrong with your truck?"

"Nothing. That I know of." I nodded at the van. "Makes me feel young again."

Rosalyn lifted her well-shaped eyebrows. "Oh yeah? You'll have to give me a ride in it sometime."

I smiled. "That I'll do."

I had one more job before I quit for the day. I drove the van. The seats smelled of cigarettes and the engine whined and lost what little power it had going up a small rise, but I had my arm out the window on a beautiful spring afternoon, and I felt fitter than I should have when I pulled into the Division of Wildlife parking lot. You were supposed to leave the animal intact for state identification so the game warden could make the count, but I couldn't really bring the whole carcass in here and throw it across this gentleman's desk, could I?

"What you got there, mister?"

I untied the rose silk scarf that Meredith had left behind in the cabin, an awfully nice scarf for someone who had lived out of a robin's-egg blue van and had picked a bad seed of a man to father her child. "I take full responsibility," I said.

"What the hell . . ." The wildlife officer got one look at the buck's putty-colored testicles and about gagged. But I was all about rules and doing right by them and making the best of what time I had left on this merciful earth.

STRANGER

A FTER packing up the apartment and helping her sister deal with their father's estate, Elaine was flying back to Denver. Her father had died peacefully in his sleep at the age of seventy-nine. He had been strong and healthy right up until the end. He walked a mile a day at a brisk pace; he drank celery and carrot juice, watched his weight, and kept his mind active with everything from crossroad puzzles to practicing piano to the occasional nine holes of golf; and he played a sharp game of poker with the other "youngsters" at the Jewish Community Center in Philadelphia. His blood pressure and cholesterol count had been that of a teenager's, and his doctor expected him to live another decade or two. On the dark side, as her father put it, he liked his cigars and his martinis. But he hadn't died of smoking or drinking; he'd gone out just as he said he would: "They'll take me when I'm not looking, without a fight." And they had; he'd died right in the middle of the seven hours he slept a night.

Elaine's Aunt Winnie, her father's sister and a spry seventy-seven herself, had walked across the hall from her condo and found him lying on his back, one hand across his stomach. "He looked like he'd just eaten a good meal," Aunt Winnie said. Elaine thought that everyone was trying to make his death appear so serene because her mother's had been so violent. She'd died at forty-eight in an automobile accident when Elaine was in her senior year of high school.

Sitting now in the waiting area for her flight home, she glanced at the Philadelphia newspaper and then heard the ticket agent's voice on the intercom. The news was not good. The flight coming from Chicago had been delayed by bad weather and would be at least an hour late landing in Philadelphia. She slumped in her seat. She just wanted to get back to Denver. Richard and Katy—or "Caidee" as she spelled it now, their thirteen year old —had already flown home a week ago. As it was, she'd be coming in late at night. She'd made a reservation on the last possible flight of the day because she wanted to pack up as much of Dad's stuff as possible and not leave her sister, Rachel, with the entire mess. She'd decided she would need to make another trip back anyway. There was too much to sort through, including all the clippings from the local theater productions he'd been in. She read each of them, going back to the forties, when her mother had been with him in *Oklahoma!* Elaine's expectation had been she'd race through all the old photographs, accounts, bills, medical and insurance records and pave the way for Rachel to finish. But she'd been painfully slow, and frankly, at the end of two weeks, she felt as if she'd failed to make meaning of the details that profaned death into tabulations and schedules, receipts and scribbled notes, worn shoes and dusty suits.

Her father had never remarried. Plenty of widows and divorcées had been after him, but he rejected their interest. "Marriage is for life," he told Elaine once, "and in my case, death." The gloomy sentiment drove Elaine crazy. He could have remarried and had a full life, even perhaps another family. Instead, for the past thirty-one years, he'd kept a shrine to his dead wife. Her pictures were everywhere in the condo. In his later years he became even worse, referring to "We" all the time, as though Elaine's mother were still alive. When Elaine and the family visited from

23

Colorado and he had his only grandchild in front of him—Rachel and her husband had never had children—he told stories not about when Elaine and Rachel were young but about his life with Elaine's mother: the ballroom dancing they did so suavely (foxtrot champions), the husband-wife golf tournaments, the charity balls they organized. "We were quite the team," he boasted to Elaine in a phone call, just before he died. She held the phone through his reverie hoping for him to ask about Caidee, let alone her and Richard. But he didn't, and she could see now that he'd been bowing his head at death's door all this time waiting to knock.

SHE awoke to the announcement that her flight would be delayed another hour. She'd fallen sound asleep; her head had lolled back on her left shoulder, her arm flung out as if she'd died in battle.

Reflexively, she touched her collar for any sign of drool; it had been that kind of sleep—deep and insular, from which you returned as if kidnapped. She sat up and started off to the bathroom. An older woman with white hair and thick tinted lenses in square frames stopped her.

"Your husband," the woman began, and gave Elaine's hand a friendly squeeze, "will be back in a moment."

"Pardon?"

The woman wore pink slacks and white sneakers and had a large straw bag that said "Grand Cayman." Fragile, slight, about the same age her mother would have been if she'd lived, she squeezed Elaine's hand again. "He's coming right back. He had to take your wallet for a minute to buy some travel items."

Elaine immediately plunged her hand into her bag, then dumped the contents of the purse out on the floor, combing frantically through the items—keys, lipstick, sales slips—her checkbook!—but no wallet. "Who?" Elaine said. "Who took it?"

"I don't . . . I thought—"

"What did he look like?"

24

"He was tall, blond—"

"What was he wearing?"

"A dark suit and a blue tie, I think. My goodness, I thought—"

Elaine quickly scraped everything back into her bag. A suit and blue tie. Every businessman in the world fit the description. "What else?" she said, her voice shrill. But she couldn't control her impatience, directed now at this woman who shrank from her. How could she have just watched someone take her wallet?

"He was carrying an overcoat on his arm. I'm so sorry. I didn't even look which way he went. He was so nicely dressed, and he . . . I thought he must be your husband," the woman said, obviously distraught now. "He kissed you, after all."

"What?" Elaine asked. "*What* did you say?"

"He kissed you. Right there," and she pointed to Elaine's right cheek, close to her lips. She touched her cheek and felt incredulous that this had been done while she slept, a violation disguised as sweetness.

The elderly woman said she was going to Miami, a flight that was scheduled to board in ten minutes. There was no time to search the airport. The best thing would be to call Richard at work and have him start the process of canceling their credit cards. He was teaching today, so she'd have to leave a message for him on his phone, or with the department secretary, and how could she succinctly explain that a stranger had kissed her while stealing her wallet? She felt the burn on her cheek, his lips creeping toward the moist corner of her mouth.

A ticket agent came up to her. The elderly lady from Miami had brought him over while Elaine had been trying to remember her calling card number—that card gone too.

"I understand your wallet is lost, ma'am."

"Stolen."

The agent nodded noncommittally.

"I saw him take it," the older woman spoke up. Elaine felt grateful for the witnessed support.

"We can have security look into it."

"I have to make my flight. I know it's delayed but I don't want to miss it just to have . . ." She was about to say just to have nothing happen, because she knew nothing would. The airport police or whoever was in charge would get information from her about something she'd not even observed. The woman who had seen it all, who had been an unwitting participant, searched nervously in her own handbag for something to write her name and address on, as directed by the ticket agent, so she could make the last boarding call of her flight. She gave Elaine a hug— it felt awkwardly inappropriate—and looked back over her shoulder once before she disappeared into the Jetway. Elaine summoned enough generosity to smile back at her, then sat down with her purse, gutted of its wallet, her license, pictures of Caidee, credit cards from too many stores—she'd been meaning to consolidate —emergency phone numbers, her AAA, library, and insurance cards, a picture of her mother and her taken at a photo booth in Atlantic City when Elaine was eight years old and that she'd kept in her wallet all her life.

She looked for a tall man carrying an overcoat over his arm, dressed in a blue tie and a dark suit. Hundreds of them, of course. A crowd of travelers safely on their way. That's all, nothing else.

THE airline gave her fifteen dollars in food vouchers and ten dollars in cash. "We're not required to do this," the woman at the customer service desk told her. "But we certainly understand and sympathize with your predicament." Her plane, coming by way of Chicago and held up by weather, was now two hours delayed, so the gesture was less altruism than an appeasement to the restless passengers, most of whom just continued sitting in the waiting area. Elaine had made her way to customer service, then to security, filled out papers, and said what she knew. Which was nothing. A man had taken her wallet from her purse. She'd been sleeping. The purse had been wedged next to her in the seat. He'd apparently kissed her—though she left this part out, because she didn't want to undermine her claim. She had talked to a round-shouldered man with an airport badge and she didn't want to see anything cross his face that would indicate he thought she was imagining or fantasizing the incident. The kiss was both the least relevant part of the robbery and of course the most. Long after today, she would remember it beyond any money gone or other inconvenience. For now, it was her own private piece of news, not quite a secret—that bestowed on it too much intrigue and hinted of pleasure—just a lone fact only she would know.

"We'll contact you as soon as we hear anything," the security officer had told her, then sent her back to customer service for further assistance—the vouchers. She thought the choice of "as soon as we hear anything" instead of "if we hear something" sounded much more positive, even if she didn't believe a word of it. It was all public relations at this point. She herself worked in the marketing department for a large software company in Denver, so she knew all about making a concept appealing. You sold the idea, not the thing.

Now she sat in a bar, using part of her courtesy money not for food but to have a glass of wine. She should buy some food to fill her stomach—her appetite had been off anyway ever since the funeral—but she was not hungry. The airline meal for sale would be expectantly horrible, and she would pass and perhaps order another drink. The thought of doing so, of having another glass or two of wine with the chintzy little bag of pretzels made her happy for a moment. Something to look forward to. She should also get off her stool, find a quiet place, and call Richard. Who knew how many charges had been made to her credit cards? But she was feeling lazy, knowing she would not be responsible for unauthorized purchases and dreading having to explain the whole annoying mishap to Richard. She continued to sip her wine.

A tall man sat down next to her.

He had an overcoat over his arm. But he had brown curly hair, not blond, and he wore a herringbone sports coat, not a dark suit and blue tie. Nor was it a surprise that he'd have an overcoat; it was cold and damp outside, and this was Philadelphia where people dressed more formally than they did in Denver with parkas and ski jackets. Indeed, nothing about the man looked like the description of the thief. He was what her father would have called an ordinary Joe, and after he ordered a Scotch from the bartender he turned to her and said, "Your flight delayed too?"

Elaine placed her wine back on the cocktail napkin. "Yes," she said, and left it at that. It had been a long time since anyone had tried to pick her up. She was forty-six and although she did not feel old, she didn't think men noticed her anymore, not in that way. Her figure was still good, trim. But it was her "figure," no longer her "body," and she was trim, not hot.

"I've been here since noon," the man said. "How about you?"

"A little after three."

The man—he had a strong, slightly hooked nose and his short curly hair was speckled with silver, about fifty she guessed —checked his watch. "What I hate," he started to say, and then looked up at the TV. "Oh, Jesus, we're never going to get out of here now. Did you hear that? There's a blizzard in the Midwest." He shook his head and took a long sip of his Scotch. "So, anyway, I cut you off, what were you saying?"

Elaine laughed at this, and she did not know whether he laughed along with her because he understood that he had only cut himself off or because he had no clue. It was sometimes hard to tell with men like him. The good-natured salesman type, who rolled from one segue to another without noticing much in between. She could say anything to him, she supposed, and he would listen pleasantly and meaninglessly. "My wallet was stolen," she told him.

"Oh for Pete's sake," he said, an expression she hadn't heard for a while. "That's misery. When'd it happen?"

"About an hour ago. I fell asleep in my seat and a man took my wallet." She paused a minute, to let him finish shaking his head. "He kissed me on the cheek."

Elaine waited to see his reaction. She would explain nothing further, a test of sorts.

"The kissing thief," he said. "Herman Grace," he added, extending his hand, and she wanted to laugh again—his last name. Was it real? She certainly wouldn't give a stranger her full name, but he was a man, after all, and on much safer ground here. "So anyhow," he was saying, "it takes all kinds, doesn't it? Next thing you know we'll have apologetic murderers and counseling prostitutes. What's the world coming to? Criminals bussing you on the cheek. That must be some sort of new age mugging."

"I don't think he meant it as a sensitive gesture."

"No," Herman Grace said, shaking his head. "You're quite right. There is nothing the least bit kind or caring about what was done to you. I've taken your comment about being robbed and kissed and made it into fodder for chitchat. I stand corrected."

At least he believed her.

The bartender came over and asked if she wanted another glass of wine. Reflexively, she checked the remaining cash in her hand. Always a good budgeter, Richard had said about her, and the thought of Richard made her unhappy with responsibility: she should be calling him to inform him of the theft, checking in about Caidee too.

"I'll have another," Herman said, holding his empty glass aloft. "And for the lady too, whatever she pleases." He turned back to her, his mouth, it seemed, suddenly full of extra teeth. "You don't mind if I buy you a drink, do you?"

"I should really check on my flight."

"Me, too," he said. "Me too," but neither of them made a move to go, and when their drinks arrived, he slipped the bartender a twenty-dollar bill and told him to keep the change— a conspicuous, even vulgar gesture meant to impress her, she decided. She checked her face in the mirror behind the bar. Her hair curled smartly at the neck. Her eyebrows were darkened, her cheeks lightly—very subtly, she thought—rouged. And her eyeliner modest, restrained compared to, for instance, the spook show of Caidee's eyes. No, she didn't look like someone waiting to be picked up, not in her black turtleneck and gray skirt, her unpolished nails and stylish if discounted camel-hair coat that she'd gotten at a factory outlet mall in Denver. She looked, she thought, like her mother did before she died, if she hadn't dyed her hair and had let the gray show through like Elaine. It would soon be all gray. "Where are you from, Herman?"

"L.A. Born and raised. And trapped there. You?"

"From Denver."

"Terrific skiing. We try to make a trip there every season."

So, he had a family. He was not wearing a wedding ring and there was no mark from where he might have slipped it off. Now she was curious. "Do you have children?"

"Grown," he said. "Two boys and a girl. My daughter, she's at Haaavaad."

"You must be very proud."

"I certainly am," he said and took a swallow of his Scotch.

"And your wife? Is she back in L.A.?"

"Divorced." He drummed his fingers on the bar, smiled— defensively chipper?

"I'm sorry," she said.

"No need to be. We waited until the kids were grown, did our duty. Ten years of love, ten of stale bread." His eyebrows twisted a bit. "I'm not trying to pick you up, you know."

"Oh?" It was all she could manage.

"Am I insulting you?"

"Of course you are. I suspect you know that, though."

"You needn't worry about me. I'm harmless."

She considered him for a moment while he lit a cigarette, offering her one, which she refused. She never smoked. "What exactly *do* you want?"

"To talk. Just to talk."

She put her drink down half finished on the napkin. It was time to go.

"In which case I don't know anything about you," he said.

"Pardon?"

"You want to be anonymous. You would have told me something about yourself if you didn't."

She should leave instantly and decisively, but the wine made her legs feel as if they were kicking lazily through water at the bottom of the barstool. "If I'm not mistaken, you didn't ask."

"Because you weren't going to tell me. If you were, you would have told me your name when I told you mine."

"I must be out of practice. I don't make a habit of talking to strangers."

"I can see. Otherwise you would at least have given me an alias."

She looked at him for a long moment, then laughed. Alarmingly, she was finding herself less afraid of him. "What line of work did you say you were in?"

"I'm a private investigator."

"No, you're not."

"That's right, I'm not. I'm in the electronics industry. Semiconductors."

"Now I believe you, Mr. Grace."

"Is it Mr. Grace, now? We were on a first name basis a minute ago, at least unilaterally."

"A minute ago you were asking if I wanted to be picked up."

"If memory serves"—he put his glass against his forehead to feign concentration—"I was saying the opposite."

"You were thinking it. Am I wrong?"

"I was thinking you are very attractive, sure of yourself, and guarded, as you should be. I was also thinking you wouldn't believe me if I told you I have never done this before."

"Done what?"

"Approached a woman at a bar."

"You're right. I wouldn't."

"Let me ask you a question or two," he said. "Is that permitted?"

"Yes."

"Your name?"

"Elaine."

"Elaine," he said, as though examining her name like a small, pleasing, striated rock. "What is it you do?"

"Marketing, software. But don't ask me anything too technical. I depend on R and D to give me the details and then I spin them into gold."

"I'm sure you do." He picked up a pretzel from the bowl of party mix the bartender had left them and slowly chewed, then took a long drink. "I want to tell you something, Elaine. You won't mind, will you?"

"That depends."

"That's the sensible answer. But you needn't be afraid. I won't offend you."

The bar had become noisier, almost six o'clock now, and she could see by the crowd at her gate that her plane had still not arrived. She put her palm over her empty glass of wine, her second glass, to keep herself from ordering more. That was her limit usually, two glasses when she and Richard went out for the evening, but the idea of limits had suddenly become just that, an idea. She studied his hands; he had strong smooth fingers and clean nails. She appreciated a man who gave his fingernails attention. She stared at the white half moons of his cuticles, then raised her eyes and said, "Tell me. I'd like to hear."

"I'm not here on business. My children lured me here, perhaps that is the best word. They are fed up with me and have tried an intervention of sorts, to no avail. That's what I was doing in Philadelphia and that's why I am leaving alone. The intervention failed. They are furious with me. This is my fourth Scotch and my second pack of cigarettes in as many hours. Airport delays are unstructured, unhealthy time and I am as weak as I've ever been." He stared out the window a moment at the parked planes. "What nakedness would you like to tell me, Elaine?"

Names were being called over the paging system, Mr. Simon Agler, Mrs. Alsa Hong, Ms. Susan Lewis . . . Elaine heard them dimly along with the announcements of flights; the electronic beeping of courtesy carts going by; cranky children screaming at being dragged another inch through the miserable terminal with its delayed passengers. Right now the dirt of her father's grave would be running muddy from the rain, while a thief somewhere was picking through her assets, discarding credit cards, throwing her wallet with the photograph of her mother and her in Atlantic City into a filthy dumpster behind a warehouse. Her mother had hated the cold and damp, and on such mornings her father would warm her sweaters over the old steam radiators in their house on Belmont Street.

If her mother had remained alive, Elaine might not have made certain mistakes—entered into a disastrous first marriage or cut off friends when she needed them most. She might have told her mother, as she never did her father, about the "struggle" with the boy in college—what would flatly be called date rape now. She might have drawn more comfort and courage for this second part of her life had her mother lived and had her father not expected her and her sister to handle everything on their own, because Mother's death was mostly his loss. And yet she had loved her father all the more desperately after her mother died, jumping to him, her only remaining oar.

"My father just died," Elaine said. She was thinking about Herman Grace's grown children surrounding him, pleading with him to save his life. The image had an exquisite pain, so much love and so much stubbornness, so much trouble and so much spilled hope.

"I'm a man who still carries a handkerchief. May I?" and she let him dab at her eyes—she had started to cry. He worked

33

tenderly, as if his fingers themselves were gloved, touching her cheeks with the soft cotton cloth, fresh and clean as a white veil.

"Can I help you get somewhere?" Herman Grace asked, because he could see when she stood up she was slightly unsteady from her two glasses of wine.

"I'll be fine," she said, but then leaned into him anyway, and he put his arm around her shoulder. He smelled of aftershave, Scotch, and smoke, a not unpleasant combination at the moment, and she listened to his breathing—heard all the discordant sounds of his life commingling into a stand against oblivion.

They walked silently toward her plane. She held his arm for comfort more than support, and she felt safe next to him. At the gate, passengers were gathered around the ticket agent's podium.

They went over and listened. The flight had been cancelled, stuck in Chicago. People were angry, asking why they hadn't been told sooner. "We got the information to you as soon as we received it," the ticket agent said, a thin man with droopy eyes. One other flight this evening was scheduled for Denver, but that was on a different airline and presently at full capacity, the ticket agent said, studying his monitor. "Everyone will be rebooked on flights tomorrow morning," he told them. "We can't control the weather. I'm very sorry, but if you need assistance with arrangements for staying overnight we can try to help."

"'Try,'" Herman Grace said. "Key word. They're not obligated to do anything because it's weather related."

She stared in disbelief at the scrolling red letters on the board that said Flight Cancelled. "I can't believe this. I can't fucking believe this." Herman Grace looked away, quieted, she wondered, by her profanity. "You'd better check on yours," she told him, though she did not want him to leave her alone.

"I did," he said. "It's still cancelled."

She stared at him. "Still? What do you mean?"

"It was cancelled hours ago. I've been—how shall I put it?—reluctant to leave the airport. I didn't want to face my children, and I didn't want to go to an empty hotel room. And then I met you."

She knew now he was asking her to spend the night with him, and she was thinking that she could do it and live with the guilt or not do it and live with the relief and that the two choices didn't seem that far apart in consequence. She had assumed such parallel lines would never converge—and they never had for her. But, as Richard was fond of saying, she was in a state. All the more reason to behave badly and irresponsibly, not be accountable for her actions from the shock of her father's death, her stolen wallet, her cancelled flight . . . .

None of this equaled the clarity of knowing that what she was about to do was wrong.

She could—should—take a cab to Rachel's house and spend the night. Her sister would surely be glad to drive her the next morning to the airport, as she had done this afternoon. She could even sleep in her father's apartment, the bed where he died, a communion of sorts, maybe finding a macabre peace in his penultimate resting place. She certainly had resources, unlike Mr. Grace. "I need to make a phone call," she told him. "Where should I meet you?"

"Same old, same old." He pointed to the bar where'd they been. "Shall I order you anything?"

"Water, please."

"Me, too," he said. "The healthy choice."

Her cell phone was out of juice, and she didn't want to ask Herman Grace to use his. She went over to the pay phone and made a collect call to Richard, prepared to hang up if he didn't answer after three rings, long enough to fool herself into believing she tried.

"Hello?"

"Richard," Elaine said, and could feel herself saying his name as if she had just dropped all her heavy bags in front of him with utter relief.

"Where are you, Laine? What's wrong? You're calling collect."

"I'm still at the Philadelphia airport. My flight's been cancelled. Oh, Richard, what a day it's been."

"I was just about to go out the door to pick up Caidee after her swim practice and go straight from there to the airport. What happened?"

"My wallet was stolen. I'm so sorry, I should have called earlier."

"Your wallet? Are you all right? Were you hurt?"

"No, no," she said, imagining his worried face. "I'm fine. I was sleeping. It was stupid. He took it from my bag by pretending . . ." She looked over at the bar. Herman Grace waved to her and she back at him.

"Laine? Are you going out on a later flight?"

"There are no others tonight. I'll have to fly back tomorrow morning."

"You'll stay at Rachel's, right? Can we reach you there? I want to know you're safe. It will be good to be with your sister after such a miserable day."

"I think," she said, and fingered the coin return, letting it slam closed, "I think I'm going to stay near the airport. The flight leaves early."

There was a pause, and she thought that Richard didn't believe her, but he said, "That's a good idea perhaps." She nodded, as if she'd gotten a forged permission slip. "But what will you do for money?"

"What?" she asked, understanding clearly what he had said.

"Money for a hotel. Oh!" he interrupted himself. "They're paying for it, the airline. I get it."

"I'll call you in the morning, all right?"

"Are you sure you don't need anything? I hate to think of you there without a cent."

"I'll be fine. Give Caidee a kiss for me. I miss you both."

"I love you, too. And, Laine, be good to yourself. Your father and all." She touched her cheek where the thief's lips had been and felt a bluish heat, ran her finger up near her earlobe where Richard liked to kiss her and felt Herman Grace's mouth there.

When she got off the phone, she didn't look over at Herman Grace at the bar; she didn't want to show anything on her face. She went into the bathroom and sat on the toilet and listened to more names being paged . . . Mr. Callahan, Ms. Wilkens, Mr. Pintauro . . . a dull drone of missing people. She looked at herself in the mirror for a long time after she brushed her hair: her brown eyes, such pretty, warm eyes her mother would always say, like little poems.

She walked out of the bathroom, joining the dwindling crowd—people on their way home or to hotels overnight or back to where they started. There were only two men sitting together at the bar, younger men. She stood in the middle of the concourse and watched both ways, and then kept her eyes on the men's bathroom for a moment. She went into the bar and sat down to wait; he was no doubt in the bathroom himself.

The bartender, the same one who had been there before, came over to her. "The gentleman said to give this to you." He handed her a business card. Elaine looked at it: Herman Grace, Tritronics Electrical Systems. She turned the card over: Is it cowardly or honorable of me to leave? Try to think well of me. I always will of you. Love, Herman.

The bartender had his back to her and was washing a glass. Elaine stared out at the terminal—the people passing through. When she'd been young, her whole family would watch the show "To Tell the Truth." She'd sit with them on the couch with its rose-patterned brocade fabric, running her finger across the delicate petals, the sturdy stems, the sharp thorns, imagining the touch of a boy's spine. One night, while her parents held hands and she shared a pan of popcorn with her sister, the show's host had declared to the three contestants, Will the real thief please stand up?

Beside her was the bottled water Herman Grace had ordered for her—she'd only noticed it now—poured into a glass, with a slice of lemon. Elaine looked down and smiled to herself. Her sweet, gentle mother would have said, you're smiling from ear to ear, darling, why?

ABSOLUTE
ZERO

E VERY morning before school, Connor ran four miles in the desert with the Marines. They did push-ups and bear crawls on the lawn in front of the recruiting center and shouted *Oo-rah!* at the top of their lungs. He'd shaved his head, his scalp as smooth as his mother's, only she was going in one direction and he . . . well, he didn't know where he was going. Since he was only seventeen, a year younger than most of his graduating high school classmates because he'd skipped eighth grade, he'd have to have his mother's consent to join up. So far she'd been lucid enough when it came to this particular matter to shake her head no and vigorously refuse. "Over my dead body," she said, not without irony. "I will stay alive as long as it takes to see that you don't throw away your life."

She wanted him to go to college at Arizona State and live with his Aunt Lyla and Uncle Sebert in Scottsdale. His sister, meanwhile, pregnant and single, would inherit the house until Connor turned twenty-eight, when he would receive his part of a trust fund. Connor figured by that time he might be dead himself. He was philosophical about it. When Sergeant Kenner, the Marine recruiter, tried to reassure him that he wouldn't automatically be sent to a war zone like Iraq or Afghanistan—after all, Marines were stationed across the globe—Connor said he would volunteer. Sergeant Kenner studied him for a long moment. "You, my friend, are exactly the kind of person that makes a leader." He further explained that the Marines didn't go after people like the Army. "Proud men come to us," he said. "They want to be Marines, and we're here to help them meet that challenge."

Connor had to admit no one had ever called him a leader, and he was flattered, manipulated he knew, but nevertheless enamored. He started showing up at the recruiting station and hanging out with the other potential recruits, called poolees, and the occasional soldier home from active duty. These were infantry grunts who had come back from Iraq and would soon be heading out again to Afghanistan. They made room for Connor at the card table—penny ante—in the rec area with its chin-up bar and free weights. They nicknamed him "Con," such an obvious diminutive yet no one had ever called him this. They included him in their touch football games, more like touch with hockey checking, and swarmed him when he caught a stretched-out, fingertip touchdown pass. They even pimped his ride, the Geo, sort of: buying him a chrome license plate holder with a placard that said THE CON. He put it on the front of the Geo and felt ridiculously proud of it and their acceptance.

Eventually, when they took his presence for granted—he was spending more and more time here—they told stories about Iraq, of dead bodies rotting in the sun and bursting apart before it was safe enough to clear them; of children missing limbs and spitting at them when they tried to help; of attacks by hajis—what they called all Arabs—dressed in military uniforms only to blow your head off in the span of a handshake; of Iraqi houses with trip wires in their front yards that wiped out whole patrols; and the comparatively mundane complaints: three weeks in the field without a shower, blistering sandstorms, scorpions and sand fleas. Did that mean they hated what they did? No, they hated those people who didn't support them, the anti-war scum. It didn't matter if the protestors said they were on their side but against the war. They were traitors.

Connor's mother, meanwhile, was one of these traitors. She'd made sure his name was taken off the list of eligible high school students so military recruiters wouldn't call. She had regularly covered the back of the Geo with anti-war bumper stickers —OLD HIPPIES FOR PEACE, WAR IS NOT PRO-LIFE—before Connor scraped them off. And until she became too weak to do so, she'd gone every Wednesday to Patriot Park at the corner of Central Avenue and Washington Street and joined a peace vigil. If there was one thing that drove her crazy, it was his wish to become a Marine.

"It's your father, isn't it?" she asked him. "Is that what this is all about? You're looking for acceptance from other men because you never got it from him. I'm right, aren't I?" She rarely spoke about Connor's father, who had left the family when Connor was five. He hardly remembered the man. He'd last heard from his father when he wrote from Florida on Connor's eighth birthday, some big land deal he was working on there—he'd bring Connor down soon and they'd go deep sea fishing. Connor sent him back his first poem: *Moo moo goes the sad cow. Neigh neigh goes the pretty horse. Heh heh goes the zoo daddy.*

His intention to become a soldier was the only subject that got his mother revved up and focused. Whereas she might ask him to go to the store and get her more . . . and here she'd brush her finger against her front teeth, finally coming up with the word, or so she believed—*cleanser!*—her brain cells worked with furious intact precision at trying to stop him from enlisting. "You have to promise me," she told him. "You have to promise right now that you won't do this to me."

"I can't promise," he said. "You know I can't."

"Why not? I'm your mother. Doesn't a condemned person get a last wish?"

"Jesus, Mom. Stop already."

"Just do it," his fat and pregnant sister said. "You owe it to Mom." They were all sitting in the living room. His mother's wig, this one a reddish copper color, was askew at a rakish angle.

"Stay out of this," Connor had warned. "You can't talk." That is, talk about making mistakes. His sister's one-night stand in a club had resulted in a child she insisted on keeping. He was going to be an uncle, his mother was dying, his sister was unmarried, and all he wanted was to make his mother sign the papers on the coffee table in front of her.

THE seer had not been in school for weeks, and Connor wondered if he had died. Even in school, you didn't so much see him as sight him, drifting from the music room like a gossamer silver thread to another part of the building. He was rumored to read by passing his hand over a page, and he never carried books. He usually sat inconspicuously in the back of the class. One girl had claimed she'd literally seen him fade into the wall.

Wingard thought the seer had potential. "Maybe he's just sick again. Let's visit him after school."

"You know where he lives?" Connor asked.

"I'll find out," Wingard said.

Connor slammed his locker closed. His last class of the day was senior English, and he had to sit next to Heather Ward. She was always asking him how-do-you-feel-do-you-want-to-talk-is-there-anything-I-can-do-for-you? "I'm fine," Connor would say. His little secret. He couldn't be mean to people. Inside, however, he was un-nice, hateful, murderous, hacking bodies in the hallway, a bloody ax held high through a wild strangulated scream of carnage. "Thanks for asking, Heather." Like a choir boy or a priest or a sage. The seer. Let him figure this out. Everyone said he could read the future as fast as a comic strip.

Wingard was waiting for him in the parking lot with an address he'd wheedled out of a friendly student aide in the office.

They drove two miles to the east side of town and pulled up to a cheery looking bungalow on a quiet street. The seer's mom was delighted they'd come by. She'd never met them, but that didn't seem to matter. "It's so wonderful of you to visit! Sandy will be so thrilled." Mrs. Seer—they didn't know the seer's last name; in fact they hadn't even known his name was the androgynous "Sandy"—led them down a narrow hallway with pictures of the family on vacations. "Sandy, you have two friends here to see you." She turned and spoke to them. "He hasn't been feeling much like talking the last couple days, so you'll have to keep the visit short. But I know it will cheer him up to have you here."

She left.

There in the bed, with railings on the side, hooked up to a war room of beeping monitors and wearing an oxygen mask, lay the seer. His eyes shifted to them, then returned to the ceiling. A scruff of his dirty blond hair fanned out in back from the strap of the oxygen mask. Connor could hear him taking deep gurgly breaths. Sometimes his mother breathed like this too, but without such desperate rattling. This was the sound of a single hoof tapping out time on a dark cobblestone street. Connor was speechless in its presence.

Wingard elbowed him. *Say something. Tell him why you're here.*

The seer couldn't have weighed more than seventy-five pounds, and that was being generous. He wore gray pajamas with thick wool socks. He looked cold, but this was Phoenix, the desert, the happy sunshine state of Arizona, where Connor's mother was dying too and this person in front of him had wasted away, his pajama sleeve rolled up to display a pale veined arm no wider at the bicep than the wrist.

The seer's mother appeared again. She was carrying a tray of sodas and cookies. "I thought you two might be hungry," she said. "We have milk also, but I'm guessing you want the good stuff." She smiled. She was the least sad person in the room, Connor was sure of it. She put the tray of cookies and soda cans—choice of Mountain Dew, Dr. Pepper, Sierra Mist—on a small wooden desk, and then left.

A voice delicate as a straw wrapper floating to earth came from behind Connor. "I'm sorry, but do I know you?" The oxygen mask was off. The seer's lips had sores with shiny ointment spread over them. Wingard took a step toward the door, his horror showing.

Connor cleared his throat. "Not really."

Wingard whispered, "Let's vacate."

"And you're here because?" The seer's voice had changed, the featheriness replaced by a sweetened irony, a fluted whimsy. "Help me sit up." He motioned for Connor to come closer. When he put out his hand for Connor to help him, Wingard said, "Posthaste," and fled the room.

Connor stood there. The white translucent hand hung in the air, until Connor finally took it, surprisingly warm for what he'd expected would be cold marble, and then carefully leaned him back against his headboard. The sodas sweated under the overhead light.

"Ahh, repose," said the seer. His thin eyebrows were burned albino white by sun or illness.

"I heard you can see the future," Connor said.

The oxygen mask went back on. After a few stringy wet breaths, the seer took it off and said, "Tomorrow is Friday. The sun will set in the west. The *Heteropterus morpheus* lives thirty-one days. Does that help?"

"I knew it was a hoax." He wanted to hurt somebody. Could you hurt the wind? Could you damage the absence of flesh? "I thought you could tell me something about what I should do after I graduate."

"Channel seven, please," the seer said, and motioned for Connor to turn on the television high up on a metal bracket in the corner of the room, just like in a hospital.

Connor got the remote from the desk with the sodas and turned on Channel 7. It was Oprah. "I love the Angel Network," the seer said. He watched Oprah walk down the aisle to the cheers of her adoring fans. Connor put his hand on the doorknob.

"Watch this part," the seer said. Oprah called people up onstage and told them they were getting free cars. It was the Pontiac giveaway show. Hadn't that happened years ago?

"Is this a repeat?" Connor asked.

"It's all a repeat," the seer said. The audience was opening their gift bags and finding car keys, too. They were going nuts, their faces lit up with monstrous joy, a frenzy of stupid happiness. "I never noticed you in school. You have very little presence," the seer informed Connor.

"My mother's dying," Connor told the seer, looking into his watery blue eyes that had lost their focus on the television.

The seer waved for the TV to be shut off. "Listen," he said. His voice suddenly had strength, heft, *basso profundo*, as if coming through speakers on the wall. "You should know better than to come here."

"I thought you could help me."

"Are you listening?" The voice was becoming weak and fluttery again.

"I'm listening."

The seer patted the bed for Connor to come sit next to him. Connor did so, gingerly, lowering the safety bar and putting his weight on the edge of the spongy mattress. The seer, light as a ghost, slanted toward him, as if he might roll down a hill and be lost.

Wingard called through the door that he needed to leave. Time passed. Minutes? An hour? Mrs. Seer tapped musically on the door, came in, smiled at Connor and pursed her lips with thoughtful satisfaction at her slumbering son. She took away the silver tray with the untouched sweating sodas and the lemon-iced cookies, as if this happened all the time—her doomed boy sleeping beside a visitor who couldn't seem to leave.

The room darkened, the air circulated, the seer's breathing became so soft that Connor wondered if he'd slipped into uncon-

45

sciousness. He put his ear to the feathery boy's chest. He heard a slow swishing, as if someone were moving a broom back and forth in an inch of water.

OUTSIDE, Connor slung his backpack over his shoulder and kicked the door of his car, his mother's really, since she didn't drive anymore. The Geo had a dent from getting T-boned and had never been fixed. You had to bash it with your foot to open it and then slam it like a vault door to get it closed.

He gave the Geo, purple with metallic bruises, another kick.

"What'd he say?" Wingard asked.

"Get in." Connor was giving Wingard, who had been waiting impatiently, a ride home.

"You were in there for like forever. What happened?"

"Nothing happened." In truth everything had happened, but nothing he could explain.

"So why'd you stay?"

"I felt sorry for him. Why'd you leave?"

"I couldn't take it. He was like a mummy or something. I thought he was going to put a spell on me."

Frankly, Wingard exasperated him. Fueled by a daily intake of six bowls of Reese's Puffs, he constantly networked with other World of Warcraft bangers. He slept by his computer and talked about people named Orgrim Doomhammer and Jaina Proudmoore as if they were blood relations. He'd been trying to get Connor interested in the brain-sucking game since they'd been sophomores.

"He's just a sick kid," Connor said about the seer. "I felt okay there with him."

"You were in there for an hour. I was in the kitchen with the old lady. You think that was fun? She was talking my ear off about her church and Sandy's faith and how we should really go watch him play guitar with the choir. 'He's a miracle, Salvatore,' she told me. Nobody calls me Salvatore."

46

"Why'd you tell her your name then?"

"I didn't. All right, somehow she got it out of me. The whole family's a bunch of aliens! So were you, what, holding his hand or something?"

How did you know? He had taken the weightless boy's hand after a while, unbidden, listening to the soft hissing of the aluminum tank filling the seer's lungs with a hundred percent pure oxygen; he had pictured the seer's red blood cells slurping up the fuel, growing darker and richer with every breath. It had been a long time since he'd felt so peaceful, and if it hadn't been for Sandy's mother knocking on the door, he might have stayed there all night.

They pulled up in front of Wingard's condo, where he lived with his mother and stepfather. "You coming in?" Wingard asked. The condos were older ones with tar-pebbled roofs that baked in the sun. A skein of yellow citrus tree leaves floated on the surface of the unused pool. Wingard with his pale freckled skin (not unlike the seer's when Connor thought about it) had proudly declared he'd never stepped foot in it.

"I've got to go," Connor said. "I'm having dinner at Sergeant Kenner's."

"*Again?*"

Connor shrugged, made a vague gesture that he knew Wingard would detect as insincere.

"You're *crazy*, man. Why do you want to hang out with those guys?"

"You're one to talk. You sit in front of your stupid computer communing with trolls and gnomes all day."

"You hate violence. You're a goddamn vegetarian, for Christ's sake. You're going to die in some country where they hate our guts. Hey," Wingard said, suddenly looking proud of himself. "I get it. You have a *death wish*."

For once, it seemed, Wingard's brain had not, in fact, completely deliquesced from playing Warcraft twenty-four seven.

IT was not the first time Sergeant Kenner had invited him to his home, a wistful, low-slung ranch house in the foothills on a couple acres of parched land studded with prickly pear cacti and bleached-out yucca that poked up like feather dusters. He'd been here three times before, mostly, he suspected, at the urging of Mrs. Kenner, who felt sorry for Connor because his mother was dying and always complimented him on his "bravery" and good manners, in the same breath. He *was* exceedingly polite—the good Connor who wanted to kill someone but would undoubtedly say, "Excuse me," before he did.

The Kenners had a seventeen-year-old daughter named Jody. She was Korean. Well, she was American actually. They'd adopted her at birth, and she spoke contemptuously to her parents, mostly about how much she hated school, how little interest she had in what she called "world affairs," how much weight she had gained (although she was, Connor thought, if anything too thin, and he suspected an eating disorder), and how much they, the Kenners, her adoptive parents, annoyed her. Tonight she wore torn black jeans, a low-cut black knit top with crisscrossing spaghetti straps, and plum-colored, ankle-strap sandals with stacked wedges. Her bottom lip was pierced with silver, her nose studded with gold, and she laughed crudely at the table whenever her parents tried to ask her a simple question such as what had happened to the fifty-dollar check she'd (somehow) cashed that was meant for her school choir retreat.

In the three times Connor had been over to the Kenners' house, Giigee, as she called herself, had finished exactly one meal with them, barely. The other two had resulted in her being sent to her room, not to be seen for the rest of the evening, as Connor and the Kenners watched TV on the sofa together. The third time, she had made it to the end but then threw a butter knife across the table in the direction of her mother. "That's it," Sergeant Kenner had said, and walked around to (Connor hoped) rip Giigee up from the table and kick her out the door or to social services or boarding school or a psychiatric facility or junior boot camp. But, no, Sergeant Kenner pointed to her room, stocked, Connor knew, with iPhone, iPod, iPad, and TiVo, and told her not to come down until she thought long and hard about her behavior.

My God, Connor had thought, the sergeant was a pussycat —or a pussy, as the word got thrown around so frequently at the recruiting station about wannabes who had "fagged out," after "almost" signing up, unofficial talk, of course, which Connor was privy to and took as a warning that he'd better not do the same. But here, in this house, Sergeant Kenner appeared to have no backbone, as emasculated as any man in America. Why would he let Connor see him like this?

Now they were attempting dinner again. Would Giigee give her father the finger as she had last time? Would she spit in the bowl of caramelized carrots as she did when her mother asked her to go easy on her pungent perfume that wafted with deadly astringent force like some biological weapon through the dining room? Would Connor just sit there and watch this as if he'd been a member of the family since birth?

"And what did you do today, honey?" Mrs. Kenner asked him now. She had lit some tall lavender tapers in polished copper candleholders and placed linen napkins in matching copper ring holders on fleur-de-lis gold-banded dinner plates. A basket of warm and sweet Hawaiian dinner rolls waited in front of Connor. Fish was on the menu tonight, some kind of snapper, imported to this landlocked state. Last time they'd had meatloaf and peas, a dish he thought only existed in fifties sitcoms. Before that Mrs. Kenner had made a Mexican casserole, which Giigee had disliked and nudged away with the glittery red talon of her pinky.

"I went to see someone," Connor answered. Why not? What did he have to lose? "He's a kid who's ill. I think he's going to die." At this, the table went a notch quieter, some perceptible noise cancellation that vacuumed out any false cheer. "They call him

49

the seer because he can read the future. I think he has a respiratory disease of some kind."

"Is it cystic fibrosis?" Mrs. Kenner asked, a bit too brightly for the subject.

"I'm not sure. Anyway, I sat with him for quite a while. It was very . . . I don't know . . . serene."

"You're a very good friend to go see him," Mrs. Kenner remarked.

"Connor's a good man," Sergeant Kenner added. He ate close to his plate, more as if he were shoveling in rice than taking bites. "He's going to make one helluva Marine. I'm proud of you, son."

"But I didn't go see him because I was his friend. I've never spoken to him before."

Giigee made some sort of hissing sound, a tire deflating, though Connor wasn't sure it was directed at him or just her general exasperation. He was used to her sounds by now, hisses, tragic sighs, impertinent burps, bellicose snorts, and tried to ignore them. "I thought he could help me. I was going to ask him about my mother. I did tell him my mother was dying. But I didn't ask him what I wanted to."

"You poor dear," Mrs. Kenner said, and reached out to pat Connor's hand. "More salad anyone?"

"What I really wanted to ask him," Connor went on, realizing that he hadn't quite prepared himself well enough for the question and that the seer couldn't have helped him anyway, "is whether I'm a murderer."

Giigee spit out her food. "Oh. My. God."

"Whether I'm killing her," Connor tried to clarify. "My mother, that is."

Mrs. Kenner laughed nervously. "I can't imagine how I would feel in your situation, but I know all sorts of thoughts must cross your mind. And there's nothing wrong with expressing them either. I think we all know that grief makes us have irrational ideas, don't we, Nelson?"

"I don't know," answered Sergeant Kenner, shoveling food faster into his mouth. "You're the psychology grad. But it sounds right to me. I wouldn't worry about it, son. We know you don't mean it."

"I do mean it," Connor said. "I'm killing her before she dies."

Sergeant Kenner picked up his head. "Con, it can't be easy. But there's no need to be offensive. I'm sure you love your mother a whole lot more than you can say."

"I don't see the contradiction," Connor said. Giigee was watching him intently.

"Exactly," Mrs. Kenner said, "and that's what you're expressing with your feelings—"

"But I don't know if I'd call what I'm doing an act of love. It's more like an act of God. God behaving badly in me."

Mrs. Kenner exchanged a glance with her husband. Connor knew what that glance meant. The boy was sicker than they thought, not just sad, but disturbed—yes, that was the word, and he would just barely qualify for the service, though not if he went on like this in public. He would have liked to explain that he had deprived his mother of his company these final days of her life, and that he was causing her heartache by not assuring her he had a future other than one as a soldier in some murderous foreign land and that he wasn't allowing her to die peacefully with the illusion of her house in order, and that he had no kindness he could fake on her behalf, and that, in this way, he was the agent of her death. It was unpretty all right, and he wished he wasn't responsible for such distress and that he wasn't killing her spiritually as well as physically. He would have liked—or tried—to make this clear if he thought for a moment Sergeant Kenner and his wife would have understood. He knew, though, they wouldn't, and he was not surprised, given all they'd been through with Giigee, when Mrs. Kenner cheerfully observed, "Well, time for dessert, kiddos."

He was surprised, however, when he and Sergeant Kenner were having their customary pool game after dinner in the converted garage and Giigee slunk in barefoot and announced she wanted to play. She had never done this before, always disappearing during or shortly after dinner.

She had changed into a more modest outfit, a ruffled skirt sprinkled with wildflowers and a light pink blouse, opened a respectful two buttons at her smooth tan throat and just above her snug pointed breasts. She looked composed, young and womanly, someone whose hand you might ask for in marriage from her father.

"Why don't you kids play," Sergeant Kenner said. "I'm going to hit the sack." He started for his daughter, as if to give her a kiss goodnight, then thought better of it and turned and left.

"Eight ball," Giigee said right away. "You break."

Connor did but failed to knock in a single ball.

"Five ball in the side pocket," Giigee declared. It was a difficult bank shot requiring passage through a tight channel of balls. He couldn't see why she didn't go for the easy fifteen ball teetering on the edge of the corner pocket.

Then he understood. She ran the table. Connor stood with his pool cue in hand, shifting it from right to left, chalking the tip, murmuring sounds of approval. He hardly knew what to say. She shot with such aggressive confidence that he blinked at the explosive fission of the cue ball smacking the others. Whether with her legs spread like a gunslinger, or with the cue behind her arched back, or with the nonchalance of someone dropping letters in a mailbox, she called and sank every shot. For the game winner—corner right pocket—she stretched across the table. Her blouse slid up her lower back, and the single eye of a tattooed turquoise octopus peeked out at him.

A scratch.

"I've never seen anyone play pool like that," Connor said, dumbfounded at the display.

"But, you see, I lost. I scratched." With her vermillion nail, she flicked the eight ball against the felt bank. "I always blow it." She appeared sad at this confession.

"You lost on purpose. I saw you shoot the cue ball straight in."

"On purpose? You think there is such a thing?"

"I don't know," Connor said, finding her suddenly fascinating. "Why are you so mean to your parents? They're good people."

She shuffled over to him in her bare feet and ran her hand across his smooth scalp. "You should grow your hair out and dye it strawberry. It would look cool."

"You didn't answer me about your parents."

"What does the word 'good' taste like?"

"Pardon?"

Giigee backed him up against the rack of pool cues on the wall. "Open your mouth. I'll show you what 'bad' tastes like and you can make it all good."

THEY lay down on a couch, his pants around his knees, her ruffled skirt pushed up to her waist, her bra, which he fumbled to get undone, hanging from her neck like a sling. She grinded against him, but his erection, which had proved so ready at the prospect of sex, now wilted at the act. After a while she stopped moving. "You think I'm ugly." It wasn't a question. "Don't you like my body?"

"Your body is fabulous!" he said, sounding, he knew, like a talk show host praising a guest's new movie.

"So what's wrong then?"

"I don't know . . . I guess I'm nervous."

"Relax then," she commanded, pushing his face against her tits, but after sucking and licking and stroking and imitating the slew of porno examples on the web to the best of his ability, he sat up.

It was late. He had to get home. "My mother, she's not well . . ." A mishmash of excuses came pouring out of him. Giigee, unlike what sympathetic girls do in books and movies, didn't reassure him or tell him not to worry about it; she instead stood up, got dressed, and went through the side door without another word, leaving him sitting there with his pants literally around his ankles.

He drove home, after giving the Geo an extra hard kick, cursing the miserable vehicle that spewed black exhaust smoke.

His mother was half asleep on the couch and trying to speak through a haze of medications. She had lost more weight and her nightgown had slipped off her right shoulder. "Is Suzie here?" he asked her.

"Suz, yes, she's outstanding," his mother said. He guessed this meant she was upstairs. Her parts of speech were decaying as fast as her organs, leaving holes in her sentences, spots in her vision: words disappeared from the page like snatched coins. She lost track of her meds and became confused about the hospice people who visited, making flapping gestures of apology in the air.

He put the sleeve of her nightgown back up on her shoulder. "I have to get up early," Connor told her. His mother shook her head, laughed and squinted in pain, a sign that the morphine was wearing off. He'd have to give her another pill. Her cancer had spread to her brain, outwitting the latest round of chemo. The doctor had said she had only a one to four percent chance of surviving, calling it a "smart cancer."

She pointed to her heart and the puckered scarred skin around it. "You love me."

"Of course, Mom."

"I want you being happiness." This happened too, especially late at night—her words no longer stayed in orbit with one another and became free planets.

She started to cry; she always did whenever he sat with her long enough. Sometimes he just stroked her back because she seemed to like this. Her emotions came jumpily to the surface, and she would cry and laugh out of any sensible order. Earlier, when Giigee was fruitlessly trying to arouse and suck him into compliance with her mouth, he had decided that the seer was the only other person he knew who truly comprehended that the coldest ice-blue temperature on earth, the absolute zero of loneliness, could be found in the gap between living and dying flesh.

Her hand was cooler than the seer's and sought the heat of his own.

He saw the papers authorizing him to enlist on the coffee table where he'd left them for the last few days. He saw, too, that his mother had scratched her signature on them. *I want you being happiness.* Spittle dribbled out of her mouth, for she had fallen asleep holding his hand, and though her body had shut down and she would lapse in and out of fitful dreams, her fingers, as if unwilling to cooperate, clamped onto his without surrender.

In the morning, he drove to the recruiting station and waited for Sergeant Kenner and others to show up. Usually, there were about five of them, counting himself and the other poolees who did their calisthenics in the parking lot out front, and then headed off in the van to the dirt trails that snaked through the desert, where they tromped past barrel cacti, mesquite trees, and cholla, hoping a rattlesnake, out for a morning sauna on the rocks, wouldn't slither across their paths.

But neither Sergeant Kenner nor Staff Sergeant Hernandez showed up. He stood around with two other poolees, until Wingard called and said he needed a ride to school.

Connor was relieved. He hadn't looked forward to facing Sergeant Kenner after his abysmal experience with Giigee. For all he knew she was telling her father right now, out of some vindictive rage, that he'd raped her. At school, he tried to get her out of his mind and was glad to have the distraction of working with

Wingard—who mercifully didn't bring up the seer—on theater sets for the senior class's production of Othello. Afterwards, he quickly left, before Wingard could catch him and drove back to the recruiting station. He had the signed papers with him and while he still had the nerve he wanted to give them personally to Sergeant Kenner.

A note on the metal front door said the office was closed and would reopen tomorrow. It was handwritten and there was no other explanation.

Connor looked around. Trucks roared past in the undulating heat on their way toward the interstate. His dented Geo parked at the curb looked as if it had been the victim of a can-stomping melee. A woman and her toddler walked by on the sidewalk and glanced at him, the little boy continuing to turn his head and watch Connor until his mother yanked him ahead, as if not wanting her child to stare at the solitary young man waiting under the green-lettered sign that said Marine Corps Recruitment. She pitied him perhaps, or feared for her own child going off to war, or was afraid of Connor or just impatient. He didn't know. He felt he had to deliver these papers to Sergeant Kenner, and if he didn't he'd never do another decent thing with his life or anything that involved sacrifice. It wouldn't have made any sense at all to her, but he was doing this for his mother.

He drove to the Kenners' house. He'd simply run up to the door and hand Sergeant Kenner the papers. If Mrs. Kenner answered, he'd give her the envelope to give to Sergeant Kenner. If Giigee answered . . . he didn't know exactly what he'd do. He'd deal with that scenario when it happened.

But as he turned up the dirt road between the two saguaro cacti marking the entrance to the Kenners' land, he saw smoke, and then he saw the astonishing sight of the Kenners' home in smoldering rubble. A single fire truck stood by hosing down what had just last night been the converted garage where he had attempted to make love to Giigee. No part of the structure remained standing except the brick chimney.

A cop stopped him before he could drive any closer. Connor opened his window. "What's your business up here?" he asked.

"What happened?"

"You can pretty much see what happened, my friend. Maybe you should turn around now. We're not letting anyone up here."

"Was anyone hurt?"

"Everybody got out all right." The cop, whose radio crackled with urgency, studied Connor's battered car. "You have some ID on you?"

Connor gave him his license, and the cop went to his cruiser to check it out. When he returned, he asked, "What's your connection to these folks?" Connor realized the cop thought he might be involved. This is what arsonists did, right, or at least some of them—returned to the scene of their crime so they could admire the magnitude of their destruction.

"I know Sergeant Kenner. I've got some papers for him." He was about to say he'd been here last night, but he suspected this would only cause more alarm. "They're enlistment forms." The cop seemed to soften at this.

"Well, you don't want to bother him now. You better see about giving them to him later."

Then Connor saw Sergeant Kenner himself, a forlorn, hunched-over figure at the back of what had been the master bedroom, poking through the charred ruins of his house with a metal rod. "Can I please just speak to him for a moment?"

The cop, who looked like he wanted to be anywhere but here reeking of smoke, glanced at the pad where he'd written down Connor's name. "You got a phone number where you can be reached?"

Connor gave it to him. Again, he thought to say something else—that his mother was sick and they shouldn't call because it might really upset her if they identified themselves as the police, but this would cause even more suspicion than admitting he was here last night. His brain was reeling though, and he knew he couldn't hold out much longer without spitting out something that would get him in trouble. "Can I please just give Sergeant Kenner these papers?"

"I'll hand them to him."

"I want to give him my sympathies too." And he did: he liked Sergeant Kenner and felt sad for him. He'd been good to Connor in a straightforward sort of way that uncomplicated his life. And unlike Mrs. Kenner and just about everyone else, Sergeant Kenner never treated him as an object of pity.

The cop relented. "Just don't touch anything," he said and waved Connor past. He could see the cop in his rearview mirror keeping an eye on his car.

He parked the lurching Geo at the end of the wide gravel semicircle and walked around the perimeter of the foundation to where Sergeant Kenner was examining the ground like a man in search of a contact lens. He didn't hear Connor approach, and finally Connor cleared his throat and said, "Sergeant Kenner?" The sergeant glanced up in bewilderment, as if trying to place Connor, then gave him a small tired wave and went back to searching the ground. "Sergeant Kenner, I'm very sorry about what happened." Connor cleared his throat again. "I really hate to disturb you at this time, but I have my consent papers for you. They're finally signed."

"That's good, Connor."

"Do you want me to bring them by tomorrow? I was hoping to hand them over to you today. I know it's a bad—"

"We have Jody in a safe place," said Sergeant Kenner, his voice weak with exhaustion. "She's going to get the help she needs."

"Sir?"

"She's under watch now. We should have done something before this."

It dawned on him that Sergeant Kenner was telling him Giigee had started this fire, his crazy daughter who not fifteen feet away from where Connor was presently standing had moaned, with more fury than passion, Fuck me, fuck me. He pictured Giigee dousing Mrs. Kenner's homemade peach curtains and pleated valences with arcs of gasoline and sloshing the very sofa with its highly flammable hunter green slipcover where she'd squirmed in frustration underneath Connor.

"Mrs. Kenner is fine. She's shaken up, of course, but she's fine. She's staying at a hotel downtown near Jody." Sergeant Kenner leaned a moment on the metal pole. He had been in Vietnam and the first Gulf War and had lost part of his shoulder in Iraq, all of which Connor learned from the other Marines who said the sergeant never laid shit on anybody. "You better bring the papers by tomorrow. Sergeant Hernandez will be there then, I'm sure."

"Yes, sir." Connor started to back away.

"Con . . ."

"Sir?"

"Did anything happen last night that I should know about?"

"I . . . I—"

"Was there anything Jody said or mentioned at all that might have led to this? We want to help her. We're on her side. I'm sure you can see that. But she won't talk right now. She won't say a word. They have her on some medication that's keeping her quiet, because, well, she was just screaming her head off and biting people. But I'm looking for a key. You understand that, Con, right? I'm talking to you as a father now. I'm talking to you man to man. I'm asking you as someone who doesn't have a goddamn clue. Is there anything you can tell me about why she's destroyed our lives like this?"

As he was about to answer, hoping to speak with a strength and wisdom beyond his years, he knew his mother had died. He felt it as a touch of her lips. Thrumming with blood, sweet with pleasure, and trembling with wonder—she brushed by.

SEEING
MILES

D AVID stared at Mimi's picture, taken at his bar mitzvah twenty-five years ago. She was his cousin, a second cousin, and she and her family had come out to Milwaukee from Brooklyn for the occasion. He remembered being smitten at the ceremony. She had dark silky hair and large brown eyes flecked with gold. Slender and tall, her face had an oval shape like a prized portrait, and her hair was tucked behind her small, well-articulated ears—carved as if from soap. Her throat had a long white curve, and she sat very still in the second row of the synagogue as he read from the Torah and led the congregation in blessings. At the end of giving his bar mitzvah speech, he'd thanked his parents for being so supportive and then thanked all his relatives and friends for coming. He looked at Mimi and said, "And thank you." It was a bizarre and spontaneous moment for him in a life so far of calm, reasoned, and practiced application. Nevertheless, she just continued to stare unwaveringly at him on the bema. But he was a goner. It was his first experience of painful desire, a fervor that threatened to swallow his flesh. Nor did it hurt that he was just entering puberty, and Mimi, fifteen, was obviously there already.

She had hung back at the reception while he danced the box step with skinny and mostly undeveloped girls from his seventh-grade class, and Mimi's remove and mystery gave her a kind of regal aloofness that only worked him into more of a frenzy. She had declined to dance with him, explaining, "I'm not a good partner. I like to lead."

"That would be fine."

"Thanks, but no."

At one point, he saw her standing alone by the presents and went over to her. "Pick one," he said.

"What?"

"You can have one."

She smiled at him, straight white teeth, free of braces. "You're silly."

"I'm serious." He felt desperate to give her something.

"I can't take your presents."

"Just one."

"You *are* serious."

And then her father, Uncle Irv, had come up and congratulated David on his excellent reading of his haftorah, and that was the end of the exchange. He'd been ready to give up his newly gotten gains to her, the tower of gifts and gelt for becoming a man. My kingdom for your hand. *I'll marry you someday*, he thought.

He'd seen her a couple times afterward, at a wedding and then an anniversary party for her parents where she wore a wool plaid cap, like a cabbie, and baggy corduroy pants, and seemed inappropriately dressed for the occasion. Still, he couldn't deny that every time he saw her the same feelings flared up, though evidently not on Mimi's part. Her eyes, almond shaped and impenetrable as to her own thoughts, remained curiously distant. And soon he lost touch with her.

Now he was driving to the Denver Hyatt. Mimi was coming in from New York for a social workers conference. David himself was a psychologist with a practice in Denver, which would give them something in common after all these years. All that was good. He had brought with him the picture of her at his bar mitzvah. Of course this was twenty-five years later, and she was now a he. Miles. Mimi had been gone for two years.

MILES told him he would be wearing a blue short-sleeve shirt and yellow tie and David had spotted him right away standing beside the fountain. He wouldn't have thought for a moment Miles stood out from any other man, professionally attired and waiting to meet a lunch partner. With his dark cropped hair, he was shorter than David remembered him as Mimi—a taller girl but on the shorter end as a man. Above all he appeared neat. Well groomed, spotless nails, and with a firm handshake in place of a hug.

"My mother has been a lot better about it than my father," Miles said when they sat down at lunch. He had ordered a steak to David's Caesar salad and was taking sturdy bites. "Irv can't really look me in the eye, but Mom asks me how I'm doing. She never says anything specific such as 'How's the hormone treatment going?' or 'Your voice is getting deeper,' but she does remember to call me Miles, which my father won't. He just avoids my name altogether. I think fathers have a harder time giving up their little girls. A mother just accepts her child regardless."

David thought of his own daughter, Leah, twelve, and indeed he did have a problem imagining her transforming herself into Leon. He craved her daughterness.

"You just learn to live with people's reactions—those who knew you when. Actually, I have more confusion with people I meet now. Do I tell them about the before? Or is the before no longer me? Will they feel tricked once they find out? Or worse. I had at least one person in my caseload who learned I'd undergone reassignment. This individual, who was a bit unstable anyway, threatened me."

"What'd you do?"

"I forwarded a copy of the letter, which said some godawful things about making me back into a woman, to the police. I can't say it didn't shake me up. In any case, I have to consider every time how relevant it is to explain about my past. This may be the hardest part of gender reassignment—others."

"I can only imagine," David said. He searched Miles' face, with its thin shadow of hirsute, to see if he had any inkling of what David had once secretly thought about him as a her. He'd been riveted by Mimi, by her elusive sylph beauty, her slender jaw and sinuous lips that reminded him of graceful Arabic script. He could still see a delicate handsomeness in the man now.

"And how about you?" Miles asked him. "Did you bring pictures of your family?"

"I did," said David, and took out the leather folio and showed him photographs of his wife, Rose, and of Leah.

"You have a gorgeous family," Miles said.

"We've been trying to have another child," David told him. He had no idea why he'd admitted this to Miles. They rarely told anyone. After so much time the pursuit no longer felt new or promising. And they were thankful for just having Leah when he knew many couples who weren't even that lucky. Though he knew, too, that Rose felt more frustrated than he. For him, Leah's large and sometimes histrionic personality more than filled the house. She was enough. Just as he had always chosen to believe that he, an only child too, was enough for his parents. But Rose had spoken of the joys of a large family, having four sisters herself, and lately the subject, as she turned thirty-eight like him, had become a line signifying their places on opposite sides of a stubborn marker. More than once he'd indicated he'd like to have a vasectomy and be done with it. "It," of course, was the pressure of making a baby, which had lately morphed into the pressure of performance.

"I'd like to have a family someday," Miles said. "That was the hardest part of my decision. Bye bye to my reproductive organs."

"I can only imagine." David realized he'd uttered these words twice now and must have sounded like a dazed observer at a sideshow. He should have been less unsettled by Miles' bluntness—

what had happened to his professional training after all? He'd worked with gay men and women, even transvestites, though not someone who'd undergone a sex change. Yet he felt a personal reaction to everything that was being said. As if he were channeling the family's regrets.

"I'd be glad to adopt, if I met the right woman. Of course, that's a problem in itself." Miles smiled broadly. "I mean, am I a straight man now who dates heterosexual women, or a man, formerly a woman, who still likes lesbians? And would any of them have me?"

"You had a partner before?"

"Helena." Miles bent his linen napkin into a frown that drooped from his mouth. "End of a five year relationship."

"You must have wanted to do this very badly."

"What you're really asking is do I have any regrets?"

David smiled. "You're a good therapist, I can see."

"I am, more than I get paid for. But to answer your question, well, let me put it this way. I'd look in my closet at the pantyhose I was supposed to put on for corporate America before I became a social worker and it would make my skin crawl. I never felt comfortable in women's clothes or a woman's skin. And frankly, I'd always wanted a penis. Now I have one. Would you like to see it?"

"Pardon?" David said, flushing.

Miles reached out to touch David's hand. "I'm only fooling with you, cousin. Consider it transgender schtick."

BUT was he? After lunch, Miles suggested they go for a swim. The hotel had an indoor lap pool. "I love to swim," Miles informed David. "That's the one sport I used to do competitively. Why don't you join me?"

"I don't have a suit."

"I always bring an extra." They were standing in the atrium of the hotel under the vast open glass panels, surrounded by a mauve forest of sofas, chairs, and wall hangings. "Unless you have to get back right away."

"No," said David, because he didn't want to seem . . . what? Rude? Uptight about swimming with a transsexual? "Sure, let's do it."

They went up to Miles' room, discussing the conference on the way. Miles' presentation tomorrow was part of a panel called "Living with Your (non) Transgender Parents." His own experience with his parents' semi-denial was not atypical, he said. "I can certainly understand," he admitted. "How would you feel about your child becoming a different gender in the middle of her life? For one, you're asking parents to give up any illusions about carrying on the family name in a genetically natural way. It's one thing not to have children; it's quite another to willfully, as in my case, undermine the very capacity to do so. No wonder so few doctors will do the operation. They're asked to perform an irrevocable procedure that is based entirely on a state of mind, something they're supposed to believe in called gender dysphoria, that either removes the sex organs or constructs entirely sterile ones. I mean, I have a respectable penis, thanks to the wonders of phalloplasty, but heaven help it to squirt out a single sperm. I sympathize, I do, with my parents, with the doctors . . . with everyone. Do you want to change in the bathroom?" Miles asked, starting to get undressed. He threw David a suit.

He did. He hadn't prepared himself after all. Not for the forthrightness of Miles' remarks. If anything, he thought he'd have to draw Miles out, as he would a struggling client, a gentle questioning to establish trust. But Miles was a runaway train—I have a respectable penis. Had David ever said anything like this to anyone? And how big was Miles' penis anyway?

In the bathroom, David held up the suit, small, but he could fit into it. At least it wasn't a Speedo.

"You okay in there?" Miles asked.

"Fine," said David.

"Suit fit?"

David pulled at the crotch of the tan nylon trunks. "Just great."

When he opened the door, Miles was standing there in the hotel's white bathrobe cinched tight and with flip flops.

"Not bad," Miles remarked, eyeing David's suit. It was almost as if his cousin had been expecting this moment.

MILES, as he'd hinted, proved to be an excellent swimmer. David watched him glide effortlessly back and forth in the pool, making smooth flip turns at the wall and then shooting forward with submerged musculature into the next lap, silent as an eel. Meanwhile, David stood in the water's deep end supporting himself with his elbows on the ledge. Rose, a strong swimmer herself, had tried to encourage him to go with her to the community pool. He agreed that he needed exercise and too often got stuck in his head, the profession's occupational hazard, and that he should follow his own advice to clients to get out there and stir up some endorphins.

"Want to sit in the hot tub?" Miles called to him from across the pool. They were the only ones in the pool. They'd come down on the elevator and passed through a throng of conferees registering for the conference. David had followed Miles assuming he knew the best way to the fitness center, but now he wondered if there hadn't been a more direct—and private—route. In the popularized argot of the profession, he would have considered his cousin's behavior—the eagerness to change clothes in the openness of the hotel room, the strolling through the lobby, the offer to view his respectable penis—an exhibitory overcompensation for his fears of being insufficiently masculine. The catch was that overcompensation or not, it was making David feel like the lesser man.

"Sure," said David, and boosted himself out of the water. The trunks clung to his thighs. It was odd . . . he almost felt as if he were thirteen again, wearing this small suit, self-conscious about his changing body. Except presently his body was changing against his will—or lack thereof—into a sedentary salute to middle age. Miles, by comparison, showed all the signs of rejuvenation, if not outright youth.

In the hot tub, he got a good look at Miles' chest, which had just a little extra padding, as if filled with a layer of down, but not so much that you'd think *I'm staring at a former woman's chest*. He could see no signs of scars. The nipples appeared a bit asymmetrical and larger than they might (although compared to what? he had to ask himself). In a moment of strange elevator intimacy, David had confessed on the way down to the pool that he'd had a crush on him—on Mimi, that is. He hadn't gone into the extent of it via his hormone-erupting, thirteen-year-old psyche at a religious rite of passage overseen by a God in whom he'd stop believing. Or that he'd mentally unzipped her pink dress and never dreamed he'd have to unzip her skin to find the real person. He'd simply said, "I had a pretty good crush on you as a teenager." And Miles, standing up straight and thoughtful in his terrycloth hotel robe with its Hyatt insignia and his navy blue knee-length swim trunks, as if he were a boxer having a centering moment before he entered the ring, turned to him and said, "Admiration accepted. And returned."

Miles caught him staring and smiled. David quickly turned away, embarrassed by his curiosity and gawking.

"Enjoying yourself?" Miles asked.

"What do you mean?"

"The swimming."

"Oh. I am," said David. He had to keep flattening down his ballooning trunks.

"Is something troubling you?"

"No," he said, though he knew from his own experience with clients that he'd responded too quickly to be credible.

Miles extended one leg—hairy, David noted—and tapped his big toe against David's chest. "Sure?"

"Well, we're struggling a bit right now. Rose and I. But it's nothing serious."

"Want to tell me about it?"

"I think it's about the direction of our lives."

"Sounds like a traffic problem."

David laughed. "In a way. Rose would like another child, as I said."

"Actually you said you both wanted a child. Is that not accurate?"

"She more than I. I think she believes this is the way to move forward. I'm not so sure."

"You've been married, what? Fifteen years?"

"Yes."

"So that's a lot of time together. I envy you. It's an investment worth guarding."

"That it is," said David. And then thought how strange to be talking with his cousin in a hot tub about the intimacy of his marriage, his cousin who had just told him he had a respectable penis, and with whom, ironically, he felt completely honest in a way he rarely enjoyed these days. "I guess we'll just have to see what happens next."

"I couldn't agree more," Miles said. "I'm a poster boy for what comes next. And you want to know something? It's always a work in progress. Somehow the definitiveness of next, despite my certainty of its permanence each time, still eludes me."

They went upstairs to change, and again David used the bathroom, while Miles dressed in the less private confines of the room. David looked at his shriveled penis in the mirror, always to be counted on after swimming, but especially in a tight suit. He stretched the appendage, but it quickly retracted into its accordion mode like the face of a preternaturally wrinkled Chinese Shar-Pei dog.

"All right if I just rinse off in here?" David called through the door.

"Go ahead. I'll do the same after you finish."

He saw Miles' travel kit on the back of the tub once he opened the shower curtain. He knew all about confidentiality. What could be more important in his profession? You went to jail, after all, to protect a client's privacy. Or told yourself you would, if it ever came to that. Yet, he couldn't stop himself from looking in the bag and picking up the prescription bottles. Lexapro, Trazodone, Ativan, Paxil . . . the whole gamut of depression and anxiety treatments. It didn't surprise him. What did was the sudden pang of tenderness he felt for Miles and his vulnerabilities. He could recall when he'd first seen Mimi, and she looked so alone, maybe the loneliest and prettiest girl he had ever seen, a deadly combination for someone like him who was keen on others' wounds and on his way to becoming a psychologist, the seed watered.

"You need anything, just take it out of my toiletry bag," Miles said, and David drew his hand away quickly, as if Miles could see him. "I mean, deodorant or something."

"Thanks."

"Want to shower together?"

"Huh?"

"David, David," said Miles. "Just kidding."

"Oh, yeah," David said. "Transgender schtick. Right."

HE showered and dressed, and after Miles did the same they went down in the elevator. He was already planning what he would say to his parents who'd want to know how the visit with Mimi went, wondering if he would tell them the truth. He still couldn't believe Uncle Irv hadn't told them about Miles. Oh, yes, he could. Repression could be a formidable force. He'd once had a client who, in trying to convey the degree of denial in her family, explained that when she was fifteen she'd had a miscarriage, literally in front of her parents. They'd all been sitting on the sofa in the living room watching TV. Four months pregnant and wearing baggy shirts to conceal what she'd been starting to show, his client, faint and weak, had gushed out a bloody clot. She'd run to the bathroom, but there was no mistaking what happened— the back of her shorts soaked, the blood right in front of her mother and father. They'd said nothing. She'd quietly cleaned up "the mess," and that was the last ever spoken about it.

So it was no wonder Miles was still invisible and Mimi would live on in the family memory until the generation died out. David still had the sense that he was on a mission, a counteragent to the family secrecy. And Miles seemed grateful. He'd thanked him profusely for taking the time to meet.

"Of course," said David. "I want to keep in touch."

Miles tilted his head. "I'd like that."

WHEN he got home, the lights were off inside. Rose had left him a note that Leah was at a sleepover and that she herself had gone upstairs to think—code for napping. His wife adored naps. Whereas such naps led to insomnia for him, Rose could wake up from a luxurious repose, stretch happily, murmur indolently, and be asleep four hours later without interference. Disturb me, the note said.

He went into the bedroom. The sound machine whirred away. They'd gotten hooked on white noise, operant conditioning: as soon as the machine went on, they both became sleepy and reported to their dream quarters. It all seemed like such normalcy now after seeing Miles.

He lay down and curled up against her, and she pushed back into him. He felt the warmth of her buttocks through the thin fabric of her nightgown. He pressed his lips to the soft nape of her neck and then kissed her shoulder, biting her lightly until she said "Mmm." Then she turned around and faced him. "What was it like?"

"Different."

"Your father called. He wanted to know how it was seeing Mimi. If she's married yet or has, as he put it, a beau. He doesn't have a clue, does he?"

"No," said David, "and I'm not sure I'm going to tell him. If Miles' own father wants to keep it a secret, why should I say anything to my parents? It's unlikely they'll ever see Miles again, and everyone will go to their graves—this older generation—content with the perceived status quo."

"What's he look like? Like the photograph still?" He had shown her the picture of Mimi at fifteen and explained his adolescent crush. She'd had similar sentiments for one of her boy cousins, but nothing had happened there either . . . well, nothing, except a game of strip poker. Rose won, cousin lost, end of story. As much as she remembered at least. It was her first sight, given her family of four sisters, of a penis, which had a dampening effect on her crush: her cousin's angelic face came with one of *those?*

"I can still see her in him." He thought of the way Miles canted his head as they were saying goodbye—much the way Mimi had looked at him when he was thirteen and sent his heart then, and another organ, soaring, as if she wanted to study David from a cockeyed angle and to look pretty while doing it.

"You smell like chlorine."

"We went swimming. I guess I didn't get it all out of my hair."

"You went swimming? With Miles?"

"And I showered in his room afterward."

"Oh, my." She was unbuckling his belt as she said this, her hand slipping under the band of his underwear. He remembered standing in front of Miles' bathroom mirror, examining himself and his manhood, trying to decipher what it meant that Mimi had once been the object of his earliest masturbatory fantasies when he was thirteen. And those weren't the only ones. In the related category of his rescue fantasies, he'd saved her from burning buildings, muggings, sexual maraudings, and, ironically, considering Miles' prowess as a swimmer, drowning. Her eternal gratitude was his dying reward. Breathless, sacrificing himself, he'd come. Le Petit Mort, as the French called orgasm, so willing with their philosophical fatalism to commingle sex and death at any opportunity.

Had he always wanted to save people?

"Ohh," Rose cried.

"You all right?"

"Yes, yes, go . . . don't stop." He'd thrust into her hard, skipping their usual foreplay, bunching her nightgown up around her neck, and with his fingers splayed across her chest, pinning her down. Her cries echoed through the empty house. So rarely did they have it all to themselves. He heard his own moans, too, reverberating in his throat, his breath coming faster, his desire swift, heedless and unstoppable, and then Rose slapped him across the face, the resounding bite of her hand stinging his flesh, and he came instantly.

He rolled off her. They lay there next to each other, spent and looking up at the ceiling. He was reluctant to speak, and Rose's breathing filled the silence. Finally, he asked, "Why'd you do that?"

"You . . ."

"What?"

"You said his name."

She had never slapped him during sex or any other time. It was so unlike her. So unrestrained. He'd burst forth at the touch, but now he couldn't tell if the slap had been simultaneous or if his coming had preceded it. "I think you imagined that," David said. "Just because we'd been talking about him."

"I didn't. You called his name. It bothered me."

"I wasn't thinking about him." Or was he? Was he thinking that he hadn't told Rose about Miles' bragging about his new penis or about the sudden kiss on David's cheek that took him completely by surprise as they were saying goodbye and how he couldn't get over how soft it was, Mimi's kiss, as if Miles purposely had turned himself into her for a moment just to confuse him.

David propped himself up on one elbow and looked at Rose, her flushed face and chest, her still erect nipples, her eyes a green bemused cloud. "Well, whether I did or not, I'm sorry."

"Me too. Did I hurt you?"

"No. I was just . . . surprised."

She kissed the tips of her fingers and touched them to his cheek. "I wanted your attention. On me."

The phone rang. He got up to answer it because it might be Leah. One day, when she was older, he wouldn't feel the need to jump for the phone every time, but now he imagined terrible scenarios in the span of milliseconds. It was a hang up, a Denver number on the caller ID, and he wondered for a moment if it might be Miles.

When he came back to bed, Rose was lying on her back with her knees pressed against her chest. The doctor had told them this position didn't help. If she was going to get pregnant, if they were going to have another child after trying all these years, the little fellas would swim up in her regardless and do their job, the doctor said. But Rose did it out of habit or superstition and David allowed her the practice without comment. "Wouldn't it be ironic," Rose said now, speaking into her knees, "if after seeing Miles, it finally did happen?"

David lay down beside her and placed his hand on her flat belly after she unfurled herself. He felt the warmth there, felt something stirring, felt, he was sure, a magnificent and mysterious transformation taking place. And he felt, too, Miles' faint lips against his cheek, the same cheek that Rose had slapped, as if to startle a new life into being, neither him nor her but faceless creation.

GALISTEO
STREET

"I HAVE a granddaughter," Ben told his wife. He waited a
moment for the shock to set in. A twitching smile appeared
on Sunny's face, then disappeared completely when she saw he
wasn't kidding.

"You'll excuse me if I faint now," Sunny said.

"You go first."

She went over to the front window of their house. Outside
it was raining; it had been for seventeen straight days. This was
Oregon after all, and though he was used to it by now—twenty-
three years teaching writing at the college—he would every so
often want to run amuck into the streets and scream, Turn it off!
Turn it off, for God's sake!

"Who told you?" Sunny asked. "Did she call?"

Ben shook his head. "Of course not. Lydia would never call.
I heard through Tom. I think we should go down there and see
the baby."

Sunny turned to face him. Her hair was turning gray, as gray
as the rain outside; she'd stopped coloring it. They would both
be fifty-five next month. "You're going to get hurt over this."

"I'm no stranger to rejection," he said, and laughed grimly.
It had been ten years since his last book. The gap between suc-

cess and being forgotten had widened with thoroughbred speed and people had stopped asking about a new book.

Sunny sat down on the seat of their bay window that looked out toward the river. He bicycled to class every day along the path. He'd started teaching half-time last year—transitional retirement —and had filled his days with reading, chopping wood, and yoga classes, trying to be a good and contented man. It was the slow and considered life, mundanely consecrated, finding his way by small ordinary means—building a rock wall out back, tending his tomato plants—to letting go of the very thing that had driven him for years, his writing and all its manic glory (or failure). The cycle of exhilaration and despair, of inflation and deflation, of ambition and resignation was over. What he thought he could never give up had been let go with more ease than he imagined possible. He would die neither defeated nor miserable, just with his wings voluntarily clipped. He and Sunny never spoke about it anymore, like an old affair that had long ago been settled.

"So will you come with me?"

"We're just supposed to show up?" Sunny asked.

"I'm sending her a letter by way of Tom. He said he'd help. He'll talk to her." Ben sat down next to her on the window seat. He'd been standing for hours, it seemed, waiting for her to come through the door from her job at the library so he could tell her. She was retiring next year after twenty-five years of service, and they planned to travel more, visit their just-married son, Jonathan, and his wife in Seattle. And see their daughter, Allison, at Oberlin College where she was a junior studying music, always busy busy busy. They'd go to Greece, some place he'd never been, and Africa. Travel could fill so many empty holes.

"I just wonder if you're trying to get something from her."

"Like a visit to my flesh and blood?" And as soon as he said it he knew it was the wrong choice of words. He could see Sunny wince. A sensitive point as it always had been—this aspect of his life set in motion before they'd met, his having a child at twenty-three. "I wouldn't write about any of this, if that's what you're thinking."

"It never crossed my mind," Sunny said. "Unfortunately."

He'd written a memoir about his year-long affair with Marilyn, the only child of a famous writer. He'd published it just before she died of kidney failure from years of drinking and not taking care of herself, and one reviewer had gone so far as to say Ben Klein with his "kiss and tell bore of a long-faded adventure" (he memorized the line, of course) had helped push her into her grave.

"I'm not writing anymore, period," he told Sunny and pain crossed her face, that terrible sadness she felt for him at the death of his work. Unlike him, she hadn't forgotten what it once meant to him.

He'd never been in a place like Santa Fe with such crisp colors, the utterly luminous blue above, the iron-drenched red rock, the soft adobe facades like brushed hides and the crumbling and darker mud of the original dwellings. His first night in Santa Fe, when he'd come west after graduating from Swarthmore College in 1973, never having been farther than Ohio and wanting the experience of travel, he'd been stunned by the dense bright clusters of stars, as if thousands more had suddenly crowded in like visitors to the same hazy firmament he'd grown up with back East. He understood why artists came from all over the world to live here, the crystalline light that sharpened every piece of matter as if it were cut out with a razor blade, and why D. H. Lawrence had written, "the moment I saw the brilliant, proud morning shine high up over the deserts of Santa Fe, something stood still in my soul, and I started to attend." He too had wanted to attend. Unattached and unencumbered by debt, with a degree in literature but no specialized skills, he decided he would stay and write here. To support himself he found a job as a waiter at a hotel, where he met Marilyn who was working in the pantry. One evening they went out and talked until three in the morning—she too wanted to be a writer, though she had her famous father to live up to, who refused to acknowledge her as his daughter. A week later she and Ben moved in together to a house on Galisteo Street, and a year afterward Lydia was born.

The adoption had taken place in Albuquerque through a placement agency that Marilyn had gone to without his knowledge. Indeed Ben had wanted her to have an abortion, she refused, and that was the end of their relationship. Marilyn had recognized she couldn't be a steady or responsible mother, the reason she'd given Lydia up to a stable middle class couple from Santa Fe. Still, she had hoped to be part of Lydia's life, and the open adoption had been arranged with the provision that Marilyn would be able to see her child whenever she wished, within reason. There was no such provision for Ben, and that was not anyone's fault besides his. He signed away all rights, afraid of the responsibility, wary of Marilyn's reckless ways, and encouraged by his parents who said it would tie him down for the rest of his life.

Lydia had been only eleven when her adoptive mother, Janice, had brought her to meet Ben, after his persistent requests, at the La Fonda Hotel in 1985. It was the first time he'd seen his daughter. She had Marilyn's searing blue eyes (like her famous novelist father) and her full lips. Janice sat close to her in La Fonda's dining room but kept her face from betraying any emotion or judgment.

He asked Lydia about school. She went to a small private one and was an A student. She liked to dance, ride horses, ski, and play her flute. She'd traveled to London last summer with her mother and father and wanted to visit every country in Europe some day. As far as Ben could tell she was a well-adjusted child and thought of him as just another concerned adult party. She called him Mr. Klein until he asked her to call him Ben, and she referred once to Marilyn by name, when she bluntly said, "You and Marilyn lived here years ago. My mother always points out the house on Galisteo. That's where you had me, right?"

The question surprised him, asking about her birth. Janice sat with a rigid forbearance, as if she knew the issue would arise.

"Yes," he told her, "we lived together on Galisteo Street and that's where we had you."

But what caught him completely off guard was what she asked next. "Did you love each other?"

He glanced at Janice for help, who, with her blonde hair pinned up, her thin, plain mouth and small even white teeth, looked nothing like her smooth, olive-skinned, adopted daughter. Janice remained impassive. He was on his own. The aggressive expectancy, the determination in Lydia's surging blue eyes, told him he'd better answer honestly.

"We were good to each other."

"I need to finish my homework," she told Janice abruptly, and then they left, with no promise or mention of a further meeting. She had not sought his love or approval, nor tried to get him into her life; neither had she wished to forgive or condemn him —not publicly at least. She'd not done any of the things his therapist had suggested might happen, including sulk, preen, feign indifference, or act out her anger. She'd only wanted to know what kind of a man he was, and he'd failed the one-question test: he was not capable of love, not for her birth mother at least, and by extrapolation for her, or anyone perhaps.

"You could just knock on her door," Tom said. They were sitting on the patio of their cottage. The branches of a locust tree shaded them from the clear blue sky. They were staying at a bed and breakfast on Don Gaspar. Coincidentally, or not, it was the block directly east of Galisteo Street where he'd lived with Marilyn.

Sunny had made the reservation, though Ben knew the place was literally a stone's throw from his old house. On their last trip to Santa Fe, nineteen years ago, the first and only time he'd met Lydia, he'd taken Sunny by to show her where he used to live.

"I haven't given up trying," Tom went on. "I'll tell her where you're staying, and hope she'll call. Like I said, you could just show up, but she could do anything from let you in to—"

"Call the police?" said Sunny. She'd been listening carefully to Tom, not interrupting as Ben had when Tom listed the three reasons why Lydia didn't want to see him: he'd never been a part of her life; she was physically and emotionally drained from having the baby (a difficult birth); and she had never forgiven Ben for writing the book about Marilyn, just to make a buck, in her opinion.

"What if I called her?" Sunny said.

It wasn't what Ben expected her to say. "You'd do that?"

"I just wonder if it would help."

Tom shrugged. "It's worth a try." Years ago, Ben had gotten to know Tom after he wrote a positive review—one of the few —about Ben's memoir of his time spent with Lydia's mother, Marilyn. Now Tom's book on Marilyn's father would finally be out next year. And although there was a section about Marilyn on the two times she'd met her famous father, and a smaller section about Lydia, and an even briefer mention of Ben, Tom had had the foresight to show Lydia the manuscript beforehand and get her reaction, something Ben, of course, hadn't done for his own book (not to mention Lydia, eighteen then, had wanted no contact with him). In any case, it had been his story, not Marilyn's, and not her famous father's. That's what the critics never understood—you didn't have a choice. You had this little acre to work with all your life, great or not, Faulkner or one-book wonders like Ellison, and you kept plowing the hell out of it for all it was worth.

"This is a nice place," Tom said, looking at the French doors off the patio to the master bedroom. "I never even knew it was tucked in here. They've converted a number of these older homes to B&Bs. What else do you plan to do here?"

"Shop," said Sunny. "In a word."

Tom laughed. "No end to that in this town, of course. You were here, what, twenty years ago?"

"Nineteen," Ben said.

"Lots of changes. You won't believe all the galleries on Canyon Road now. It's wall to wall."

"When I lived here with . . ."—he had started to say "with Marilyn," then caught himself—"when I first lived here there were just some good Mexican restaurants on the Plaza, and I think the Woolworth's was the biggest merchant then. Now it's all international boutiques and upscale restaurants catering to tourists like us. I think I rented our place on Galisteo for a hundred fifty a month." *Our place.*

Tom nodded. He was tanned, his face lined with dignified creases, Birkenstocks on his feet, and wearing a billowy white shirt on this pleasant April afternoon. Ben took another sip of beer. He could hear the fountain in the courtyard, and finches flitted above the adobe wall of the patio. Tom, who had a partner, Michael, had settled here years ago and befriended Lydia. She'd wanted to make sure he wasn't going to use her to sell books (like Ben?). She'd had no interest in profiting personally from her grandfather's popularity that grew even more after he died, or having people make pilgrimages to her house to pay cultish homage. She cared nothing for fame and felt no connection to the kind of life on the road her grandfather or her biological mother had lived.

"We should move inside," Sunny said. "Too much sun—not that I don't love it. But it's a shock to my soggy Oregon skin."

"And I should be going," Tom said, and stretched his arms above his head, flexing his fingers. "Love this spring weather.

How's the writing coming, by the way? You have a new book coming out?"

He hadn't seen Tom in years and had only talked with him on the phone, and briefly at that, about making arrangements to see Lydia. "I've given it up."

"Oh, right," Tom said, and laughed. "That's what we all say."

"No, really. I'm fine about it."

Sunny stood up and went inside. She couldn't witness the confession, no matter how sanguine he sounded about it.

"Good God, man, you're only what . . . fifty?"

"Fifty-five."

"Loads of time left," said Tom, lighthearted. "You're just in a fallow period. Have you been writing anything?"

"I wrote two novels, both of them shelved—by mutual agreement between me and thirty-five publishers."

"Oh, you're just having a little pity party. Get back on the horse, my friend, and ride ahead. We all fall off."

"Tom . . . I appreciate the encouragement but I'm really okay about it. Nobody will miss me, and more important, I won't miss it myself."

"Bull," said Tom. "I know you don't believe that for a minute."

"Why don't I?"

"Because it's your blood and breath."

Ben laughed. "Is it really so noble as all that? I just stepped to the side, out of the way, and I'm not that terribly lost without working, as I once feared I would be."

"You know who you sound like?" said Tom, standing up and clapping Ben's shoulder. "Like someone who's been brainwashed in a cult. All placidly composed and happy giving away your entire estate and first born."

"I still have my very modest estate, and I certainly have my first born," and there was a thump in the air, his unintended allusion to his "other" first born, Lydia.

"You're lying to yourself, but if this is what you have to do to wipe the slate clean and write for yourself again, fine. You got blasted up pretty well over the memoir, but that was what . . . ten, twelve years ago now? Time to come back from that. Get yourself a website like the rest of us, put up some good reviews, excerpts from your books, a flatteringly outdated photo—be the trillionth person to start a blog. We're all whores for publicity now anyway. Might as well accept it."

"I'm keeping myself pure, thank you."

"Fat chance. Let's get together again before you leave."

After Tom left, Ben came into the cottage's small kitchen where Sunny was making herself a cup of coffee. "Why does everyone consider it such a threat because I gave up writing? It's not as if I'm asking them to stop, too."

"Maybe because it bothers them that you did. Because they believe in you."

"Believed. Let's go out to dinner tonight," he said, wanting to change the subject.

HE and Marilyn had only lived together for eight months, not the year's time over which the memoir took place, and Marilyn's theft from the hotel had been played up a bit in the book—she'd returned the money the next day on her own and it wasn't the big blowout argument between them that it was in the memoir— and he'd exaggerated his own involvement in their visit to her father in Virginia where the literary legend lived misanthropically with his mother. Her father, inebriated, gave her the original manuscript of one of his novels and advised her to sell it for all it was worth (which, despite her often desperate financial circumstances, she did not, donating it to a library archive). Ben, not wanting to intrude on one of the only two visits during her lifetime she would have with her father, waited in the car. Nor— his most egregious stretching—had he engaged in a midnight conversation with her father in front of the fireplace, talking writing, both of them drinking straight Scotch. In fact, Ben never met the man face to face, as he claimed in his memoir. Marilyn's time with him had been brief and bittersweet; Ben had kept the engine running, so to speak, and he and Marilyn slept in a run-down motel twenty miles away.

So yes, he'd embellished or enhanced or whatever was the prevailing term for the liberties that writers took to make a good story from the limitations of their factual lives. You could call it lying, but he hadn't done anything different from the scores of other authors who wrote about events they'd never personally witnessed, purporting to remember what so and so wore or the precise exchanges of dialogue. And even if you worked from old notes, as he had in part—he'd kept a journal back then—you still paid the price: Your subjects were never pleased, no matter how accurate a picture you presented. Close as it might come to representing their lives, it was still not the flattering photograph they would have chosen to display on their mantels.

Before the memoir, he'd published four books, one of which had been a finalist for a major award that had sent him to New York for a ceremony at an opulent hotel. Wearing a tux, he'd sat at his publisher's table. When his name wasn't called, as it was not expected to be, given the massive opus of the best-selling literary novelist as competition (his own book was a slim though penetrating volume about a holocaust survivor and his son), he received consoling pats on the back, reassuring handshakes, buttressing comments about what an honor it was to be even a finalist for such a prestigious prize—the literary Oscars! He knew, however, even as he was enjoying the flattery that this was to be his only chance.

All the congratulatory phone calls, letters, and even telegrams (this was before e-mail) precipitously dropped off. His editor, who had been calling him twice a day, did not phone anymore. Ben had once heard a poet at a cocktail party, drunk, envious, and believing himself to be overlooked, say to a more successful visiting writer, "Are you still shitting out those little poems of yours?" That's what haunted him as he tried to write after his brush with fame: the constipated little sentences that squeezed out of him—little turds of strained despair. It was then that he'd had the idea to write the memoir.

Later, once the memoir was published and critically slammed, though it sold more than any of his other books, the prurient interest trumping any moral castigation, he wrote two novels, what he thought to be some of his best work. He was stunned that his agent couldn't sell them. Perhaps he'd shot himself in the foot as far as his reputation went as a fiction writer by doing the memoir. His editor even suggested he write a sequel to the memoir, despite the trouble it had caused Ben. Numbers were numbers, the editor said.

Of course it was possible that the two unpublished novels, despite the respectful brush-offs from editors, were just bad. For a while, his agent tried to place them with university presses and when that didn't pan out—their refusals had been couched in academic language stating that "the work was not in line with the Press's mission"—she'd turned to small independent publishers who declined them too. "Not experimental enough for us," they wrote, or they were looking for material "with more of an international flavor."

One day his agent sent him a fax. She was interested in "developing emerging writers" now, and although she knew it would be a blow to him, and she admittedly didn't have the guts to tell him over the phone, especially given that his latest efforts had come to naught, she thought it best to be candid. Emerging writers. Those hot, young virgins with their sexy purring prose that passed as edgy literary work.

"Frankly," the agent's fax had continued (growing more apologetic by the line, expiating her guilt over their twenty-five years of working together), she could only sell genre work or multicultural writing or first novelists, the "emerging writers." Cookbooks were still good also. "I'm so sorry, Ben," she wrote in the faint fax he could barely read. "Please, if there's anything I can do, let me know." And that had been the end for him. He hadn't written another word, despite all his advice to students to the contrary that you should never let anyone have power over your writing but yourself.

THEY ate dinner at the Palace Restaurant. It was one of the few places still familiar to him, and he enjoyed its excessive extravagance of red leather booths and white table cloths, a former brothel in the 1800s preserved in the decor, everything, including the portions, a bit overstuffed. The leisurely meal took them almost two hours, with coffee and dessert, and then Sunny suggested they take a walk. They stopped at a bar in what had been the warehouse district on the other side of the tracks, along Guadalupe Street, now a bustling after-hours area. They ordered margaritas and Sunny said, "Maybe we should just let it be."

"I have to see her. I can't leave without trying."

"Are you making a point about responsibility? It's thirty years late for that and just as many unnecessary. You signed an agreement, all parties concurred, you moved on with your life and so did others, happily I presume."

"Not Marilyn."

"Marilyn was fated to wander the earth in the deep shadows of her father's footsteps, and get lost there. This did not happen to Lydia. She had a regular life, with loving parents, and she benefited from their mature guidance, which you and Marilyn could never have provided."

"I have to see her," Ben said.

"God, you're a stubborn ass."

"I thought you always loved that about me."

"When it's made good use of." He knew she was talking about his determination as a writer. Try as he might to ignore the remark, his face must have shown otherwise.

85

"All right, all right, I'll call her in the morning," Sunny said. "I told you I would."

"I owe you."

"You always owe me. Just don't forget you have your own grown children who don't make you grovel for their love and acceptance. You've said barely a word about them, by the way, and every time I bring up their names you change the subject back to you-know-who."

She wore the silver and turquoise drop earrings she'd bought under the portal of the Palace of the Governors where the Indians sold their jewelry. She had a constant stiff neck from a herniated disk; she refused to have the recommended operation, her stoic New England background, and perhaps a good dose of fear that she'd be worse off. They'd been married twenty-seven years and only once had the marriage almost ended, when he'd retreated so far into himself and so hostilely batted anyone away, that she had moved out for a while. He had blamed it on the writing, and she had blamed it on their stuck marriage—it was time to get serious again about each other or get on with new lives.

"Ben Klein?" He looked up. A young man, bearded and wearing a baseball cap, was smiling at him, hand extended. "It's Gavin. Gavin Mitchum."

"Gavin . . ." The name and face suddenly came into focus— though he hadn't had a beard then. He'd worked with Gavin at a literary conference, years ago, when Ben was still being invited to such things. Gavin had been a waiter at the conference, in exchange for room and board, and he'd been in Ben's workshop.

Ben stood up and Gavin gave him a bear hug. "What are you doing down here, man?"

"We're visiting," Ben said, and left it at that. "This is my wife Sunny."

"Nice to meet you," Gavin said. He was bursting with smiles, a little lit, Ben could see.

"How many years has it been?" Ben asked.

"A decade, take or give five years. I was a little *larger* back then. You remember what a big guy I was?" He did remember. Gavin had been so obese he had to sit sideways in one of those student desk chairs. "Lost a hundred and fifty pounds."

"Good for you. And you live here now?"

"Nah, I'm doing a conference."

"You're attending a conference?"

"I'm teaching at it," Gavin said. "Yeah, we got a writer's conference going on here, screenwriting, fiction—poets behind every potted plant. That's what I thought you were here for, came in late or something."

"I didn't know anything about it. Are you . . . faculty?"

"Fiction."

"Fiction?"

"My novel's coming out next year."

"That's wonderful," Ben said.

"No big deal. Well, it's sort of a big deal. I mean"—he tilted his can of Fosters back and took a large gulp—"they're paying me a bundle. Those fools."

"Congratulations," Ben said. "Who's publishing it?"

"Knopf. It's their lead book in the spring catalogue."

Sunny put her hand on Ben's knee under the table and gave it a squeeze. "I'm happy for you," Ben said.

"Well, I owe you *big* time. You set me on the right track. You told me it didn't matter what anybody thought, if you had it right in your head, go for it."

Ben smiled.

"And how about you? What are you working on now?"

"I'm not."

"C'mon, don't give me that. You just don't want to share." Gavin put his hands flat on the table. He had a jean jacket over a sky-blue plaid shirt, a pack of cigarettes in the snap pocket. "Hey,

I don't like to talk about what's cooking either or it goes cold on me. Totally understand. I read your last book, by the way. That piece you did about his daughter . . . Moi and Marilyn?"

"It was *Marilyn and Me*," Ben said tensely. "It was the publisher's decision. I had nothing to do with the title and thought it was terrible."

"Wanted to play on the Marilyn Monroe thing, right? Can't blame these guys. They're investing half a million in me. You know I had to go for media training. Can you believe it? They want to see how I'm going to do on television. So I was at my publisher's in New York and I'm waiting to see my editor and out comes, you won't believe this, out walks *Snoop Dogg*. I'm like, are you kidding me? What's Snoop Dogg doing here? And my editor says, 'Oh, he just went through media training with us for his book.' Can you fucking believe that?" Gavin said, practically shouting, his face blazing. "*Snoop Dogg doing media training.*" He crushed the empty Fosters can in one hand.

"You've got cheese in your beard," Sunny said.

"What?"

"I said you have food on your face."

"Hey," said Gavin, wiping at his chin, "you two enjoy yourselves here. We're cool, right, my man?" and his fist went flush against Ben's cheek, just like Ali used to do to Howard Cosell.

TOM was right—the galleries along Canyon Road had increased exponentially. Ben stopped at one with a Russian artist's work that had appealed to him from the painting in the window, an abstract landscape with fiery shapes. The price: twenty thousand dollars. The gallery assistant told him there would be a biographical volume out about the painter soon. She put together a folder for Ben, with an eight-by-ten color print of the painting, background material on the artist, and her card stapled to the inside cover—it was as thick as a college application. All he'd done was ask about the painting.

He felt the sun on his face at the top of Canyon Road where it met Alameda and he stood a moment and looked at the river flow by before proceeding to Apodaca Hill. Sunny had called Lydia's house, but there was no answer, and Ben, hovering next to her, had whispered to hang up when the answering machine went on. Then he made her try again fifteen minutes later. "Why don't I leave a message?" Sunny had said. "That's the polite thing to do." "She won't call back." "Then we'll call again."

So she'd left a message, explaining she and Ben were in Santa Fe and would like to speak with her. Could she call them at their bed and breakfast? And Ben had waited by the phone until Sunny finally declared the day practically lost and went out. He could obsess, she told him, but it would do him much better to get some fresh air with her, buy a newspaper and have a coffee. "I'm just going to wait," he said, sounding churlish even to himself.

"I have my cell phone. Don't do anything foolish without me," she warned.

But she must have known as soon as she left he would walk up this way, to Lydia's house on Apodaca Hill. Gavin's gloating had not affected him as much as it had her. "What an arrogant lout," she said last night after they went back to their cottage, not mincing words as usual. Ben had shrugged. "You can be angry, you know," Sunny said. "You don't have to act unaffected for me."

"I'd rather just fuck, if that's okay," and that's what they'd done, rapaciously, the French doors open and the cool air blowing across his back, the months of sodden Oregon weather drying up inside him as he thrust into her, possessed by his youth here long ago.

"My Lord," Sunny said, her fingernails lightly scratching the small of his back afterward, as if tickling out the last of his vital fluids. "I think you might have untied my tubes with that one."

A baby reference.

All such allusions, intended or not, led him to making his inexorable way to Lydia's house on Apodaca Hill. He'd memorized the address as soon as Tom had pointed out the listing under her husband's name in the phone book ("You didn't get the information from me," Tom had said).

Two dogs came down the road, their tails wagging. The houses stretched back and dotted the once empty foothills. Lydia's house was in the next block, and when he stopped in front of it, a one-story place with a fenced front yard, he petted the two dogs that had escorted him up to her fence. They were both black labs, probably from the same litter, and he realized they were Lydia's, waiting patiently for him to go through the side gate that had been left open.

The front porch had a bicycle out front and a milk box, and someone had recently started digging four holes on the north side—a swing set? The baby was too young for swings. Maybe Lydia's husband had a child from a previous marriage. Ben didn't know. He hadn't wanted to pepper Tom with too many questions. He was already on shaky ground here, and now he was walking up to the door. Did this make him a stalker of his own daughter? A stalker perhaps, though not of a daughter. She'd never considered him her father and had every right to question his urgency to see her now.

The door itself had a tiny grated window, the kind you might see at an old inn. He knocked lightly. He stood with his shoulders back, prepared for the little square window to open. The dogs, who'd loped in the yard after him, waited by his heels to be admitted too. He rang the bell. There was no answer.

THE weather suddenly turned cold on his way back. Before he reached Paseo de Peralta and made the turn onto Don Gaspar, snowflakes had started to come down. Seventy degrees just an hour ago, the climate had changed with the swift capriciousness of spring that occurred at seven thousand feet. Sweaty and yet shivering from the cold, he opened the door to discover Sunny sitting on the couch in the front room, and next to her—he knew her immediately from looking at his own flat nose and dark eyebrows—were Lydia and her baby. He could see she had come unprepared for the weather too, wearing a cream-colored thin blouse and tan slacks. Sunny had brought out the extra blanket from their room and they'd swaddled the baby, who slept peacefully in Lydia's arms. Her name was Samara, Tom had said.

"Hello," Lydia greeted him, and her voice was so much fuller now than when he'd met her as an eleven year old. Her hair was shoulder length, straight and highlighted with reddish gold like Marilyn's had been, not his own spongy curls that his daughter, Allie, would pat her hand against, saying over and over, *boing boing boing*, practically her first word. Sunny sat close to her, her knees tilted in, their shoulders angled toward each other like mothers did when there was a baby between them, and he stood and waited to be invited past the invisible boundary that marked his remove.

"I thought I'd stop by," Lydia said, "and show you Sam." So they were calling her Sam; he liked boys' names for girls; it made them strong, he thought, showed the world you couldn't mess with them, and let them be girls too. Sammy, her friends would call her, and he pictured a whole life for the child, this beautiful little girl with her shock of brown hair like a thatch of topside roots.

"Ben," Sunny said, in a prompt for normalcy on his part, "why don't you keep these two company while I get the tea I made." She stood up and Ben sat down near, but not in, her place.

"I'm so glad you came," Ben said.

Lydia nodded. "I thought it was time."

A long silent moment passed while they both looked at the baby. He was so afraid to say anything wrong, though words flew through his head: *regret, allow, intend, intrude,* and whole phrases: *can promise you, start from scratch, from hereon . . .*

"I really can't stay long. I just wanted to say hello while you were here."

"Thank you," Ben said, and tried to keep the desperate gratitude out of his voice. "I just came from your house."

"You did?"

"I was afraid I wouldn't get to see you."

"I'm sorry. I haven't been very . . . receptive. I really don't have any bad feelings. It was just, you know, messy to get involved, and I didn't want to hurt anyone, my parents in particular. They already had Marilyn to contend with, who would stop by without warning and be all strung out and expect them to take her in until she got back on her feet, which they always did, bless their hearts. She made them feel like they had to because of me. One troubled parent, much as I loved her, was enough to deal with."

"I never wanted to make trouble. I don't now."

"Oh, I know," Lydia said, "but still . . . I guess I'm just a very private person."

"Yes," Ben said, "and I would never—"

"So though I understand our connection and how important it might be for some people—"

"For some people?"

"I think it would be better if we don't have any further contact. I wanted to tell you that in person. I don't want you thinking I'm angry at you, or that I hold some kind of grudge. You didn't do anything wrong. You and Marilyn were young and you had a decision to make, and maybe if I'd been neglected in any way it would be different. But I had everything, and it just gets, well, messy, like I said. My husband has a big family and I have cousins and we're all sort of set, if you know what I mean."

"Set," he said, and thought of a table with all the places reserved and shiny with silver. He saw she was wearing a gold cross. He was Jewish, nominally at least, a little detail of how separate they really were. "What are you afraid of, Lydia?" he asked, and saw her eyes blink rapidly, her brow knit with precisely the same pattern of creases as his own. "I won't be a burden. I only want to know you." He longed to reach for her hands, but her fingers, thinly sculpted, another cubist piece of Marilyn thrust crazily before his eyes, were wrapped tightly around Sam.

"What if I don't want to be known?"

"Won't you give me a chance? Our knowing each other is important, don't you think? Even for practical purposes."

"Is there some medical background I need to know about?"

"No, no, I just mean I can be helpful."

"I'm grown now, Ben," she said, and hearing his first name from her jolted him, the casual aplomb in her voice, the indulgence.

He touched her wrist gently. "I shouldn't push. You probably want time to think about all this."

She smiled wanly.

Sunny came back with two cups of tea. She'd been delaying as long as possible, Ben knew, and had made her entrance when she heard the rising plea in his voice, her cue to calm him or to keep him from begging, though he felt beyond humiliation.

"This will warm you up," Sunny said. "We don't seem to have honey or sugar, I'm sorry to say."

"Actually, I think I'd better be going," Lydia said. "The snow and all. I want to get home before it gets too thick on our hill. Once it does, we have to park at the bottom and walk up and that's no fun with this little bundle." She looked down and stroked the baby's head. "I'm sorry," she told Ben.

"You don't owe me an apology."

"Nor you me."

He nodded, his throat thick with words that would die there. Lydia stood up, and Sunny took the blanket. "She's so beautiful," Sunny said.

"She has your nose, I can see," Lydia told Ben. "I can send you pictures."

"Please," Ben said. "That would be wonderful."

"Here," Sunny offered, "wrap her in this for the ride home," and she gave Lydia her soft blue sweater.

"The car warms up fast. We'll be fine."

"Do you want me to get it started?" Ben asked.

"We're okay." There was nothing she'd take or let either of them do for her. She was fiercely independent, he could see, like Marilyn, though not self-destructively so.

"I was wondering," Ben asked, "if I could just hold her before you go?"

Lydia hesitated a moment, then said, "Of course," and handed him Samara. He felt her lightness in his arms, the wondrous floating firmness of a baby, the small bones you could touch like piano keys. Samara looked up at him, a thin smile of tiny blown bubbles on her pursed lips.

"I've read all your novels," Lydia told him.

"You have?" He'd expected nothing like this to be said.

"Tom gave them to me. I really loved them."

He carefully gave Samara back to her, and then stood awkwardly a moment at the door while Sunny gave her a hug goodbye. Lydia stretched up and kissed him on the cheek, her own face damp.

"Can we walk you to the car?" Ben asked.

"Sure," Lydia said. He took Sunny's hand and they followed her out. He held on to the car door—a wind had come up—to make certain it didn't shut while she was putting the baby in her car seat.

"Well," she said, "goodbye again," and got in the car.

So this was it, he thought, as Lydia drove away. He would not see her again. He would try, he would write back every time she sent him pictures, he would draft long letters, he would offer money as he had over the years (always refused), he would plead for her to come visit them in Oregon, he would dream of Sammy going to the college where he taught (though no longer by that time) and about her growing up and knowing her cousins, Allison's and Jonathan's future children.

She said she had loved his books. It was an absolution he'd never expected.

"Come back inside," Sunny coaxed.

"In a minute." He stood awhile, then started to walk around the block to where he had lived with Marilyn on Galisteo Street. The snow was coming down heavily now, and his feet slid in the hard-soled shoes he was wearing.

He stopped in front of the low-slung adobe house and looked at the closed curtains of the room with its beehive fireplace where Lydia had been conceived thirty-one years ago. He tried to see himself inside the four small rooms of the house, a young man then in love with the possibilities of art. He'd only wanted to do good work. Marilyn had encouraged him. She knew better than anyone what he dreamed of, and in turn Ben had said he would always take care of her. They made promises, naïve in the face of their ages. One night Marilyn had taken steaks from the hotel kitchen, wine from the bar, a cherry pie from the coffee shop, and a flower arrangement from the lobby, a full-course purloined dinner. "Let's do something really devilish," she suggested after they'd eaten the illicit feast, and they went into the living room and made love several times in front of the beehive fireplace, his erection resuming almost instantly after each sweaty coupling as they tore at each other. She'd drawn blood from his earlobe. That was Lydia's beginnings, and he could never have known then how much he would desperately want this child to love him as the father she didn't need.

Sunny came down the sidewalk, her coat pulled tight around her shoulders. She was walking in a straight and determined line, carrying a cup of steaming tea for him. She would keep him company while he stood in front of this house on Galisteo Street and remembered everything.

INDIE

His picture would appear in the paper, scrutinized for any sign of dementia. People would read between the lines for hints of indiscretion or scandal in his background as to what had motivated him. They'd find nothing. No illicit love affairs resulting in blackmail, no crushing gambling debts to do himself in over, no terminal illness that he couldn't bear. Not a thing would be amiss.

He hadn't even planned on doing this. Oh, that was untrue. He had, he had. But not in front of the students. He was sorry; it wasn't like him really. He'd snidely told Kelsey Dunn to "shut her pie hole" in a moment of frustration at her interrupting his concentration, and sorry, too, that he'd alarmed anyone by warning Matthew Morgan to remain in his seat, afraid the boy would stop him, unable to face the humiliation of remaining alive as "that teacher who'd held the gun to his head."

He'd initially planned to carry out the task after school (though he would have liked to consider it more a deed than a task, imbuing the act around its edges with a corona of historical significance). Drive to the lake or to an isolated and wooded area in the foothills. But he knew that would entail a search for a missing person, and although he had been missing from himself for some time, he didn't wish to be officially designated as such and cause

Margaret the extra hardship of agonizing about his whereabouts before his body was found. Best to get it over in a conspicuous place, and what could be more conspicuous than in front of his class?

Too conspicuous, in fact. He'd been staring blankly at his students' quizzes when he reached down and felt the outline of the gun in his briefcase, the .44 caliber Colt black powder revolver. One hundred fifty thousand of the sidearms had been manufactured during the Civil War. Their durability and better firepower—the South had preferred the .36 caliber Navy model —had helped the Union to prevail. Or so he liked to suggest to his students in the reenactment club. He had hoped using such a weapon would lend his action a hint of noble sacrifice, but of course that was folly. He was not, and never had been, a soldier; he'd bonded with an army of men long dead, wearing their blue uniforms and firing their muskets. He read their words in ancient diaries, imagining their battles from Shiloh to Sharpsburg; he collected their regalia and mementos of battle, and remained as ripped apart in himself as the war had rendered the nation.

It would be humiliating for Margaret. Her husband of thirty years a "dedicated high school teacher" who "had snapped" after "holding his class hostage" in a "bizarre incident." He could write the story himself: "a terrifying ordeal for the students," "a frightening experience for the parents," "a complete shock to his family." Honestly, he'd wanted the opposite: privacy, oblivion, indifference; he'd wished to slip away without a splash, just like an old caiman. Or that wonderful last shot in On the Beach—the submarine, the last human habitat left in a nuclear toxic world, descending without a wake into the sea.

But he'd made a spectacle of himself now, fucked up again, as he was coming to think of his existence in these latter years, though there was no evidence of such failures, just the twisting pain he lived with all the time, the miserable discharge of dread and disappointment into his guts, as if from an unsalvageable rusting ship (he could not stop thinking about the oceans—those immense bodies of water that both swallowed one up and promised rebirth).

He had the little pink pills the doctor told him would help, and he had the schedule of exercise classes Margaret had highlighted for him, and he had the cell phone number of a "good man of faith" who wanted to aid, and he had his rightful mind, lest anyone excuse his behavior as that of a madman, and he had his family, of course. Yes, the family, their love, the children and grandchildren, and, if he could only bear staying alive, the great grandchildren too. All the years of watching their blossoming, bountiful lives . . . he'd had it all.

9

Gabriel Hap thought Mr. Adams looked well, considering. Their teacher stared at the white phone next to the bulletin board after the sheriff's voice came over the classroom's loudspeaker asking him to pick it up. The phone was only to communicate with the office.

"Would you like to pick up the phone, Mr. Adams?" asked Kelsey Dunn, as if she were his secretary. Mr. Adams had no response, which wasn't a surprise, since he'd been standing there for an hour with the gun against his head. Gabriel didn't actually know what would happen if any of them tried to leave, but based on what Mr. Adams had said to Matt Morgan about not moving, he suspected they weren't free to do so. The problem, as Gabriel saw it, was God's anyway. Their fate rested in His hands. At least that's what he believed most of the time. At their Young Fellowship meetings they'd discussed destiny. The youth pastor, Chad, said that God knew every person's fate but had given people free will to act independently, whether that be for good or evil. When Gabriel asked how you could have a destiny but still have choices, Chad said, almost too quickly, as if he'd gotten this question a thousand times, that it was a blessed paradox and had to be accepted on faith. God wanted Man to make the right choices even if those choices were predetermined. You could make bad choices, which were part of your free will, but you could make positive choices to follow Jesus' commands and be in accord with God's grace.

"So," Gabriel had asked, "free will is bad choice and destiny is good choice?"

"Not exactly," Chad said. "Both are your decisions, but only God knows which ones you'll choose."

"Then why doesn't He tell us what to do?"

"Because He wants you to figure it out," Chad said.

Gabriel decided Mr. Adams was in one of those "blessed paradoxes" right now. How else could you explain the behavior of a teacher who was one year away from retirement and had never so much as come on the radar screen as far as the crazy stuff teachers did, like Ms. Evers last year, their tenth-grade English teacher who wore a cheerleading outfit to class for a week straight, a joke at first, but then she wouldn't stop, her pleated maroon skirt getting shorter and shorter. Or Mr. Norton, the married technology teacher who was seen groping his student teacher in the parking lot and then got fired. Those were at least explainable, even Ms. Evers who just wanted "inappropriate attention," as it was communicated to them in an assembly after she got booted too. But with Mr. Adams it didn't figure. He went to Gabriel's church and his wife was in the choir. His kids were grown. Only last week, Gabriel had seen Mr. Adams and his grandkids helping out at the church's charity car wash.

And wasn't Mr. Adams worried about Judgment Day? Gabriel had accepted Jesus as his savior when he was thirteen. He didn't do drugs, he didn't drink or smoke, and he never cussed. He prayed every morning and evening to walk in Jesus' footsteps, but he did, however, spill his seed at least four times a day, and despite what the sex-ed teachers said about such behavior being perfectly normal, he expected to go to hell. He would just as soon go now. Which was why he stood up from his seat and walked straight toward Mr. Adams.

8

Elissa Lorge watched as groups of students outside snaked their way along the perimeter of the school's fence. She concluded the entire building was now fully evacuated, fifty minutes after Mr. Adams had put a gun to his head and thirty-three minutes after Kabir had glanced in the classroom door's window. The policemen, the SWAT team that had surrounded the school seventeen minutes after Mr. Adams first lifted the gun to his head, were locked and loaded at every conceivable position, including belly down on the grass right outside their classroom windows.

Before this, she had counted the number of times Mr. Adams had shuffled his quizzes from right to left—six times—and vice versa—eight times—and the frequency with which he had sipped from his coffee cup—fourteen swallows—which was in line with how long, on an average, it took him to usually finish his morning coffee. She had also counted the words in each of Mr. Adams' post-gun utterances, which divided by two, the number of times he'd actually spoken, added up to eight, an ominous sign because reticent murderers usually proved more cruel. Of course it was quite possible that Mr. Adams was not going to kill anyone, including himself, and that the eleven times the gun had moved from the center of his left temple to a slightly lower region at the top of his jawbone to his eardrum to the orbital arch of his eye, a total radius of not more than eight centimeters, possibly indicated he was losing his nerve. Elissa would be relieved if he did. She did not want to go through the aftermath of such a tragedy, as everyone would term it, because it would mean extra counting (and no doubt more enforced therapy).

Not counting at all meant, of course, she'd have to go to her room, close her blinds, lie on her bed, stare up at the ceiling, cross her arms, and watch those same old boring reruns of her stepfather holding a knife to her mother's throat and telling the bitch, as he had put it, that he was going to cut off her fucking head. While Elissa screamed in the corner. Ho. Hum.

"Mr. Adams," came a voice over the school's intercom, "this is Jack Cunningham with the Severton County Sheriff's Department. Can you please pick up the classroom phone?"

7

What Roland Fineman was thinking about, besides the fact that his father had quit his job as an accountant in midtown Manhattan and moved everyone to this small Colorado town on the Front Range because he believed it was paradise, was finality. What did it really matter that Mr. Adams had a gun pointed at his head? Hadn't Nietzsche written, "Men are even lazier than they are timorous, and what they fear most is the troubles with which an unconditional honesty and nudity would burden them"? What could be more unconditionally honest than standing in front of your AP history class and putting a gun to your head? And talk about "nudity," as in baring your soul—here it was in the flesh, but did anybody in this class of hicks, jocks, phats, spooners, and huggers really appreciate Mr. Adams' guts? He doubted it. Kelsey Dunn was apoplectic with concern, no doubt dying to get in there and do some "peer counseling," if only Mr. Adams hadn't told her a few minutes ago to shut her pie hole, a retort Roland found positively and insanely lovely. He wondered for a brief moment whether he should stand up there in solidarity next to the man. He could quote Nietzsche: *My death I praise to you, the free death which comes to me because I want it.* Boom!—the gun would go off.

Was that relic even loaded?

"No can do, Mr. A," Dan Brock said. "We can't just turn our seats and let you shoot yourself—or us."

"Why not?" Roland put in.

"Excuse me?" Brock said. The last time Roland had talked to Dan Brock was when he left his copy of *The Power of One* at home and asked Brock if he could share his. "You can have it," Brock had said. "I'm not going to read it anyway." The only other exchange had been Brock asking Roland why he used so many big words.

"If he wants to shoot himself, that's his choice," Roland said. He saw that Mr. Adams had lowered his gun a bit, as if from the strain of holding it in place.

"What the hell are you talking about?" Dan Brock asked.

Brock mostly sat in the back of class with his aviator sunglasses on, when he wasn't sleeping. Roland was fairly terrified of him. He'd already sent a couple of kids to the hospital while playing football, a sport Roland despised but couldn't help appreciate for its unbridled destruction.

"'Nihilism stands at the door.' Wouldn't you agree, Mr. Adams? From 'whence comes this uncanniest of all guests'?" Roland saw Mr. Adams' eyes flicker—was that in recognition of the tele-meta-philosophical level they were communicating on?

"Why don't you shut your trap?" Matthew Morgan told Roland, and then to Mr. Adams, "Were our quizzes that bad?"

"You idiot!" Roland burst out, unable to control himself. "This is nothing to do with us. It's . . . it's about the *Overman*. Right, Mr. Adams?"

"You're not helping," Dan Brock said, through clenched teeth.

"I'm not trying to help, you jerk," Roland said. "I'm *accepting.*"

"Be quiet! Shut up, all of you! He's standing there with a gun at his head, I'm fucking pregnant, and you're all mouthing bullshit!"

"Ariana?" Oliver said.

"Yes, your goddamn selfish bastard of a brother is the father!"

6

Dan Brock was just coming out of a dream when he got nudged by the team's center, Matt Morgan. In the dream, he'd been sitting in front of two college coaches, one from Texas A&M and the other from UT Austin. He found it kind of strange that they were both interviewing him at the same time in a Texas hotel room, but everything else was real, just like it had been for his brother Kyle who played quarterback for UT until he got in the car accident that left him a vegetable. He wasn't supposed to refer to Kyle as a vegetable, or even think it, and never, *never* say, "Hey man, you're a vegetable, did ya know?" His parents must have thought he was stupid or something. He'd never say that to Kyle. Sure, he thought it, but you couldn't help that. The guy had a feeding tube and round the clock nursing care and his mobility pretty much consisted of jerking his head involuntarily. Sometimes, Dan stared at him and tried to see the person who'd broken the state high school record for passing yards, the star who'd gotten a full scholarship to Austin, the brother who on a trip to Eastern Colorado, just the two of them, before he left for college, pulled over on a back road, and let Dan drive, closing his eyes and pretending to nap just to show how cool he was about it.

Now they had to turn Kyle's head so he'd slobber out the other side of his mouth.

"Make your brother proud," their dad told Dan last year when he started as a linebacker. Parents on the other teams had complained. This was football for God's sake, not hockey. Dan was too mean, too crazy. The refs constantly blew their whistles at him: "No illegal hits!" "It was legal!" he'd argue. And it was. He didn't do helmet hits, just good old flying tackles, vicious enough to get him a penalty anyway, especially when he stood over his conquests afterward with his fists clenched. He didn't care. He was trying to kill somebody, maybe even his brother, better off that way.

That's what the A&M coach had said to him in the dream, "You're a murderer, Dan Brock. Look what you did to your brother." But the coach had a smile on his face. Creepy. Shit, he thought now, seeing that Mr. Adams had some sort of a long-barreled pistol pointed at his temple. What was he planning to do with that frickin' thing?

"You think we should jump him?" Matt Morgan whispered.

Dan Brock stared at Mr. Adams. He was looking at a spot on the back wall, like they told you to do in speech class so you wouldn't get so stressed by watching people's faces. Mr. Adams, who was low key and the only teacher that let Dan sleep in the back of class, had once said to him, "I used to hate everyone when I was your age too, sometimes I still do." He wasn't fair game.

"Let's roll," Matt whispered again, just like they'd said on that plane that went down.

"Make one move, Mr. Morgan," said their teacher, as if reading Matt's name from a roll sheet, "and this gun goes off."

5

The thing was, Vivian Hernandez thought, if I get out of here alive, will I be any different? She'd always heard that when you went through something traumatic and survived, it changed your life forever, mostly for the better. You appreciated every day, you liked your parents and little sister more, and you didn't care about having to shop at Kmart for your clothes. But she wasn't sure this was really going to change her life; they'd been sitting here for twenty minutes, nobody was getting up to leave or trying to talk to Mr. Adams, except Kelsey Dunn who had just said, "Mr. Adams, whatever is wrong, we *can* get help," and Mr. Adams had answered in a fairly bright voice given the circumstances, "Please shut your pie hole, Kelsey," and gone back to standing at attention with the gun at his head.

Everybody was texting back and forth. She wasn't allowed to have a cell phone. Her parents thought it would distract her from school, and they still believed it meant gangstas on streets looking to deal, where she'd come from in East L.A. That, after all, was why they'd moved to Colorado. They had relatives in Northern Colorado and her dad had found a job working in maintenance out at the meat packing plant. Her mom cleaned homes just as she did back in L.A., but they had a bigger house here, even if the odor from the nearby stockyard made you gag on a hot summer day.

Kabir had looked in the window of the classroom door a while ago and seen what was going on and then disappeared. His eyes had gotten huge. She hoped he'd gone for help. Kabir reminded her of her father, who was always afraid of doing something wrong and getting sent back to Bogotá, even though they were citizens now. Americans were suspicious of Colombians, he said, so they had to set a good example here, because of all the drug business. Kabir often had the same look on his face as her father did, worrying for some trouble he didn't even do, a shame he carried with him just for being here. She wanted to tell Kabir to lighten up and not put his face so close to the exam paper, pressing his pencil down as if drilling his answers into the test. But he was too shy to even speak to anyone, and anyway, she was the same.

"Would you all please turn your chairs around with your backs to me," Mr. Adams said.

4

They'd never used loaded weapons for the drills that they did in their Civil War Reenactment Club. Mr. Adams had strict rules about that. In fact, Jerry Worthington had never fired a gun in his life. But he did know that the particular gun Mr. Adams had, a six-shot Colt .44 revolver with a range of nineteen yards, long enough to reach any of them in class, had the power to penetrate seven three-quarter-inch white pine boards, because Mr. Adams had demonstrated that once using the same gun, blowing out their eardrums in the process.

"Mr. Adams?" Kelsey Dunn asked. "Is this a joke?" He didn't answer. The barrel was flush against his temple. He was rigid. Was he trying to make a point? It didn't really go with their lesson. They were studying World War I, the Treaty of Versailles. True, Mr. Adams wasn't above a prank now and then. He'd once written comments on their papers backwards, some kind of weird skill he had, so they had to look in the mirror to read them. But was this a prank? It didn't look as though he was punking the whole class.

Everyone turned to Jerry. As if he knew. How would he? They just dressed up in these uniforms and slung rifles with bayonets over their shoulders and marched around and learned about battles. *What's going on?* Kelsey Dunn whispered to him. *I don't know,* he whispered back.

3

Ariana was looking over the chart of Indie royalty that Oliver had passed her in history class. Oliver had put her at the bottom, somewhere below Shannon Grayson who had bought all of the band Bitzie's demo tapes off eBay last summer, evidently giving her a secure place in the hierarchy. She noticed Oliver had made himself a bishop. Ariana, meanwhile, was some kind of lowly handmaiden. At the top were Hallie and Ishmael, the king and queen, even though they'd graduated last year. Hallie was in art school back East. Ishmael was still in Colorado working as a busboy at a Mexican restaurant. Ariana wasn't sure how you could be a busboy and still be king of the Indies. At least Hallie had something to show for herself. She was a great painter. But Ishmael's band hadn't worked out. Oliver evidently disagreed. "If you're really Indie," he'd told her, "you understand that it's all about attitude, not what you accomplish." Success, in the conventional sense, was just such bullshit, he said.

"So why do this stupid chart?" she'd asked him.

"Just for fun," Oliver had told her, with his simpering little smile. Oliver wore small green frame glasses and tight Capri jeans —he was above the gender thing, he said—but the jeans made him look like Anorexic of the Week. Oliver was also Patrick's younger brother who was Ishmael's best friend and the bass player in their now defunct band, The Turnkeys, and Patrick and Ariana had dated for a while, until it was clear Ariana didn't know enough about Indie bands and obscure poets. Like she cared. The chart was stupid anyway. Indie royalty. What a laugh. Oliver was a little wannabe power grubbie. A snot, too.

He'd told her yesterday when they went shopping together at the thrift store that he didn't like the term Indie anymore. Hipster was the better word. Not the old beatnik dudes with their silly berets and bongos or the hippies reeking of sandalwood incense, but the new kind of cool hipsters who could do fashion at the lowest possible cost, like the black suede boots he'd gotten at the Back to the Rack clothing store down in Denver and the velvet jacket with blue satin lapels and its nipped-in waist.

"Ugh," he'd told Ariana, when she tried on a flannel shirt at the local thrift store—she'd stupidly agreed to go shopping with him. "That's so Nirvana and Pearl Jam." She took it off. Why did she let this twerp control her? He'd told her Mothman, a band she loved, was no longer acceptable as Indie because they'd appeared on MTV. "Kiss of death," Oliver informed her.

"You're just incredible," said Ariana.

"Thank you," Oliver said, taking it as a compliment. Ariana had rifled through the bins of t-shirts two sizes too big, since she was four months pregnant with Patrick's baby and that was the only reason she was hanging out with Oliver, hoping to enlist his help in breaking the news to his brother, once she got up the guts to tell either of them. Patrick had come up from Boulder his first week after freshman orientation at college and called her. She'd thought they'd broken up but allowed herself to be flattered into screwing him at her parents' empty house for the weekend. She hadn't heard from him since, and she kept thinking she should do something decisive, but she couldn't get past staring at the number for Planned Parenthood in the phone book. Her parents— her father was a retired Air Force colonel—would simply kill her.

"Oh, my God," Denise Alexander said, who sat next to Ariana. They were waiting for Mr. Adams to stop shuffling the quizzes, which he'd been doing forever. Mr. Adams had finally stopped, but he had a Civil War pistol pointed at his head.

2

It had happened again. Kabir felt the warmth spread across his groin and into his underwear. Kelsey Dunn in her white shorts, with the flaps of her back pockets snugly buttoned, had simply walked up to Mr. Adams' desk after collecting all their quizzes. The light from the tall classroom windows had revealed the outline of her panties. It was the same as two nights ago when he'd been watching a program on the History Channel—his parents restricted his TV watching—and a "flapper"—part of American culture from the 1920s—was dancing and swinging her beads, her loose breasts jiggling. That was enough to do it, his first ejaculation. While watching the History Channel! His mother would be mortified. His father would find it amusing perhaps and say that at least it had been an educational experience. But how could he tell either of them? Back in India no one talked about sex, not where his parents were from at least.

He decided Kelsey Dunn was staring at him oddly.

He raised his hand for permission to go to the bathroom, but Mr. Adams was busy moving around the quizzes that Kelsey had just brought him. He didn't even look at Kabir when he left the room.

Stripping off his jeans in a bathroom stall, he tried—unsuccessfully—to wipe away the sticky fluid that only spread like glue. He thought about throwing the underpants away, but the trash can was empty and it didn't have a lid. The last thing he wanted to do was stuff them in his pocket, so he flushed them down the toilet and watched as the toilet burbled and gulped and sucked them away with a roar.

He thought again about Kelsey Dunn. She was that kind of nice American girl in this small Colorado town an hour north of Denver where his parents had emigrated two years ago. He was only fifteen but had been placed in the eleventh grade because of high test scores and the insistence of his father who didn't want him, their only son, to delay getting a head start on college and finding a good job, preferably in engineering or higher mathematics. Kelsey always questioned him in her sweet American voice about India. She had read two novels by Indian writers over the summer and would like to discuss them with him sometime. She had always wanted to go to India the way other kids dreamed of traveling to Europe or tropical islands.

He would nod politely at such pleasantries, not believing for a minute she was seriously interested in him beyond his importance as a cultural symbol. This did not stop him from picturing his mother having tea with Kelsey while they spoke about the wedding arrangements for Kelsey and him, his mother in her sari with a gold necklace and bangles up her arm to protect her from evil. He had little time to dwell on such a fantasy, because returning to his classroom and glancing in the door's window, he saw his teacher Mr. Adams holding a gun to his head. The confused looks on his classmates' faces indicated that this was not an idle demonstration. Several of them noticed him, including Kelsey, whom he thought mouthed *Get help*. And he recognized, too, the paleness and vacancy on his teacher's face, the same as when his Uncle Bhanu lost his home and business to a flood in Bihar and held a knife to his own throat until Kabir's father talked his younger brother out of killing himself.

He fled to the office, the fate of his new America trailing behind him.

I

Did he say anything? What were you thinking while he stood up there with a gun? Were you scared? Did he tell you *why*? No, everyone would answer to this last question. Yes, we were scared. We were thinking about our lives, they might say, if they could answer honestly. We were thinking about ourselves. And wasn't that the same for him? He was thinking only about The Absence, which he'd been thinking about for a very long time. He could not imagine a more selfish act. After all these years of living alone in The Absence, of sparing Margaret and his children and friends, wasn't he making up for lost time with this most public and heinous exhibit of self-serving misery? These young people had done nothing to deserve him laying himself out in such ugly pain before them. But he couldn't reverse course now. For someone who abhorred public displays of emotion, he had become a baby again, crying in front of his class.

He could certainly picture an afterlife, but it was one for his students, not him. Kelsey Dunn would become a missionary or maybe work at a foodbank; Kabir Gupta would no doubt fulfill his parents' dreams of being a mathematician; Elissa Lorge would go on for a PhD and more therapy over the death of her mother; Roland Fineman would try his hand at advertising after failing as a poet; Gerald Worthington would run his father's hardware store until the day he died; Vivian Hernandez, never a contrary word out of her, would attend Yale on a full scholarship; Dan Brock would blow his knee out playing football and go into real estate with his buddy Matthew Morgan; Ariana, after a miscarriage, would become director of a women's shelter; Oliver Yeager would move to the Bay Area and finally and officially come out.

He had a future planned for all of them but had somehow missed Gabriel Hap, that boy from a pious ranching family. He hadn't expected Gabriel, always so accommodating and polite, to be the one who got up from his chair and came toward him. He really had not given the boy much thought. He doubted anyone ever had, even his parents. Gabriel Hap sat in a middle row, handed in his completed assignments—that was the best one could say for them—offered answers to only the most obvious questions, and was always thrilled to see his teacher at church. "I'm so glad you share a love for the Lord," Gabriel bashfully told him once afterward. He wasn't brownnosing either. But Gabriel Hap didn't know that he attended only for Margaret. She sung in the choir and enjoyed being among the other worshippers on Sunday. Whether she actually believed in prayer or not, he couldn't say. They never discussed it. The Absence grew greater for him at such times, and when he closed his eyes and heard the pastor's words, he saw the warring tribes of the Bible tearing one another's flesh from the bone. Why had he thought the Civil War was so different? It was not. It was one of the most lethal and brutal battles between men, savagery really. Six hundred thousand dead, twice that many gone from disease, fifty thousand amputees. And yet he could not stop glorifying it in his head. Those courageous men in blue and gray; armed with muskets and sabers in iron scabbards; their front lines strong behind the Chevaux-de-frises barricades; their feet bloody, bruised, and swollen from marching. He had wished to die for one side or the other.

And so it was Gabriel Hap who came forward, his hand out, his fingers extended, his eyes beseeching. What did the boy want? The gun of course. But was it to be a hero? Or to genuinely help?

Neither would happen. Gabriel, the young man's future clear now, would go to war. He would learn to kill. He would talk about a day long ago in his history class when his teacher held a gun to his head, and how he alone stood up and tried to take the weapon away. A shot blasted through the window, blew out the back of his teacher's skull, and stopped only after piercing the blackboard. His teacher jerked once and fell.

"The point was," Gabriel Hap would explain to his young recruits, "you can't hesitate and survive." Sure, people had questioned his judgment, and some said Mr. Adams was actually lowering the gun to put it down, but the point was . . . "the point is you have to know you're doing the right thing and not second guess. That gun was aimed at me," he would tell them, "and the SWAT guys knew it and took the opportunity." At that final moment there were words on Mr. Adams' lips, but Gabriel would always say they weren't meant for the living.

NATURAL CAUSES

THOUGH he'd retired from the geology department, Francis still came in occasionally to pick up his mail, and the first person he met in the hall on this afternoon, carrying a plate of cookies, was none other than Penny Aulderbrough.

"How are you, Professor?" she asked. "Francis, I mean. I guess I shouldn't stand on ceremony now that I'm faculty too. I'm not implying that we're equals—"

"It's all right, Penny," said Francis. She was in her late thirties and had come back to college for an advanced degree in geology after her divorce from a lawyer in Dallas. Always bubbling with excitement over some project, or stuffing people's mailboxes on Valentine's Day with affectionate hand-drawn hearts taped to candies, she rode around town on her single-speed bike wearing a floppy blue suede hat, her coarse and abundant red hair punching out the sides. Long limbed and a bit gawky, she had a terrible habit of cracking her knuckles at staff meetings. On one occasion when she'd come to a party at his and Mary's house, she'd rushed through the door with her skirt askew at the hem and a shawl of coarse ropey material that appeared to be a work of wildly geometric macramé.

Now she wore a stiff leather skirt more the look of a rubber apron for butchering, and true to its hide-like appearance, when she bent a knee against the front, it dented rather than wrinkled. "Have one," she said, offering him a cookie. "I made them for Carl's lecture. I didn't see you there, by the way."

"I had to miss it," Francis said, though he hadn't any good reason to do so, except for the mild resentment of being neglected by his former colleague. Carl had increasingly directed his research toward the more cosmic field of planetary geology, the subject of his public talk, having lost interest in analyzing the ore of Colorado's Western Slope for its chemical and mineral properties, as he and Carl had always done as a team before.

"Are they good? I think I burned them a little around the edges."

Francis bit into one. "They're just fine, Penny."

"I was going to make oatmeal raisin cookies but talk about rocks—and gas!" She smiled crazily at this, but it did not stop her. "I thought he gave a wonderful lecture. Carl is so *animalized*." He was sure she meant to say animated. God help her, he thought. "I bet Carl has a copy he could give you. Oh, I'm certain he could!" She always spoke with excess exuberance, and frankly he didn't know why she hadn't gone into a dramatic discipline like theater rather than science. Through sheer hard work and the kindness of friends in the department, she'd finished her dissertation on a geological time table of fossils in the marsh areas of Colorado's South Platte River Basin. More astonishing, she'd been hired to teach three sections of introductory geology. No one quite had the heart to turn her out after eight years of hanging around the department's halls and being the unofficial greeter. She baked treats and oversaw the holiday celebrations, organized the annual picnic and softball league games, all duties she had gladly volunteered for during her student days and continued now. "But anyway, how *are* you?"

Her eyes. They seemed to spin with sympathy like plates on sticks, wobbling to a stop and fixing on him with penetrating regard. No one had searched his face so closely for an answer in months.

"Would you like to have coffee?" he asked.

HE couldn't imagine starting over. "You're talking yourself out of the possibility even before it happens," his daughter, Ilene, who lived in San Diego with her family had told him. "I can understand your being scared to get involved with someone after only a year and a half, but Mom would want you to . . . she wouldn't want you to be alone."

But his daughter was wrong. Mary wouldn't care if he was alone. He and Mary were going to get divorced. They had, in fact, been talking about the subject at the moment of the accident. Driving to a sectional meeting of the Geological Society in Lincoln, Nebraska, Mary informed him this was the last time she would accompany him on one of his trips. She didn't see herself continuing to live with him in Colorado, either. She had looked in the mirror one day and wanted to find more of herself. Her first step had been changing her name back to Ingleman. No longer Mary Jenkins. She was Mary Ingleman again. She wished to paint more and practice her flute and travel to quilting shows. When she pictured herself it was painting in the sunroom of a small bungalow all her own. But why? Why for God's sake? he had asked her. What had happened suddenly that she couldn't still do all these things while being married? "Is there someone else?" he asked.

Mary shook her head sadly, as if the possibility were too remote to even consider.

They had decided to take a back route to the conference off the interstate. Mary was saying she'd been a nurse and that home-care was something she could do for a little extra money, and maybe they needed to be apart for this last act of their lives, it wasn't so terrible to be alone—

A Cadillac came barreling through the intersection and hit them broadside. Glass exploded into Francis' face and mouth, and then their car rolled. When it stopped, his cheek pressed against the roof, nuggets of glass bejeweled him, and Mary lay next to him, halfway out of her seatbelt. "Are you all right?" he asked. "I don't think so," she said, and these were her last words.

The ambulance arrived twenty-five minutes later on this county road outside Bertrand, Nebraska. He endured the ride to the hospital with the Cadillac's seventy-six-year-old driver who had been gabbing away to her equally elderly companion and had missed the stop sign and would only suffer minor injuries.

He called Ilene first, then his son Brian in New York. He told them Mother was dead. He had no way to soften the truth; he was in pain from a ruptured disc, an injury that later would lead to ongoing back problems, despite surgery, and his decision to retire earlier than planned from the university. His face sprayed with glass and their suitcases destroyed along with the car, he had only his own bloody clothes from the accident to wear that a nurse washed out in the sink and sent him home in. The slivers of glass could not be removed right away. His skin would have to push them out over the next twenty-four hours.

That night, talking to Brian who worked as a medical technician, he sounded overly rational: Fifty percent of him grieved for Mary; thirty-five percent pitied himself; and fifteen percent hated the doddering, yakking old lady in the Cadillac who had killed his wife. Everyone said the way he portioned out his feelings indicated he was in shock. And perhaps he was. He couldn't deny it. But he was certain he could not tell Brian and Ilene that their mother was killed mid-sentence talking about leaving him.

"I ALWAYS get a triple shot in my latte," Penny was telling him now at the Starbucks counter on campus. "Not that I need it!"

He wouldn't disagree with this statement. They found a table in the corner with a checkerboard painted on its top. "Do you play?" Penny asked.

"Checkers?" Who didn't play checkers? But it was something he hadn't done since his children were young.

"C'mon," she said, and jumped up, returning shortly with a box of black and red checkers. She set his side up too. "You go first."

He moved his black piece. She moved hers. He moved again. She moved. He saw an opening and jumped her piece, but it led him into a trap, and she got a double jump. In no time she had three kings and had wiped out all but one of his pieces. "Don't you love it!" Penny said.

"Well, it's been awhile," Francis said. "Obviously I'm out of shape."

She eyed him in a way that indicated she didn't agree. Her hair, minus her customary floppy hat, was tied up in a snug bun and didn't look as if it needed to be tilled with a harrow today. She had a bit of aqueous green in her brown eyes, and when she swept the checkers back into the box with her pale and freckled forearm, the gesture had a certain delicate grace he hadn't noticed in the usual jerkier movement of her limbs when she went down the hall as if flagging down an emergency vehicle.

"Do you believe in second chances?" she asked. "Oh, holy Moses, that is *soo* corny. But I mean, well, you know . . . do you?"

SHE was actually only twenty years younger than him, not twenty-four as he had originally thought, as if it made a difference. He still had trouble and would have whether she was his age or a *Penthouse* pinup bursting with ripe youth. "Hey," she said, "don't worry. I can't perform, come and stuff, myself a lot of the times."

What did she mean, "a lot of the times"? How many lovers did she have?

And as if to answer his thoughts, she added, "I mean, whenever I do have sex, which is by no means that often, and then there was the whole Barry thing."

The "Barry thing" was her ex. He didn't care much for her needs, physical or otherwise, as she put it. "You're already way ahead of him and we've only spent twenty minutes together," and this was ego boosting and arousing enough to gain Francis a hardness of purpose and he thrust into her while she moaned softly and rhythmically, a lilting tide of passion, not at all like her more typical and public shrieks of pleasure upon the smallest interactions with people. She held his head against her chest afterwards and murmured or hummed, he wasn't sure which, and the fullness and length of her body—Mary had been what would be called petite—both unsettled and excited him so that he pressed against her again. "Oh, wow," Penny said, an expression that Mary would never use—not a child of such times and its vernacular— and she got up on her knees, raised her bottom in the air, reached down to pull him up behind her, and then placed his hands on her hips. "There," she said, and then, "Don't you love this?" and he didn't know whether she meant this doggie position or sex in general or if she had some uncanny insight into just how barren of physical intimacy had been the last several years of his marriage, how simple and voraciously satisfying it was to pound against her backside, her soft pale flanks, and watch her red hair bob against the pillow and hear her rutting squeals.

Finishing, he collapsed against her back, and she slowly lowered herself onto her stomach. It was then that she told him her age, forty-one, not thirty-seven. She'd fudged a little, she said, just in case. In case of what? he asked. "You know, in case," and he understood that she meant in case someone should come along. She'd had a few affairs with "others" since she'd moved here from Dallas eight years ago. He was curious about these "others." Graduate students? Professors? Aliens? But he couldn't bring himself to ask and she showed no inclination to tell him. "I guess I haven't always known what I wanted," Penny said. They talked in the dark. She told him of her father, a powerful judge who served on the federal bench and was a man of the arts, too, writing poetry and composing music, someone she could never seem to impress, as could her two brothers, one a successful lawyer himself, the other a surgeon. She was always the "slow" one, the girl who couldn't snap out the answers at the dinner table to questions of current events or math. "It was like a game show living in my family," she said, "and I was the perpetual loser they kept bringing back on the program for laughs. Even my mother was brilliant in her own way at interior decorating. So I decided I'd just be everybody's favorite water girl, carry out the bucket during halftime, support the team. Then I married a lawyer who I thought was just like my daddy, except he enjoyed pointing out the difference between his genius and my stupidity and humiliating me. My family had always been protective of me and affectionate, even if I couldn't keep up. This guy was just mean," and she slapped herself in the face to demonstrate, so hard it shocked Francis. He took her hand and held it. "Don't," he said, "don't do that to yourself." He meant beat herself up, literally and figuratively, but of course he'd been doing the same to himself. "You must miss her," Penny said, looking at the picture of Mary and the kids on the dresser. "I used to feel like a big oak tree when I was around her. She was like this little sprite. I've always had that problem with smaller woman. They make me feel even clumsier than I am." She reached down and felt between his legs. "Ooo, bonus round!" He couldn't believe it himself. "Ladies' choice," she said and pushed his shoulders down, climbing on top of him. Her breasts and erect nipples hung down in his face and when he reached up to hold them, he didn't think of oak trees but of being parched and aching and of closing his eyes and oranges and grapefruits and mangoes being dropped into his open palms. "Squeeze them," she breathed in his ear. "They're for you."

In the middle of the night his back started to act up. It hadn't bothered him during sex, but now he felt the pain sliding like a musical whistle along his spine, pinching notes of discomfort out at different vertebrae. He took a Vicodin. He tried to take it only when the pain became overwhelming, but perhaps he wanted one tonight just to calm himself down. He sat on the toilet seat and let his eyes focus on a photograph of Mary at the end of a kayaking trip on the Colorado River at lower Gore Canyon. They'd learned a few basic moves in a class, then spent much of the day trying to perfect their rolls on the class-two rapids of the cold river. By the run's end they were soaked but happy, maybe happier than they'd been in a long while. They stayed the night at a bed and breakfast in Radium, cozying up to each other and—if his memory served him—having sex for the last time in their lives. He would have expected things to get better after that, but they didn't, and he and Mary drifted into separate lives, his work, her activities—she was always busy with many things as compared to his one. In the photograph she stood beside her upended kayak, which towered above her like a huge trophy fish. He remembered smiling at her as he took the picture.

He felt the initial effects of the Vicodin, the slipping focus of attention on his muscles, the breaking up of clustered pain like a gang of thugs dispersing. He drifted back to the Phanerozoic eon and then further into the Proterozoic period with its glacial periods, Earth a large snowball at this stage, and then, why not, four billion years earlier into the Cryogenian era from which no known rocks existed today, and here he stopped, taking out his tools and extracting a sample of rock core and speeding it back to Carl, a gift from the farthest reaches of time. And he saw himself, in all his newfound protean capacity, pulling Mary alive from their car, protecting her from strata of compressed rock, his healthy back resisting the shattering forces of matter and sheltering her under its protective hollow. When tears came, they were painless, compliments of the Vicodin, dropping from his eyes in a slow thaw.

Penny was snoring. He hadn't expected to hear the soft whistling noise of his daintier Mary, but this uninhibited bellowing of great gulping slumber took him aback. She was lusty in her appetites, all right, and she took up so much more room in bed than his wife, this other woman. When he lay down, a sudden revulsion made him turn away from her and hug his side of the mattress.

BUT whatever estrangement and perhaps self-disgust he might have felt that first night soon disappeared, and he found himself planning his days around her.

"I had a mad bad crush on you," she told him after a few weeks, "but I knew you were happily married and if I did anything about it, well, that way was mayhem. I speak from experience." Oh, why did she have to say such things! What "experience"?

"When I was younger," she thankfully explained, "and going to school in Austin, there was a professor there, my freshman English instructor who had long shaggy hair which now, in looking back, I think was just dirty, not sexy. You know how crushes go, especially if you act on them and get to know the person. You wonder why two weeks, a month, a year later you ever felt that way. You can't find anything in the data that remotely adds up to justifying this consuming obsession." She saw his face fall. "Oh, not with you, Francis. You're not in the crush category."

"But just before you said—"

"I meant before before. Not now. I was eighteen years old then and full of baloney about the madness of romantic love, which was easy to project onto Mr. Shaggy with his handy quotes from poets who'd died of their own brilliance and too much drink. I'm so much more careful now. Those kinds of impulses don't whack me at the knees anymore. We're a relationship you and me, not just a couple of . . ."

"Couple of what?" he asked; he could hear the desperation in his voice at trying to follow through on her thought.

She cocked her head, her large hoop earrings dangling. "Couple of what what?"

"You said we're not just a couple of . . . then stopped."

"Right, we're a couple!" And he had to let it drop. She bounced around the kitchen, chopping away, whirring, mashing and liquefying ingredients in a food processor she had brought from her apartment to his house, where she now slept at least four nights a week. She didn't like to eat out as Mary had, and she preferred he not assist her in the kitchen as Mary always required. Better to just sit in his chair and watch the news or read. He found himself submitting docilely to her instruction, encouraged by her coming over between food preparations to pull up her skirt, straddle him, and lower herself on his now always ready penis and then hop off and be back to cooking. She wore shorter skirts and more sleeveless blouses than before. Even her hair seemed to have taken on a lustrous and shapely character, and he'd press his face against it to inhale her scent for the long hours when she was off teaching. He also noticed more men looking at her in appreciative ways on the street.

Once, during an early and plentiful snowstorm when it was impossible for her to ride her ubiquitous Iron-Mike bike to school (and she would usually pedal under the most inclement conditions, dragging the thing alongside her if necessary), he came to pick her up from the university after her classes. She walked out to the parking lot with Carl, throwing back her head at something evidently hilarious that Carl was saying, and Francis saw her touch Carl's arm, and then again she reeled back in laughter. It was like watching a silent movie at the drive-in—her and Carl's guffawing tête-à-tête projected to towering heights. Carl, who was married to a radiologist in town, happily Francis always thought, received a fluttering little finger wave goodbye and then Penny skipped to Francis' waiting car. "Oh, how happy I am!" she said, when she got in. Her teaching was going well. She'd just gotten evaluated by—surprise, surprise!—Carl, who frothed over her spontaneity, intelligence, and organization in the classroom, "a completely stellar performance," he'd informed her. "Isn't that wonderful?" she asked Francis, her face flushed, precipitated air still coming out of her mouth on this frigid day. "He said if I keep going like this there might be a chance for a tenure-track position if one should open."

"I'm sure the budget won't allow for that," Francis informed her.

"Why do you say that?"

"Because times are terrible for higher education in this state. We're losing people to retirement and they're not being replaced. My position was never filled."

"Well, that was different."

He stared at her. "What do you mean?"

"I don't know . . . oh, I don't want to get into it. Are we having a fight?"

"No, but I'd like to know what you mean."

"Carl said it was a possibility. That's all. And I've never even pictured it before, that I could be a full-time tenured professor. You should be happy for me, Francis. Don't you know what this would mean to me?"

"I do know, and I'm glad Carl thinks so."

"But you don't."

"I just think times are tough now in our field to get hired."

"No you don't. You just don't believe I'm good enough. You think I'm a bumbling idiot who doesn't know a thing."

"I don't think that."

"You've never even seen me teach. You've never observed me."

"That's true, I didn't—"

"Do you know what Carl said? He said they weren't replacing you because students had lost interest in your area."

He felt a sharp pain run along his back, a fast ferret of misery racing up and down and pounding a ball-peen hammer along the way. "You didn't have to tell me that."

She was crying now; he'd never seen her cry before, and it was like sex in that way, surprising to see someone so transformed, a sodden running of mascara and eyeliner, her cheekbones falling into a melting wax of heartbreak, her terrible sobs. "I'm sorry," she said. "I'm so sorry."

"I am too," he told her. "I was . . ." He had such a hard time admitting it. He so rarely had told Mary any of his feelings, for which she either resented or appreciated him, he truly had no idea—such was the dearth of their confrontations like this one. "I felt so jealous just now when I saw you with Carl."

Her face sprung up from her hands, that red-headed manger on top of her head which he had come to love and long for and see first in his mind when he missed her during the day. "You were? Oh, Francis, why? I'm just happy. Can't you tell? I'm just so in love with everyone and everything and it's because of you. I don't want Carl. I want you. I have this strength now. Oh, please don't take it away from me, from us."

"I won't," he said. He pulled the car, a used Volvo that he'd bought after the accident, into the parking lot of Wendy's. He took her in his arms and kissed her eyes and cold cheeks, while she made her little moans of agreement and the windows fogged up, and then she ducked below the steering wheel, unzipped his pants and did what no other girl in a car in his six decades of life had ever done for him before.

THE holidays approached and Ilene called and said she was sending Francis a ticket to come out for Thanksgiving. "No ifs, ands, or buts," Ilene commanded, who had once described her life in San Diego as sailing, shopping, and sunning. His daughter told him she was going to get their cousins in L.A. to come down and of course Philip's parents who lived in San Diego would be joining them.

124

"I can't come," Francis said. "I'm sorry."

There was dead silence on the other end of the phone, as only his eldest child was capable of. "Why not, Dad?"

"I have plans. I'm getting together with some friends." He coughed.

"Are you getting sick?"

"No, no. It's just a tickle in my throat." From lying, he thought.

"You could have told me before I bought the ticket."

"Ilene, you should have told me you were buying a ticket."

"I asked if you would come out back in October. You said you'd love to. See me, see Philip, see the kids. Remember them? Max and Isaac. They're two little boys about four feet high who really would love to know their other grandpa."

Gramp Francis, they liked to call him, at Ilene's suggestion. Could any appellation sound more elderly?

"I was hoping . . ." Ilene started. "Well, never mind."

"What?" Francis said. There was always at least one "never mind" when he talked to her.

"I had arranged for someone special to join us. She's going to be very disappointed." He said nothing. "Aren't you the least bit curious who she is?"

No. "Tell me."

"Do you remember my roommate Karen Schmidt from college?"

He vaguely did. "Certainly."

"Her mother lives here in San Diego now. She's recently widowed. Karen's father you might remember me telling you suffered a long illness. I don't have to remind you what Karen looks like, do I?"

He presumed that meant she was "hot" by today's terms.

"Well, her mother is the original, if you get what I mean. And she was always incredibly sweet to me when I used to visit Karen. She was really looking forward to meeting you, Dad, and frankly I'd like to see you more than once a year now that Mom is gone."

Guilt. Heaps and shitloads of guilt. Pile it on. Bury me in steamy manure piles of guilt. Oh, why not just tell her. Tell her about Penny, he thought. Tell her he was dating, hell, cohabitating with, fucking the brains out of a woman who was only two years older than his own daughter and had him playing board games until his eyes became bleary from rolling the dice, tell her that his arms and legs floated around in an exercise room on Tuesday evenings when he did Tai Chi with Penny at the local health club, and for Thanksgiving, tell her that the reason he couldn't visit—a googolplex of guilt rained on him in whipped Thanksgiving potatoes—was because he and Penny were staying in a yurt nine-thousand feet high in the snowy mountains of the Colorado State Forest.

"Dad?" said Ilene. "Are you still there?"

Yes and no, he thought. The person he was just a few months ago wasn't here; Penny had expanded his life to hitherto unimagined proportions. He believed this was a good thing most of the time.

"Can't you get out of it?" Ilene asked, a scratchy plea in her voice. "It's just some friends, right. I'm sure they'll understand that you forgot you'd planned to spend Thanksgiving with your family."

Penny? Was she his family now? This girl—woman—whom he used to watch moseying down the halls of the department looking for companionship in the guise of offering her help as if she were one of those hospital ladies with a cart of goodies for the sick. He'd pitied her, unmarried, alone—that nest for hair! Riding around town on her old bicycle and high black rubber boots slapping at her calves. And now he couldn't stop thinking about her all day, the flirty little sway of her bottom when she bent over the counter humming and reading a recipe and he came up from behind. The notes she left for him in the morning: *Coffee's brewing, think of me . . . Have you ever wanted to go on a safari? . . . Don't forget ballroom dancing tonight (and do your stretches, it will help your back!).* He shuddered at the possibility that he had loved her more, or at least more intensely for this short period of time, than he ever had Mary.

"I'll make it up to you, Ilene. How about Christmas?" He would bring Penny out to meet her, and maybe Brian would come from New York. That's what he would do. He'd settle it right then. He'd own up to this breast-beating love for a woman who put him in toe dividers and gave him pedicures with her little home kit of files, clippers, sloughing lotions and mentholated oils, smoothing the edges of his battered toenails with a pink emery board.

"You promise?"

"Count on it," Francis told her.

HIS back didn't permit him to ski, but he could snowshoe, or so Penny convinced him, and they'd strapped on their snowshoes at the trailhead and clopped in the half mile to the Dancing Moose Yurt, as it was gaily called. Because of Francis' bad back, she'd packed in all their supplies, forging ahead on her snowshoes like a seasoned trapper.

A large circular tent-like canvas on wood supports and built on an elevated deck, the yurt contained a propane stove, mattresses, pillows, dishes, candles, tables and chairs. Outside were a food storage box and an outhouse. "Isn't this amazing?" Penny said. He had to admit it was if you liked three feet of snow outside your door and nothing to do but sit, talk, read, and play cards for four days. He and Mary could go for extended periods doing what might be called the adult version of parallel play: reading, gardening, eating, and solving crossword puzzles, with few words exchanged. But with Penny, he could never take silence for granted, and he wasn't sure if he was up to the challenge of so much interacting in one small rounded yurt.

"Let's get some firewood," she said, which meant he would get the firewood. He stepped outside and immediately sank in the snow up to his knees. He had to don his snowshoes for a simple twenty-foot walk to the woodpile, much like an astronaut couldn't count on gravity.

He brought back an armful and Penny sent him out with a stockpot to melt some snow to boil water.

There was no running water or electricity of course, so they cooked by candlelight. She assigned him chopping duties, fired up the propane stove, and then told him to get more wood outside for the fire. He brought in another armful. "Are you tired?" she said, seeing his flushed face in the door.

He wouldn't admit to it. She took his stamina for granted, physically, sexually, mentally; he wasn't about to disillusion her now. "Just a little winded," he said. "The altitude."

"Oh, absolutely!" Penny agreed.

Despite the spare conditions, she had hauled in the ingredients for a dinner of marinated duck in red-wine sauce, roasted red potatoes, and an arugula salad with asiago cheese. They sat down at the pine table to eat by candlelight. She reached over for his hand. "I love you," she said, the first time such words had been spoken by either of them. "Do you love me?" What a simple question that demanded an untroubled response, but in his hesitation, as with the single moment of his and Mary's accident, all would change.

Shadows flickered across her stricken face in the candlelight. "Francis?"

Down to its smallest detail, she had researched, planned, and executed this holiday to perfection. What could be more intimate than being together in Dancing Moose Yurt while raccoons, porcupine, deer, and bears tramped around outside, and you had only each other for safety, companionship, sex, and love. And yet he could feel that Mary was somehow in this yurt with them disapproving of abnegating his self to this woman who controlled, munificently as she did, every waking hour of his life now. Mary would expect more, even had she lived and had they separated, not faulting him for his pleasure but for surrendering his will, a sin of convenience, and a long slow sob came out of Penny's mouth when he said, No, he didn't love her, he wasn't sure that he ever could, he was sorry, perhaps they had rushed too fast into things after all. . . .

They left the next morning, snowshoed out through clusters of frosted blue spruces and stands of aspens with their pale gray trunks spindly as the bare legs of children. They stopped in solemn unhappiness to stare at the intact body of an elk, no sign of a kill on its body. "It died of natural causes," Francis said, needing to break the icy quiet around and within him. They'd spoken not a word during the hour of their mushing to reach the trailhead.

"There's no such thing as natural causes," Penny snapped at him. "Your heart bursts, your lungs collapse, your kidneys fail, your bowels give out—it's always something specific." Oh, she could be sharp of tongue—and mind—when she wanted to be. "Just because they can't find what kills you doesn't mean it doesn't exist. I used to fuck this guy," she told Francis, and his head dropped toward the blue shadows of the snow while she went on. "He was a friend of my brother's, a physiologist. There's always an organ failure, he said, or a germ or rupture behind every death, no matter how the newspaper or coroner phrases it. Even the oldest man, Francis, even the oldest man dies for a very real reason."

They drove in disquieting silence out of the forest and onto the main road. Near the bottom of the canyon, as the road flattened out and started to turn toward town, Penny said, "What happened? What did I do?"

"Nothing," said Francis, "you did nothing. I just need a break, that's all."

"Why now? Why spoil this wonderful trip? I mean, terrible! Terrible trip. It was wonderful until you said that . . . couldn't you have waited at least until we got home? What kind of person says such a thing at that time?"

"I wasn't planning on it."

"You've been so happy, Francis. I know you have. Tell me you haven't! You told me you used to walk into town to get a newspaper every morning and a cup of coffee, and you'd fall asleep in your chair at six o'clock watching the evening news. Goddamn it, you're telling me that's something you're afraid of being *rushed away from?* I know what you saw. You looked right at me last night and you saw another fifteen, twenty, maybe even thirty years of life and it scared you, didn't it? You saw you'd have to live like a full man too, with new blood passing through your veins, and you choked! You saw that I could give you that, didn't you?"

"Penny, you . . . I don't know . . . you have some large ideas about yourself."

"Oh, I'm crazy now. Is that what you're saying? I have this delusion that I'm this great big important person to you who was filling up your world, is that it? Well, *yeah*, I do, and I was!"

"I have kids—"

"Don't use them as an excuse! They're grown up!" Her fist came down like a mallet on the Volvo's dashboard. He pulled off the road at a turnout under a steep rock face glistening with rivulets of snow. Sunlight sparked off the melting streams like flakes of mica. It reminded him, disturbingly so, of the slivers of glass that had embedded his face.

"Listen," he tried to explain, "I'm only saying that I haven't even told my own family about us yet, and we're already spending holidays deep in the woods with lynxes eating snow hares. I just think it's too much too fast—"

"Take me to my apartment."

"Oh, come on, Penny. Does it have to be all or nothing? Can't we be two reasonable people who have a bit of a time out from each other?"

"Children have time outs. Mature adults usually walk into something with their eyes open and keep their wits about them.

They don't reject people in the middle of a beautiful forest for no reason other than they're cowards."

"Fine," he said. "I'm a coward then."

She sprung around toward him. "Are you having an identity crisis? At sixty-one years old? Is that possible?"

"I'm a coward, I'm a child, I'm not mature, I'm in the midst of an identity crisis. You're determined to make it anything but a simple matter of us having our own space."

"You know something, Francis? I really, really, *really* despise that phrase *having our own space.*"

At her apartment she got out of the car, slammed the door, opened the back of the Volvo, dragged out her backpack, threw it on the ground, and then banged the rear hatch shut. He watched while she went inside, his back searing with pain.

She called the next morning and asked when he would be out.

"Is this really necessary? Just come get what you need. Please," he said, "it's just a break."

But when he came back from picking up the mail that he still received as an emeritus professor at the department, perhaps hoping to run into her as he first had, every trace of her was gone, her clothes, her jewelry, her cosmetics that crowded out his Di-Gel and Zocor on the bathroom counter, her bicycle, and board games. He thought to go over and apologize, take her roses, but when he looked around at the furniture she'd rearranged and the Chinese herbs that now stocked his kitchen cabinet and the books on socially conscious investment, all to the good, he just felt tired and went to take a nap, something he would never have done with her here.

AT Christmas he visited Ilene and her family in San Diego. He got down on all fours like a lion and let the boys climb over him. What could be more fun than hanging from grandpa's neck like spider monkeys while he lumbered his body across the polished wood floors and commenced monstrous roars of menace. They would not leave his side for the whole week, jumping up on his lap for him to read them a favorite story about an irrepressible talking dog who reminded him not a little of Penny with her frenetic energy.

Brian did not show up, but spoke to them by phone and told his father that he had made EMT-2, which meant more money and challenges as a medical technician. Francis poured out his approval, perhaps too much, for Brian became quiet at hearing such gushing. Too much Christmas cheer? No, they couldn't have known, either of his children, that he had adopted Penny's mannerisms, her effusive praise and overexcited celebration of the least event under the smallest pretext. Certainly he was proud of Brian, but the boy was right to ask him, "Are you drunk, Dad?" because though he hadn't touched a drop during Christmas dinner he clearly was not acting himself.

Ilene, tanned and fit as always, a more serpentine version of her mother, pulled him into the study and shut the doors on the evening before he was to fly back to Colorado. He'd been out in the hall talking with Philip about water usage, a subject of rare mutual interest between them, Philip a hydrologist, and Francis knowledgeable about water levels in the reservoirs and lakes of the West. Two days earlier they'd all had Christmas dinner, and the trumpeted mother of Karen Schmidt, Ilene's college roommate, had been placed next to him. She was a slender blonde in her late fifties he guessed, with turquoise jewelry and high arched eyebrows and perhaps a Botox injection of late and a tendency to make wry, mortally insinuating remarks out the side of her mouth about being fixed up at her age—no hiding there—an honesty she had no doubt developed from years of watching her husband die of pancreatic cancer. No time to waste; no reason not to get to the point. Francis had little to say in return, and after a while she grew tired of trying to draw him out with thoughtful questions and moved over next to Philip's parents, chatting with them for the rest of the evening. The match was a failure, and he could see in his daughter's somber face her disappointment. He thought this must be what she wanted to speak to him about, this and his high excitable bursts of helium-like glee that came out of nowhere and had descended on Brian for one, celebrating his promotion to EMT-2 as if he had just been appointed Surgeon General.

"Dad, I know what happened," Ilene said, and it took less than ten seconds to tell him she knew that Mother had wanted a divorce, and that he didn't have to keep it from her anymore.

"I'm sorry," he said, something he'd been repeating all too much lately—to his children, to Penny (in his messages on her voice mail, unreturned, and his e-mails, unanswered), and to Mary, dead for almost two years now.

"You're not to blame. Mother wanted . . . I don't know what Mother wanted."

"How did you find out?"

"She told me. She said she wanted to leave you and that she was afraid it would really damage you and she wanted advice. That's when I knew something was wrong. Why would she ask me for advice? What did she expect me to say? She acted as if she were talking to a girlfriend about it."

"Maybe she thought of you that way," Francis said. "In a good way, I mean." He so longed for a Vicodin. He had promised Penny he would not take it anymore. What a silly promise! He was in pain! What the hell did she know about his pain? How could any reasonable person want someone to keep himself from feeling better? But it was a measure of his utter—could he dare call it this—devotion to her that he'd agreed to follow her regime of alternative healing, none of which he was practicing now but still didn't permit himself a simple pharmaceutical analgesic out of some misbegotten loyalty.

"You can't go on blaming yourself," Ilene was telling him. "Mom didn't know what she was saying." He looked at his daughter and her oh-so-bruising faith in him. She could not imagine how he could possibly make someone unhappy.

"I don't blame myself," he said. "I wish we would have been talking about something else when she died, but I don't blame myself."

There, he'd confessed, and he saw the horror on Ilene's face, the twisting grief and rage—at whom? Her mother? Him for telling her?

Her mother and father's last words to each other had been about their dead marriage. He'd cursed his daughter for sure now.

But she ran over and threw her arms around his neck, his grown-up spider monkey of a daughter, and told him not to worry; he would never be alone, she and Philip would take care of him. And he thought of Penny and her swishing calypso bottom while she cooked, and of her bobbing red hair—that beacon in the distance!—and how mightily he would seek its luminous grace.

THE LAST
COMMUNIST

M Y PARENTS always had visitors. They would come in the
evening and sit in folding chairs on the back porch of our
small house in New Brunswick. They greeted me—an only child
—with the warmth of aunts and uncles. "How are your studies
proceeding, Manny? Are you making good progress in school?"
Except "good" sounded like "goot" and "school" like "skoo." I
hated the name Manny, after my dead grandfather, and insisted
everyone call me Matt, an all-American name for a boy born in
1954, but our visitors didn't know or remember to do this. Speaking the language was hard enough for them in their accents that
thickened on their tongues like cornstarch the longer and more
intensely they talked through the night with my parents.

Every summer my mother and I would go to the Lake Kiniwa
Hotel in the Catskills, outside Liberty, New York. My father would
stay behind to run the grocery and come up on weekends. Dora,
my mother, waited on tables at the hotel, and in 1970, when I was
sixteen, I worked as her busboy. The guests who had once num-
bered in the hundreds amounted to less than sixty, two stations
worth of customers. Few children stayed at the hotel anymore,
perhaps just a grandchild or two coming up on weekends. Some
of the guests were the same ones who had visited our house over

the years. They would cup my chin when I came over to clear their plates and pinch my cheek for good luck, even though I was bigger than my father, which wasn't saying much, since he was only six inches taller than my five-foot mother.

I was all too interested in money, according to my parents. My "preoccupation," as they referred to it, came to a head early in the season that summer of 1970 when Mr. Borwitz, one of our guests, died of a heart attack after dinner. The next day his daughter arrived to claim her father's things; I didn't hesitate to mention that it was the end of the month and neither my mother nor I had been tipped for our services. Mr. Borwitz's daughter, a tall blonde wearing a silk scarf, whipped out two one-hundred-dollar bills, a premium on what we could normally expect. I presented the money to my mother, who was not pleased. "How could you?" she asked. "You run up to a grieving woman with your hand out *begging?*"

"First of all," I said, "I wasn't begging. It's our money—"

"It was a tip!" my father, Isaac, interrupted; he'd driven up for the weekend. "A gratuity, which, by the way, I don't agree with. Either you pay someone what they deserve—"

"*Second* of all," I said, stopping him before he went off on one of his lectures about the dignity of the worker, "she wasn't grieving at all. She was all business, complaining about how much crap her father had brought up with him and how would she ever get it all in the trunk of her big fat gold-trimmed *Cadillac!*"

"Go to your room, Manny!" which was what they called me when they were mad or wanted to make me mad.

"I don't have a friggin room!" I screamed back. I shared one with my parents on the third floor of the hotel.

"What's happened to your compassion for others?" my mother implored.

"A *khazer*," my father muttered.

I was a selfish person, not quite a *goniff*, a thief, but close, and although my secular parents scorned religion, the opiate of the masses, after all, they didn't hesitate to employ old world Yiddish for its unmatched tonal accuracy in evoking disappointment.

"Bad move," Irwin said, when I told him of the incident. I'd known Irwin all my life. He was the other waiter besides Dora at the hotel, and we'd been neighbors until he went off to college. Twenty years old, he'd just finished his sophomore year at the University of Michigan. He'd gotten a low number in the draft lottery and wasn't sure what he was going to do; his student deferment would no longer keep him out of the army. "Maybe Canada," he said, when I pressed him.

"What about being a conscientious objector?"

"That wouldn't work for me. It's the conscientious part they might have trouble with—I'm not the most peaceful person." He looked grim when he said this.

"You should have just pocketed it," Irwin said, when I told him about getting the money from Mr. Borwitz's daughter. He gave my shoulder a squeeze.

Every Tuesday, Nick and I—Nick worked as Irwin's busboy and was a local kid from Liberty—placed newspapers written in Russian on about half the seats of our stations. Though I couldn't read it, I knew that this was the equivalent of the Daily Worker, only with less stateside news and more of the Mother Country. I can't say how many of our guests were actually members of the communist party, but a number of them spoke Russian as fluently as Stalin, whom they still defended. I'd taken to arguing with Mr. Peach—yes, that was actually his name, though it had been changed from the original Petrosky—about how he could possibly support the killing of millions of citizens. Stalin's crimes were well known by this time. Hadn't even Khrushchev changed the eponymous city's name to Volgograd, for good reason, since Stalin was a mass murderer?

"And what of the attacks on Negroes in this country, Manny? You haven't seen the news? Fire hoses and dogs, bombings and beatings—you call this democracy?"

"At least we have the right to protest," I said. "In Russia you'd be arrested and never heard from again."

"Let me tell you something," Mr. Peach said, leaning on his cane. "The worst is yet to come."

"Which is?"

He tapped his cane on the hotel porch. Ten feet from us a card game went on, but no one paid attention to our argument. "I tell you this country will be ripped in two."

I don't think Mr. Peach was referring to the Vietnam War or racial strife. Rather it was his dream of the revolution: workers pouring into the streets and freeing the masses from capitalism, of which, sadly for my parents, I was its chief exponent.

I CAME close to drowning that summer. I'd gone down to the lake in the evening after I served dinner and shortly before dark. No one went to the lake anymore. Only frogs and water bugs disturbed its glassy surface. Dragonflies buzzed above me as the sun started to set behind the white oaks and birch trees, their branches casting shadows across the water. I hadn't bothered bringing a bathing suit because I wasn't planning to swim—just paddle a canoe around until I got tired and could sleep through my father's snoring.

I took off my shirt and paddled in one smooth motion, enjoying the burning in my muscles. An old handball wall and a sagging badminton net stood on the opposite shore, nearly overgrown with chokecherry bushes. When I got to the lake's center, I sat a moment, listening to the crickets and watching the fireflies come out, eating the handful of blackberries I'd picked on my way down the path. I lay back in the canoe, closed my eyes, and then opened them a minute later to see how much darker it had become. My hand strayed below. I thought about Sheri Savitz who had bent over to pick up her pencil in civics class. Her pink sweater had risen above the waist of her skirt and revealed the top of her matching pink panties. Not good—not up here at least, without any girls my age and only a summer of frustration ahead, so I stopped and stripped off the rest of my clothes and dove in the water to shake myself free of the memory.

I tried to exhaust myself swimming as furiously as I could in no particular direction. And when I wearied of that, I dove down to the slimy bottom of the lake, grabbed a hunk of muck, slapped it against my chest, and then shot back up like a missile piercing the water's surface. I must have done this about fifty times. Finally after almost an hour and now tired enough to sleep, I looked for the canoe, but it was gone—having drifted back to the far side of the lake, a good hundred yards away. I turned on my back and tried to float and stay calm. I'd completed a Red Cross swim class, in case I wanted to be a lifeguard at the hotel, but of course our elderly guests rarely swam in the pool and the camp for kids had long ago been disbanded. So I knew what I had to do, yet when I looked behind me I saw that I'd gone in circles. In the dark I'd lost my reference point on the opposite shore. And then I got a terrible cramp in my leg that was so painful it affected my whole right side. I used my left arm, but that only made me go in even tighter circles. Panic set in. I started breathing faster and took water in my mouth from favoring my left side too much. You're a strong swimmer, I kept telling myself, stay calm, breathe evenly. But when I checked my progress and saw how far I still remained from shore, fear washed over me. My leg, aching with pain, threatened to pull my whole body under.

"Hey! You okay out there?"

My body stiffened immediately. It was a girl's voice, familiar but too distant to recognize.

"No," I said.

"What'd you say?"

"HELP!" I shouted.

"Coming!" the voice said. I didn't think about being naked. I didn't care that I had no idea who was coming for me. I couldn't concentrate on anything other than the seconds passing. Then I heard the other canoe and grabbed hold of its solid bow.

ABOUT Irwin. We'd both come up to the area since we were young, attending the red-diaper summer camps and belting out the words to "Joe Hill," "Union Maid," and the "World Youth Song." Once, when I was eight and Bobby Melk teased me about being skinny—he had called me Road Map because the veins showed through in my chest—Irwin, twelve years old, the same as Bobby, punched him in the nose. Irwin was "confined to quarters," but when pressed as to why he had punched the boy, he wouldn't say. He didn't want to be seen as heroic in defending me, because this somehow diminished my stature, and he didn't want to rat on the kid, because this diminished his. So he would only explain he'd done what was necessary. I finally told the counselors the story myself. Then we had a long group meeting at the baseball field about all of us being brothers and sisters and sharing beliefs in the common good and "from those with the most ability to those with the most need," a variation of a speech I'd heard all my life. Bobby Melk mumbled an apology to me. Irwin was asked to apologize to Bobby—in front of the group. Irwin stood up and though we could have expected anything, he put two fingers in his mouth and blasted a whistle, at which Rusty, the camp's Irish setter, came racing down the hill and sat at rigid attention in front of Irwin, an astonishing show of canine fealty.

"Irwin," the counselor said, not knowing what to make of Rusty's sudden presence, "don't you have something to say to Bobby?" But Irwin snapped his fingers and Rusty twisted in the air like a hooked fish. Then Irwin put his hand out flat and motioned down, and Rusty put his snout on his front paws and crawled toward Irwin as if in jungle combat. We red-diaper campers cheered; Irwin must have been training him all along. The counselor's plea for self-criticism and apology was drowned out, and Irwin, who had forgiven me for telling what happened, waved to us over his shoulder as he bolted into the woods with Rusty.

He was sent home the next morning to his parents, our neighbors. Of course that made him a martyr and started a movement of its own at the camp: Why had Irwin, our young comrade, been "expelled"? Why did he have to apologize to Bobby Melk, the camp bully (who later that summer wound up getting caught stealing)? Didn't Irwin represent all the good things the camp was trying to teach us about fellowship? Indeed, just being associated with Irwin shot up my prestige at the camp, and in the absence of the real person, I mythicized his exploits, and invented some, by flashlight late at night.

So it was a great surprise to discover that my rescuer proved none other than Irwin's fourteen-year-old sister, Julie, who'd just arrived that evening with her parents. She'd been sitting alone on the bank of the lake.

"You're shivering," she said when she reached me. "Get in."

True, I was shivering, but not from cold as much as embarrassment at being saved by a fourteen-year-old girl who'd had a crush on me for the last several years. "I'm good here."

"Don't be silly, Manny." When she leaned over I smelled peppermint chewing gum on her breath. I tried to rest my elbows on the side of the canoe, as if we were just having an idle conversation at the edge of a swimming pool. "I won't look," she promised, but there was more chance of me walking on water than getting into that boat naked with Julie. She'd obviously been watching me swim around, perhaps even followed me to the lake, and grateful as I was to be alive, I was irritated too.

Eventually Julie gave up trying to persuade me and paddled, as I held on to the stern and kicked along. When we got to shore, I asked her to turn away while I got my clothes from the other canoe, which had drifted to the lake bank. I had the distinct feeling she failed to obey my request as I streaked toward the boat, my buttocks flashing white in the moonlight.

THE next morning my mother fainted while serving breakfast. She dropped her service tray of twelve bowls of oatmeal. In the kitchen, I heard the loud crash and rushed out. I'd worried this would happen. For weeks, I'd pleaded with her to let me carry the tray, but she insisted she was strong enough. She would not, or could not, carry it one handed above her shoulder and had to hold the wide tray in front of her as if presenting a big birthday cake. Her face would turn red, she'd huff and puff, her back would creak under the strain, and she'd barely make it to the tray stand. I would chase after her, but she'd shoo me away: "This is my job, Manny. If I can't do it right, I shouldn't do it at all."

"Don't be stubborn," I told her. But she wouldn't listen. She didn't want to be dependent on anyone, even her son. For years she'd schlepped at the store helping my father, cashiering and pushing around stock. She was her father's daughter, my grandfather a Russian Jew from Odessa, who'd made his living as a tailor and hadn't stopped working even in his seventies when nearly sightless he could only sew by touch.

Irwin was already at my mother's side when I got there. She'd recovered enough to sit up. All around her were the shattered bowls, the metal lids, and gobs of oatmeal. Seeing her there dazed, her white apron between her spread legs, terrified me.

"Mom," I said, kneeling down. "What happened?"

"I got dizzy, Matty." She never called me Matty. Manny, or maybe Matt when I reminded her. "I saw stars—just like they say!" She tried to make a joke out of it, but nobody was laughing. The guests had gathered around.

"Please give Dora some air," Irwin asked. They shuffled back a few paces.

"She needs a doctor," said Mr. Drach. "Anybody a doctor?"

No one answered. They were all communists, no high rollers here.

I got up and went to the serving station and poured a big glass of water. I held it to her lips. "Thank you, sweetheart," she said. "I must be dehydrated."

"You ready to stand up?" Irwin asked her. My mother nodded. Irwin motioned for me to get on her other side to help. Although my mother was a small woman, I was surprised at how heavy she was when we tried to lift her. Dead weight. She didn't have any strength in her legs. We supported her until Mrs. Fishman pushed a chair under her, and she sat down again. "Just give me another moment," she said. "Then I'll be ready to go." She drank some more water.

Irwin went to the kitchen for a mop. I kept my eye on Dora while the chef started to dish up more oatmeal. After a while, she stood up on her own. "I'll take over, Mom," I announced. I'd expected her to protest. I was only sixteen. But Miriam, the owner, who had come in from outside, nodded her consent. My mother didn't argue.

SHE rested during the afternoon, while I served lunch without a hitch. Irwin's busboy, Nick, the local kid from Liberty and sixteen like me, hustled between our stations and kept up with both jobs. But of all times, Miriam insisted that Nick and I polish two bus boxes full of flatware, a messy, smelly job. "Dora is ill," I complained to her. "Can't this wait?"

"It's been waiting all summer. There's nothing you can do for your mother right now. Let her have a good long rest." Talk about your lapsed socialist. I'm not sure Miriam gave a damn for the Movement. She'd hosted the group for years, and despite their dwindling numbers, she counted on their core business. My mother was supposedly a distant cousin of hers, but we weren't exactly treated like family. We had a small and hot room (I'd gotten two fans from the storeroom and put them near my mother to keep her cool) and were asked to work seven days a week. This was no union job. I didn't care because I was young and glad for the work, any job, but I worried for my mother. It was no secret that my father's grocery, in an increasingly downtrodden and crime-ridden section of New Brunswick, was barely making it, squeezed out by the larger supermarkets that had opened in the suburbs. His customers were the poor and elderly who walked to and from the store. They paid in food stamps, and when those ran out at the end of the month, my father extended them credit.

He prided himself on never being robbed and informed me the best protection a person can buy is generosity, but this didn't keep his shelves from growing sparser, his creditors from leaning on him, and the other merchants from going out of business like swatted flies.

As Nick and I worked away at the silver, Julie came into the dining room, a moment I'd been dreading. She was wearing a red bikini and looking for a can to curl her hair. "You have one?" she asked pleasantly, her voice bright, her green eyes shining. I said I'd check in the kitchen. I dawdled a moment looking through the trash for an empty vegetable or fruit can the right size.

"Here you go," I said, when I found one and came out with it.

"Thanks, Manny." I shrugged. Matt, Manny, what did it matter? I'd almost drowned and was standing in front of my bikini-clad savior, her breasts substantially larger than when she used to come to my house and ask if she could play golf with me, a capitalistic sport if ever there was one that I'd taken up and devoutly played every Saturday. Or she'd come over with a plate of cookies. Or a quiz she wanted me to take in a teen magazine to determine if I was more a feeling or thinking person. This had been going on for the last two years, and now she was, as they say, developed, curvaceous and tanned, her lips a frosted pink. Nick dreamily rubbed a silver cream pitcher as he stared at her. Technically she and I, at this time of year, were only two years apart—her birthday in May, mine in July—but we were miles apart otherwise: I was going into eleventh grade, she into ninth, a huge gap in teenage time. It wasn't so long ago that I'd watched her set up her stuffed animals in the backyard with nametags while she practiced gymnastics in front of them.

"I'd better get back to work," I said.

"See ya," Julie said. Barefoot, her hips wriggling in her low-slung bikini bottom, a scalloped shell of sun-bleached downy hair fanning out from the small of her back, and trying to balance the can on her head, she made her way out the door.

"Wow," said Nick.

"She's fourteen," I said. "Just."

Nick smirked. "Just right, you mean."

"Not cool," I warned him. I was grateful Julie hadn't mentioned anything in front of Nick about saving me from drowning. "Let's quit polishing," I told him. "We've got to set up for tonight." The hotel, more from tradition than demand, kept kosher, separate plates for lunch and dinner, no *flayshadig* with *milchedig*. And we had a few guests, mixed among our fellow travelers (and even some of those), who were observant. I set out the dinner plates and silverware, folded the linen napkins like swans tonight—I could do hares and doves too—and nestled them in the goblets, then I went to check on my mother.

BUT before I could get there, I became distracted by loud voices on the porch. Irwin, who had just come back from picking up clean tablecloths for breakfast because the laundry delivery truck had broken down, was going at it with Mr. Hower, also one of our visitors in New Brunswick, but someone I'd never cared for. He often drank and became loud and argumentative—obstreperous, my father called it. I'd gone to a number of protests with my parents, until I told them I didn't want to go anymore, and Mr. Hower was always out in front. Usually we'd join a larger group, farm workers, strikers, civil rights marchers, and fit in alongside them, beefing up their numbers, until someone, specifically Mr. Hower, would unfurl the Communist Party banner. People would suddenly part from us as if the Red Sea had opened. Mr. Hower would inevitably call them weaklings or cowards or phony baloneys, or on one occasion, though my father disputed it, "proletarian pussies." I knew I'd heard right. And I didn't trust him.

Mr. Hower had stormed off and Irwin was breathing hard, as if he'd been in a fistfight, not just an argument. Mrs. Krantz and Mrs. Lieber, both widows, squinting up through their thick lenses at six-foot-two Irwin, were telling him not to pay any attention.

"What happened?" I asked.

"Nothing," he said.

"What were you yelling about?" I wasn't going to let it go. Between my mother's fainting, my near drowning, and now this nasty argument, things were getting out of hand, especially considering the hotel's usually arthritic pace.

"It was about those shootings," said Mrs. Lieber. She meant Kent State, which had happened in May.

"What was Hower saying?"

"He thought the students were expendable," Irwin said.

"You're kidding?"

"If they had more sense, they would have made themselves part of a larger movement, been better organized and kept their focus on the greater good. No one should mistake themselves for being indispensable. What bullshit. He was trying to bait me. And I let him."

"No surprise you lit into him," I said.

Mrs. Krantz said, "He's a very pushy man."

"Yes, he is," Mrs. Lieber agreed.

"He likes to get people's goat," Mrs. Krantz added.

"Does he ever!" Mrs. Lieber echoed.

"We'll stick up for you," Mrs. Krantz said, "if anyone gives you the business."

They adored Irwin, who had grown a beard at school but had shaved it off to work at the hotel, as well as cut his dark curly hair. He'd promised his mother that he would help out Miriam, though he could have made more money at one of the bigger hotels, the Concord, Browns, the Flagler, the Pines, even Grossingers.

"Er toig nit," Mrs. Lieber said, which I understood well enough to mean Mr. Hower was a loser.

I SERVED dinner that evening while my mother rested. As soon as I'd swept my station, I went up to see how she was doing. My father, who'd just arrived, a day early to be with my mother, was sitting in bed with her, both of them in their stocking feet. "See?" my mother said, patting the top of her head as if it were a good puppy. "All better." She looked pleased, and the color had come back into her face.

My father wiggled his toes at me like sock puppets. "We're very proud of you."

"We are," my mother said. "People stopped by and told me how well you've been taking care of them."

"You're growing up, son."

They looked tiny, if happy and relieved, sitting in that small double bed (I slept on a cot the size of a strip of bacon). They'd surely forgiven me for whatever disappointment I'd caused them over Mr. Borwitz's daughter.

"Sit, sit," my father asked. "Tell me what you've been doing all week."

"You know," I said, looking at my watch, "I think I'm going to take a walk."

"You just came upstairs! It's getting late."

I shrugged. "I guess I'm not sleepy yet."

"I'm sorry, son," my father said. "We should have insisted on getting you your own room."

"That's okay." I knew they'd done it to save money. One room was free, a second would have meant a deduction from our meager pay. "I'm glad you're feeling better," I told my mother.

"Thank you, darling. You were a wonderful help."

I went downstairs to the kitchen. Sometimes I would sneak into the walk-in refrigerator and just sit on a covered plastic bucket of floating pear halves and eat everything in sight: hardboiled eggs, salami, herring, grapefruit, olives, potato salad, cheesecake . . . I was always famished. My face had become leaner, my shoulders and chest broader, and I could barely close the top button of my white shirt to snap on my busboy's bow tie. Like any growing adolescent I was on intimate terms with a refrigerator, in this case an entire walk-in, and considered it my rightful compensation for seven days of labor at seventy-five cents an hour, which didn't include set-up time.

But when I sat there this evening, chilled as a beer glass, the cooler's fan silencing any noise outside of my own thoughts, I didn't eat. I just wondered if my mother would ever be able to stop working and if my father had expected this hard life, striving all hours of the day and justifying it by always saying he was "just one of the little people" trying to survive. It was as though he secretly believed his life meant more if he suffered as an example than if he succeeded as an exception. But who was I to blame them for the life they'd chosen? Sitting next to each other in bed, sharing some grand dream of a better world, planning to picket for fair housing, debating excitedly whether they should fork out the cash to print leaflets this time around or use a mimeograph machine, my father the treasurer, my mother the secretary of a nearly penniless and shrinking organization . . . and could I ever have made them happier, with any academic accomplishment or extracurricular achievement, than when I came home in second grade and reported that I'd refused to say the Pledge of Allegiance because it contained the words "one nation under God"? Who was to say their illusions were any worse than the ones I would collect over the years and lose? I felt too young to know something so disappointing, but I did.

I went outside and walked in back of the hotel to the casino, closed years ago. Julie and Irwin were there talking in the dark. I sat down next to them on the peeling wooden steps of the casino. Bats regularly flew around inside; pounds of guano were rumored to be above the rafters.

"What's going on?" I asked.

"Just talking," Irwin said. Julie was wearing white shorts, all the better to show off her tan legs. Not one to be out of step with the times either, she had on a blossom-bursting, tie-dyed tank top.

"Am I disturbing you?"

"We've pretty much wrapped it up, right Jules?" If her sulking look was any indication, Julie didn't seem to agree.

"Really, I can leave," I offered.

"Stay. In fact, you kids talk," Irwin said like an uncle. "Give me a hug, Jules?" He put his long arms around her and she weakly reciprocated. He got up and left.

"What was that about?" I asked. "You look crushed."

"He makes me so mad." She put her head down between her knees.

After a long silence, I said, "Are you going to tell me why?"

"He won't tell me what's going on. He's arguing with Mom and Dad about not going back to college. He's got more important things on his mind than college, he says. So I keep asking him what's wrong, and he goes, 'Nothing's wrong, Jules.' 'Is it the draft?' I ask him. 'No.' 'Did you get a girl in trouble?' He grunted. I guess that meant no. He's always told me everything before, everything."

"Maybe he's just trying to figure things out for himself."

Julie lifted her head and looked at me. "I didn't tell anyone," she said. "About the lake."

Now that she'd brought it up I couldn't pretend it hadn't happened. "I was embarrassed out there. I could hardly face you, let alone thank you."

"You would have made it. I just gave a lift, was all. Anyway, it's nothing to be ashamed of. I almost drowned once in Cape May. Irwin had to pull me out."

"He's good at saving people too. You've got a regular family franchise going."

"Stop it," Julie said, slapping my arm, but letting her hand linger there. "Don't tease. I'm not in the mood for it. My brother's treating me like a complete child. Everything's so 'personal.' He actually used that word when I asked him what exactly his plans were for next year. He's never been like that around me."

I was listening, but I was also wondering if she was right. Would some survival instinct have finally propelled me safely to shore on my own?

"My parents are bugging me, too," she said. "They won't let me go to Long Island for a week. My friend Cindy's parents have a house on Fire Island. We'd be there by ourselves for a couple of days while her parents traveled. I made the mistake of telling my mom that part, too—dope that I am."

"It does sound a little unsupervised."

"I knew you'd say that." She brushed the ground with the toe of her sandal. Her nails were polished a pearly white. "Forget it," she said. "Everyone's turning against me anyway."

"Nobody's turning against you. Irwin's in a bind, worried about being drafted—"

"He won't even discuss it. He just keeps saying to leave him alone. He has to figure out what to do. Go to a psychiatrist and get a letter, I told him. 'I've never been saner about things,' he told me, but he was incredibly angry when he said it."

I thought about Irwin's explosion on the porch today. Julie was right about his anger, but I'd seen something else too—fear.

She put her hand on my thigh. "Let's stop talking about my brother," she said. "How's your mother doing?"

"Better, thanks." She let her hand drop further over my thigh and leaned her head on my shoulder. I thought about her lining up the stuffed animals in her backyard. She was still a skinny little girl then, using a deodorant can as a microphone to sing to those same stuffed animals, and though that shouldn't have mattered now, our bodies having regenerated their cells several times over according to my tenth grade biology book, I couldn't do what every new cell and engorged muscle in my body wanted to. "It's getting late," I said. "I've got to get up early and serve breakfast."

"I don't eat breakfast," she said. "I don't give a damn about breakfast."

"I have to," I said. "I don't have a choice."

"Then go. Leave. Desert me like everybody else," she said, pouting and pointing her finger away, as if casting me out from the garden.

IN the morning, my mother was back at work, with my father's help. At one point, they both carried the tray out, Mother on one side, Father on the other, as if moving a sofa across the room. "Come on, let me do that," I said.

My father took me aside in the kitchen. "Leave your mother alone about the tray. She doesn't want to look helpless."

"But that's exactly how she looks carrying it like that."

"Please," he said, "she wants to do it this way."

So I kept my mouth shut. Irwin went about serving, but I noticed during a lull he was standing at his station drinking coffee, which we weren't supposed to do. After breakfast, he took me aside. He looked as if he'd lost weight since he'd first gotten here.

"What did my sister tell you last night?" he asked.

"Nothing," I said. "Just that she was worried about you."

"She didn't tell you anything else?"

"No. What's wrong?"

He didn't answer me. Not directly at least. "I want you to do something for me. If I'm not here tomorrow . . ."

"Wait—what do you mean, if I'm not here?"

"Just listen. I want you to tell my parents I'm okay. Can you do that?"

"Where are you going? Is this about the draft?"

Irwin took me to the end of the porch. Mr. Abrams, who once had to "disappear" for a few weeks after being subpoenaed during the McCarthy hearings, was playing a game of solitaire and occasionally glancing up at us. Irwin lowered his voice, just a bit. "I'm going to South America, all right? But you can't tell anyone. I'll be fine. I'll contact people as soon as I can."

"What are you talking about? Where in South America? Are you in trouble?"

"Take it easy," he said. He wrapped his arms around me, just as he had his sister last night, and hugged me hard. "And take care of everyone, okay?"

"Julie's very upset—"

"Keep an eye out for her most of all."

"Irwin, you just can't leave—what about your guests?"

He laughed and shook his head. "You would worry about that. The least of my problems, Matt."

By the next morning he was gone. Everyone was looking for him. Miriam told me to check his room to see if he'd overslept, but I knew he wouldn't be there. When there was no answer, she got a key and opened the door—an empty room, all his stuff missing. "What's going on?" she asked me.

"I don't know," I said.

His parents came down next. Mr. Winterstein was a tall man, like his son, and Irwin's mother was built more like her daughter, curvy; the ever-creepy Mr. Hower had always leered at her when she came to our house. I told them the same thing I'd told Miriam, and now my parents too, who had lined up in the hallway outside Irwin's room: I knew nothing. But Mr. Abrams had mentioned I'd been talking to Irwin on the porch and that we were "whispering."

"You must tell us," my mother said, "if you know anything."

"I don't," I said.

"Why would he take off like this?" Irwin's father asked. "We were arguing, yes, about his going back to school, but this isn't like him."

Meanwhile, our guests were clamoring for breakfast. "We have people waiting," I told the group jamming the hallway as if we were in a Marx Brothers movie. "I'll take over Irwin's station," I announced, and that's what I did, for the rest of the summer.

JUST before the season ended on Labor Day, we had a visitor at the hotel, a balding man with thick black glasses, wearing a dark blue suit and white shirt. He spent time speaking with Miriam in her office. I was down by the pool, cleaning it, and thinking that I wouldn't come back next summer, that I didn't want to work with my mother and see her sweating and grunting over this job, and that if I refused to return, money or no money, maybe she would too. My name was paged over the PA system: *Manny Hefferman, please come to the hotel lobby.*

"This gentleman would like to speak with you, Manny," Miriam said. My father was back in New Brunswick, and my mother had gone shopping in Monticello. "He's with the FBI."

"My parents aren't here," I said.

Ken Boyer, that's what he said his name was, clapped his hand on my shoulder. "Let's just talk for a couple of minutes. No big deal, Manny, right?" The term "super-friendly" came to mind, not in a good way.

"Why don't I sit in too," Miriam said. For once she seemed to be on my side and concerned about me.

"Sure, no problem," said Agent Boyer—as I would later refer to him. "But I think Manny's a big enough fellow to have a private chat. Aren't you, Manny?" It felt patronizing, his appealing to my pride and maturity, as if he were talking to a child, but there was a threatening edge to his good cheer that also backed Miriam down, and she left us alone in her office.

He placed a legal pad on the desk in front of him and laid his fountain pen—gray with marble swirling—across it. "So how's your summer going, Manny? You enjoying working up here? I understand you're a waiter now."

Since I was only sixteen and there were limited numbers of hours I could work, I just nodded vaguely.

"Got some good fishing around here, too, I hear. You fish down at that lake?"

"Used to," I said, "when I was five."

"Brookies, bass, walleyes . . . how's your friend Irwin doing?"

"What?"

"Irwin. You and he are buddies, right? Heard from him lately?" Agent Boyer spun his marbled pen on the pad, a big smile on his face.

"I haven't," I said.

"I was hoping you could help me out, Manny." It bothered me that he used my name so much. "He spoke with you before he left here, didn't he?"

"Who told you that?"

"All I want to do is talk with your friend."

"I really think I should have my parents here. They wouldn't like me meeting alone with you. I shouldn't be doing this, I'm only sixteen—"

"Seventeen," Agent Boyer corrected.

"Just a few days ago."

"You're not a kid who lies, are you, Manny?"

"I'm not lying—"

"You just did about your age."

"I forgot . . . I'm so used to being sixteen."

Agent Boyer rubbed his hands together as if trying to start a fire. "A little cold back here," he said. "Fall will be around before you know it. So what was it exactly that Irwin told you before he left?"

"He didn't say anything."

"I think he did, Manny. In fact, we know he did."

It was the first time he'd used the word "we," and it sent a shudder through me. "I want to call my father."

"You want to get your father involved in this?"

"What do you mean?" I said.

He smiled without amusement, his eyes flat. "Just what I said."

"My father had nothing to do with this!"

"With what? Oh, you mean with this?" Agent Boyer opened his briefcase and laid out a photograph of Irwin in a crowd of college students. He was holding a rock in his hand and facing a row of police with gasmasks on.

"I don't know anything about it," I said, and I didn't.

Agent Boyer nodded agreeably. "Okay, how about this one?" He slipped a larger glossy photograph out of a manila envelope. My breath caught. It was a photograph of Irwin talking with my father outside his grocery in New Brunswick. Irwin had a beard then that dated the photograph, but I didn't know how far back. It could have been as much as a year. "Irwin was our next door neighbor," I said. "He came to the store all the time. Where did you get that picture?"

Agent Boyer put the photographs away without answering and knit his fingers into a ball. "You seem to know a great deal about his whereabouts, Manny. I'm sure you can think harder about them now."

THE following winter my mother died. She'd had several more dizzy spells. Her doctors had advised her just to rest. It was most likely her diabetes or high blood pressure, they said. But one night after we all went to see the movie *Mash*, and allowed ourselves a good, if dark, laugh on a cold evening, she curled up in the back seat of our Plymouth on the ride home, claiming she was suddenly tired. She let out a sharp whimper that we thought was a sleep noise. By the time we reached our driveway, she'd died of a brain hemorrhage.

Many of the same visitors who'd come to our house over the years attended the funeral. Mr. Peach was there and Mr. Abrams, as well as Mrs. Lieber and Mrs. Krantz, although Mr. Hower was notably absent. They talked amongst themselves, offered their condolences, and told me how wonderful a person my mother was —not an enemy in the world. They drank the coffee and ate the knishes and kugel we had put out for them. My father, who hadn't stepped foot in a synagogue since my bar mitzvah (that I'd insisted on, not for the least of reasons being money), sat shiva and asked me to join him. He was worried about me, a seventeen-year-old boy and only child losing his mother. I smoked my grief away, and when cigarettes didn't do the trick anymore, I took up grass and kept myself stoned for my year of mourning. If anyone asked how I was doing, I said great, and believed it.

Julie and her parents were at the funeral, of course, but not Irwin. No one knew where he was. People suspected Canada, but I'd perhaps thrown the FBI off the track by telling them South America. "You haven't heard anything from him?" I asked Julie.

"No, nothing, zip," she said, and dropped her head. I could see the clean pink line of her parted brown hair that hung straight down her back now. She looked sophisticated in her black dress and a single strand of gold around her neck. Her parents were sick with worry about Irwin and still believed I was holding something back.

"Are you?" her eyes pleaded. "You can tell me now, if you are. It would give us all some peace of mind, no matter what."

"He said he was going to South America—the same as I told the FBI." I didn't tell her that I feared for my father and mother if I didn't cooperate, and that Agent Boyer had made it clear he knew everything about them—and me—and that he somehow knew, too, this was my greatest childhood fear: my parents would be taken away and executed like the Rosenbergs. I'd never quite outgrown it.

I turned away from her eyes, which were wide open with expectation. "He's fine," I said.

Julie put her hand on my arm, a steadying touch for her. "What are you saying?"

"Just that Irwin could always take care of himself. We both know that."

"I want him back," Julie said. "I can't stand not knowing where he is and if he's okay. Sometimes I feel crazy. Oh, *God*, your lovely mother just died and look at me going on about my problems."

I put my arm around her shoulder. She kissed me lightly on the cheek and said to stay in touch, such an adult phrase. I was almost—or yes, I was at that moment—in love with her. "I'm so sorry about your mother, Manny." It didn't matter now. Irwin was the only one who remembered to call me Matt, anyway. I would be Manny from hereon, the name my mother had died calling me. *Honor your name; name no names,* my father had always told me.

I got a scholarship to a small liberal arts college in the Northwest. The summer of my freshman year I went camping with a student group in the Three Sisters Wilderness. One night, I wept uncontrollably for my mother. A girl from my economics class, Sandra, sat by me, and didn't ask what was wrong, for which I was grateful. She seemed instinctively to understand I couldn't do anything but weep, after years of not doing so. In the morning I decided when I went back in the fall I'd switch majors from marketing to history and would become a high school teacher.

Years later, when I was married to Sandra and living in Portland with our first child, a daughter named Daria after my mother, my father called to say he'd heard from Irwin's family, who had moved to Florida. Julie had gone into broadcasting and was an anchor on a New Jersey TV station, married to, my father didn't fail to mention, a lawyer for the ACLU. "You won't believe it, Manny. Irwin's been right above us all this time."

"Above?"

"Canada! Under an alias. Michael Winn. All these years and his parents didn't know a thing!" Irwin was coming home to serve an agreed upon sentence for the bombing of a ROTC building on campus. No one had been hurt in the incident, but it was a federal building and he would have to face the consequences. Amnesty had been granted to those draftees who fled to Canada but not to radicals who took action into their own hands. My father didn't approve of such violence, but he could certainly understand the frustration that led to Irwin's act.

I felt enormous relief, mostly because I could stop hiding what I'd kept secret all these years, telling no one, not even Sandra —that I'd been sending Irwin money from the part of my mother's life insurance left to me. Nor was it for purely educational reasons that I'd gone to college in the Northwest. I'd cross the border into British Columbia, zigzag through the province, and meet him in remote places to bring him any news I had of the family. When the war ended and the threat of discovery and prosecution lessened, we eventually lost touch and I destroyed the phone numbers I had used to contact him.

That day on the porch at the hotel, after mentioning loud enough for Mr. Abrams to hear that he was going to South America, Irwin had whispered the first of these numbers and told me to memorize it, swearing me to silence. "Remember me," he said. He bent his head down and rested his damp forehead on my shoulder, adjuring me to forgive him for what we were about to do.

OPPOSITE ENDS OF THE WORLD

E VERETT whistled for his dogs. They jumped up immediately and waited by the door. Earlier that morning, two animal control officers—were they called officers?—had come by to report a complaint about Cissy and Alberta. A neighbor had filed the complaint; that's all the animal control people would divulge. If he wanted to know more, specifically the names of his dogs' accusers, he needed to send a formal request to the county.

He'd been handed a sheet of paper with friendly bright orange lettering: TIPS FOR CONTROLLING YOUR PETS. Don't leave them alone all day. Don't leave them in the hot sun or freezing cold. DO give them plenty of attention, water, food and exercise. DO remember the three R's: Routine, Reassure, Reward.

At the front door, he put Alberta on the double leash first, then Cissy, who acted the older sister, less frivolous, more cautious, two chocolate labs from the same litter. Last week, Alberta had run into a fire hydrant and knocked herself out. She stood up after a moment and gave her lean brown body a hearty shake, as if to say, *Whew, that was different.*

He identified with her clumsiness. His own stiff-legged walk. His MS. He couldn't ride a bicycle anymore. He'd loved riding, and it was the thing he missed most, but he couldn't even lift his leg over the bar to get on and off now. Swallowing his pride, he'd gotten a girl's bike, but he needed toe holds to keep his feet on the pedals. A few days ago, he'd ridden around the park; he kept falling and getting up, strapping his feet in, falling and trying again, until his ankles and feet were raw and lacerated. Lauren winced when she saw him (he'd stupidly—or intentionally—worn sandals too).

Now he walked around the lake, both dogs rasping on their leashes while other owners jogged by high-kneed with their dogs loping ahead of them on slack leashes. He moved slowly forward in his poky drilled walk, then stopped for a rest in the shade, tying the dogs to the pole of a barbecue grill. Alberta, spotting an irresistible specimen, lunged for one of the park's ducks, until she was yanked back on her chain. The more astute Cissy watched calmly on her haunches as if to scold her sister, *Haven't you learned anything yet?*

"Mr. Stottlemeyer?"

"Kevin, what are you doing here?"

Kevin, almost six feet tall at fourteen years old, pointed behind him to a bus full of children. It was the junior high where Everett had taught band. "We're going to practice for next Wednesday."

"Next Wednesday?"

"Band Day."

"Oh, yes," said Everett. He'd forgotten. The three junior high schools held their competition here at the park every May. Everett had been in charge of it before he stopped teaching.

"Is Mr. Cramer with you?"

"He's right there," said Kevin, pointing up the hill at the teacher who had replaced him a year ago.

Everett put his hand flat on the ground and tried to push himself up. He'd been sitting too long.

"Can I help?" said Kevin. He had grown at least four inches since Everett had seen him last. He played the clarinet, passably.

"I think I can manage," said Everett, but his legs, number than usual, wouldn't cooperate. He breathed deeply and tried to picture energy flowing to his extremities. Nothing. "Maybe I'll just sit here a minute more."

"I'll go get Mr. Cramer," said Kevin, before Everett could stop him. He didn't want John Cramer to find him in this position, helpless, unable to get up, maybe unable to stand. That's what he was most afraid of—that he wouldn't be able to remain on his feet once he did stand.

John Cramer, who was forty-seven, ten years older than Everett, came down the hill with a big pleasant smile on his face, his red and white windbreaker—the official school jacket—rustling. He'd heard good things about John, that he motivated the kids, got them to practice, kept their minds focused on the playing. He had them doing songs, Everett had heard, from *Phantom of the Opera*. Not bad.

"Everett, what a wonderful surprise to run into you. How's it going?"

"Fine, John." He extended his hand up for John to shake. "Just out walking the dogs." The dogs hadn't taken their eyes off the lake, the free flying geese. They'd be no help. "I've been hearing good things about the kids," said Everett.

"I'm constantly reminded of the standard I have to live up to. They don't hesitate to begin a sentence with 'When Mr. Stottlemeyer was here . . .'"

The kids ran up the hill, carrying their instruments. "Would you like to join us for practice today?" John asked.

"Join you?"

"Back to back. You take one side, I'll take the other."

His legs wouldn't have anything to do with the idea. "Maybe some other time. A little tired today," he said.

John nodded sympathetically. Everett thought it must make people more uncomfortable than if he were in a wheelchair, his stiff-legged gait, his shakiness, and most of all the uncertainty of his condition. There wasn't anything finite about it. One day he might be in remission. Another day it might eventually kill him. "I'd better go before they try to escape," John said, looking up the hill at the kids who were chasing each other in tag, swinging their instruments.

"John, would you mind giving me a hand?"

He didn't hesitate. Everett reached up and grabbed his wrist. He saw the alarmed look on John's face when his wrist was gripped with the tension of a towline.

"Should I pull?"

"As hard as you can," said Everett. He had absolutely no strength in his legs. He felt he would collapse.

He stood, shaky. John kept his grip. The legs—he thought of them as a separate entity: a corporation with its own physical bylaws—had decided to hold. He took a tentative step toward the dogs, the right leg quivering like a plucked guitar string, but it stayed in place. This would work. This would work.

"Are you going to be all right, Everett?"

"I am," said Everett. "Thank you."

LAUREN phoned as he opened the door to let himself and the dogs inside. "How's it going?" she asked.

He could hear her eating her lunch at her desk. She was director of human resources for a health care company. The company had grown three-fold in the last two years and her position was stable and lucrative enough to support both of them. They had an affordable mortgage on a modest home in the old section of town, no big expensive wishes. It had made sense to them both for Everett to leave teaching. He could devote himself to staying healthy, not tire himself out so much. And frankly he couldn't get around the school, all those steps, marching down the field, the exertion of practices . . . he would have needed a wheelchair, which he couldn't accept. Yet.

They had no children either, though he knew this was not something that Lauren wished. The MS had come unexpectedly into their lives, a burden of such consequence that it had squeezed out hopes for a family: illness was their unwanted, unplanned member, and perhaps if they'd conceived a child before its onset they would have adapted, but the focus of Everett's nurturing had become his own iffy health. It wasn't fair to Lauren, he knew, but it wasn't fair to himself to have one, not as far as helping her or (and this more than any other reason) witnessing himself possibly disintegrate right in front of his offspring's eyes. Watch my bladder go, my bowels fail, son. Watch my legs collapse, daughter. He tormented himself with such possibilities, perhaps from fear of humiliation, perhaps from just fear. "I can do the majority of the care-taking," Lauren had told him. "Or we can get help." But around this time, Everett fell down a flight of steps, and the fall was bad enough that the subject just got dropped, went underground, along with his best legs.

"I had a little trouble at the park," he said. "I couldn't stand up for a moment."

"Did you take your medication?" Every week he received a package express mail from Israel, his medication packed in dry ice. He injected himself with the serum and hoped for better things. He didn't even know what was in it, only that his physician had recommended this procedure and the stuff couldn't be gotten in the U.S. He laughed at first—medicine from Israel on dry ice, hugely expensive. Before long he was taking it three times a week, afraid now to stop for the little relief it appeared to offer.

"I'm going to."

"Don't push yourself," said Lauren.

"I know."

"That means leaving the kitchen alone."

Slowly, he was remodeling the kitchen. It was a project that had turned into a nightmare: 1950s metal cabinets ripped out; the old-style Battleship linoleum, two layers of it thick as tires, needing to be pried up to reach the wood floor beneath; a warren of lead piping dating back eighty years that had to be replaced. He couldn't have picked a worse job.

"Why didn't you start with a bedroom or something simple?" asked his father, a lawyer in Washington. "You always have to tackle the toughest thing." Everett didn't know whether the old man—still going strong in his practice at seventy-four—was talking about the MS or the kitchen. Then again, his father sometimes gave the impression Everett could beat this thing, if he just put his mind to it. Diseases that lacked known causes and cures baffled the man, a litigator who had lived his life smack in the middle of causal deployments. His mother offered more sympathy, but along with it came an entire clipping service devoted to MS developments, subscriptions to newsletters, and—her latest venture— efforts to get him to join a therapy group on the Internet.

He had gone to a number of meetings with fellow sufferers, and there was much talk of treatments and sub-treatments (Prozac for depression, Paxil for anxiety, Botox for bladder control) and living with a progressive disease, and he couldn't say that he hadn't benefited from the support and company, but he hadn't gone back, either because he was basically a loner or because, as his group might say, he was still fighting the big stupid fact of his damn luck.

"All right," Everett said to Lauren. He wouldn't put up a fight about the kitchen today. He had the floor ahead of him anyway, pulling up and replacing the rotten boards, then sanding, screening, and finishing—work that was hell on his knees and legs. He'd promised Lauren he'd get someone to do the job, but he couldn't justify it, the expense, when he was home all the time.

"Do something relaxing," Lauren said. "Paint, watch a movie. Remember how we used to watch old black and white movies in the afternoon?"

"We should do that again," Everett said. "Soon." They would close all the curtains, unplug the phone, make popcorn and curl up on the couch together, watching the movie. Afterward, they'd make love. Film noir excited Lauren in a way Everett couldn't quite figure out. Perhaps it was the toughness of the two dimensional past; she wouldn't have to hire anyone like Robert Mitchum or

Sydney Greenstreet as a nursing aide; she wouldn't have to get involved in a grievance suit; she wouldn't have to run a security clearance; she wouldn't have to mediate. These men were just brave or cowardly, noble or despicable, without needing "further evaluation." Something remained dependably heroic or evil about their character and perhaps lust, arousal, yearning, whatever it was that caused Lauren to hurry off her clothes and grab for his belt had to do with that fantasy of a whole and predictable man you could always count on. It was a question he'd given a lot of thought to recently—what exactly constituted his manhood, his completeness, now that he could barely walk? Now that he took medication with Hebrew labeling that affected his sex drive. It required a lot more work than simply sitting together on a couch watching an old black and white movie.

"Don't get discouraged," said Lauren. "It doesn't mean anything that you had trouble in the park."

"Lauren . . ."

"Yes?"

"I . . . I was terrified."

There was silence on Lauren's end. What did he expect her to say?

"I can hear it in your voice."

He swallowed a few times. He'd wanted her to be there; he'd felt so horribly alone.

"I'll be home early tonight," she said. "Will you be okay?"

"Yes," he said, and got off.

ONE afternoon ten years ago, shortly after Everett received the clinical diagnosis of his MS, Lauren informed him, "You'll always be the same person to me, don't you ever forget that." He heard her fierce loyalty seared in the statement, her promise to never leave him, her Lauren-like resolve. They'd been married for two years. They sat in a little park across from the Denver hospital. Lauren started talking to him about changes in diet, alternative therapies, exercise. Their sex life wouldn't, as some people claimed, necessarily take a hit. "And there's only a slight risk of a child inheriting MS," she slipped in.

Obviously she'd done the research and prepared herself for this result, unlike he, who had held out hope that his dizziness and fatigue had to do with anything from anemia to depression. A gentle breeze had blown through a stand of shadowy pine trees above the berm of the downtown Denver park. Unleashed dogs leaped with exquisite arched grace for Frisbees. This may have been the moment when the idea of Cissy and Alberta arose, a vision of their springing muscular canine bodies free from this particular virus or whatever it was that had his immune system stripping away the insulation of his nervous system like termites chewing a house from the inside out. "I'm optimistic," Lauren had announced, intimating he should be too. Her legs were smooth and tan from a beach trip to Mexico they'd taken to get their minds off waiting for the results of all the tests. Her small mouth remained pursed with keen determination; her hand never left his arm.

Except for hearing her later that evening crying in the bathroom on the cordless phone with her mother, he would have thought, and half believed, everything was going to be all right, and she was neither scared nor disappointed about the rest of their lives. He'd always pictured himself—son of a take-charge father—as the one who would care for Lauren in the event of illness or an unforeseen catastrophe. How humbling and disquieting to see how little say he or anyone really had in the matter.

WHEN he returned from Hardware Hank—he couldn't restrain himself from a trip to rent a floor sander, feeling better after a nap—there was a note on the windshield of the car. It wasn't a note actually, but a thick computer printout. He unfolded the pages and stared at it in amazement:

BARK BARK BARK BARK BARK BARK BARK BARK BARK BARK BARK
BARK BARK BARK BARK BARK BARK BARK BARK BARK BARK BARK

BARK BARK BARK BARK BARK BARK BARK BARK BARK BARK BARK
BARK BARK BARK BARK BARK BARK BARK BARK BARK BARK BARK
BARK BARK BARK BARK BARK BARK BARK BARK BARK BARK BARK
BARK BARK BARK BARK BARK BARK BARK BARK BARK BARK BARK
BARK BARK BARK BARK BARK BARK BARK BARK BARK BARK BARK
BARK BARK BARK BARK BARK BARK BARK BARK BARK BARK BARK
BARK BARK BARK BARK BARK BARK BARK BARK BARK BARK BARK
BARK BARK BARK BARK BARK BARK BARK BARK BARK BARK BARK
BARK BARK BARK BARK BARK BARK BARK BARK BARK BARK BARK
BARK BARK BARK BARK BARK BARK BARK BARK BARK BARK BARK
BARK BARK BARK BARK BARK BARK BARK BARK BARK BARK BARK
BARK BARK BARK BARK BARK BARK BARK BARK BARK BARK BARK
BARK BARK BARK BARK BARK BARK BARK BARK BARK BARK BARK
BARK BARK BARK BARK BARK BARK BARK BARK BARK BARK BARK
BARK BARK BARK BARK BARK BARK BARK BARK BARK BARK BARK
BARK BARK BARK BARK BARK BARK BARK BARK BARK BARK BARK
BARK BARK BARK BARK BARK BARK BARK BARK BARK BARK BARK
BARK BARK BARK BARK BARK BARK BARK BARK BARK BARK BARK
BARK BARK BARK BARK BARK BARK BARK BARK BARK BARK BARK
BARK BARK BARK BARK BARK BARK BARK BARK BARK BARK BARK
BARK BARK BARK BARK BARK BARK BARK BARK BARK BARK BARK
BARK BARK BARK BARK BARK BARK BARK BARK BARK BARK BARK
BARK BARK BARK BARK BARK BARK BARK BARK BARK BARK BARK
BARK BARK BARK BARK BARK BARK BARK BARK BARK BARK BARK
BARK BARK BARK BARK BARK BARK BARK BARK BARK BARK BARK
BARK BARK BARK BARK BARK BARK BARK BARK BARK BARK BARK

It went on for eight pages. Nothing else. He looked behind him, as though there might be a surveillance camera. What the hell was going on? He thought about his neighbors. A college student who came and went with her boyfriend rented the house to the south of theirs. Everett didn't even know her name. The house on the corner belonged to Mrs. Yemetz, a sweet old lady who wore an apron and greeted him with a big smile of false teeth. She was hard of hearing. On the right side was a young family with two cats, a hamster, a gecko, and a turtle. They were animal lovers and the kids, twin girls, regularly came over to play with the dogs and bake cookies with Lauren, who doted on them. Next to them were the Mikelsons, Curtis and Arlene, childless like themselves. Everett supposed they could be a possibility. Curtis worked out of the house, so he was home all day. But Arlene worked with Lauren at Western Healthcare and had never mentioned a thing to her about the dogs. And in person they always acted pleasant and friendly enough. They'd even had a few backyard barbecues together, although Everett had quickly run out of things to say to Curtis, who never followed up on a topic or initiated a conversation himself. "What did you and Curtis talk about?" Lauren had asked after one of their get-togethers, because Lauren really did enjoy Arlene's company. Everett had shrugged, unable to say.

He sat down and wrote to the Humane Society requesting the names of Alberta and Cissy's accusers.

THE dogs stayed especially docile and quiet the next week, as if suspecting they were the subject of an investigation. They looked up at him with their limpid gray-green eyes, an eerie transparent shade of hazel, unique to the breed: *Who, us?* those eyes seemed to ask when Everett would inspect them for signs of misbehavior after he came back from a short errand. They did appear innocent. And Everett had received no more notes, no computer printouts. Lauren had said just to forget about it. If the person didn't have the guts to accuse them to their faces, why care? And if the Humane Society investigated further they'd find out how baseless were the charges.

He spent the whole week redoing the kitchen floor: replacing the occasional damaged board with a matching one he pulled from the closet. With a drum sander, he made the old wood smooth as a pearl, then edged with the belt sander, screened and applied four coats of polyurethane. When it was done, the original cherry floor shone a rich sunny red—perfectly restored. Lauren was amazed. They stood at the kitchen threshold and admired it.

"I want to eat on this thing as soon as it's ready," she said. He felt inordinately proud, ridiculously happy. It was only a floor! And yet it filled him with the satisfaction of slaying a dragon. Hours later, after they'd gone out to dinner—the solvent fumes hung in the air despite the fans—and after they'd successfully made love, dragon slayer that he was, he stood at the threshold and admired his floor in the dark. He'd renovated it board by board, his fingers cut from prying up the stiff linoleum, his back and legs searing with pain, but good pain, acceptable pain, pain from hard work alone and nothing else. So what if one day he might not be able to walk on it; for now it was solid gleaming ground.

In the morning, Lauren woke before him, and he heard her showering. He went out to the kitchen and walked across the floor. His legs felt fine. He walked back and forth several times, then sat down in the middle.

"It's beautiful," said Lauren. She stood in the doorway in a thin white sweater and tan skirt watching him.

"Come sit," he said, and patted a place next to him.

She knelt down—she didn't want to sit all the way in her skirt.

"I'm feeling well," he said. "Really fit."

"Good," said Lauren, but he could see she didn't get what he was saying.

"I'm talking about the MS. And about us. A bigger us."

She stared at him. "Really?"

"It feels like it's going to last." He knocked on the kitchen floor, believing it. He'd been thinking about it while he'd worked on the floor, his knees sore, his back aching, the occasional crackling pain down his spine, which he had ignored. If he could lay a new floor, he could have a child. It was that simple and that preposterous.

"You wouldn't joke about this, would you?"

"No," said Everett. "I'm not."

Lauren's eyes widened; her face flushed a pretty shade of rose that swept down her neck and startled him. "I'd completely given up any hope," she said. "I mean, about a baby."

She got up and hurried into the bedroom. When she came back she held up her blue diaphragm case. "Should I?" she said.

"Sure," he agreed, unclear exactly what she had in mind.

He followed her out to the garage and watched her throw the egg-blue case in the trash, filled with all the worn boards he'd pulled up from the kitchen floor. The diaphragm case wedged itself there between nailed and splintered wood.

"I'll call you," said Lauren, "as soon as I get to work."

He'd never seen her so happy, not in a long while.

Dear Mr. Stottlemeyer:

Per your formal request we are forwarding the name of the complainants as prescribed by section 3098 of the county code. Please be advised that such disclosure does not constitute a waiver of your responsibilities to comply with all recommendations for control of your pets.

This disclosure additionally does not endorse any legal action by the Humane Society on behalf of the complainants.

Complainants: Curtis and Arlene Mikelson

He couldn't believe it! Arlene! She worked with Lauren. He called Lauren at work.

"You'll never believe this. It's them."

"Them?"

"Curtis and Arlene. They're the dog haters."

"What are you talking about, Everett? Can I call you back? I have someone in the office for an interview."

"Wait! Just don't say anything yet to Arlene. I want to think about how to handle this."

He got off and walked out front. He stared at Curtis's house. Everything was neat and organized. A cedar plaque with their name—The Mikelsons—swung from the spotless porch. Each of the trees in their front yard had a low decorative wire fence, white with half moons along the top. The grass, freshly mowed, not a dandelion in sight, rolled out from the front step like an emerald lake. A hose coiled around its caddy without a kink. Never so much as a leaf on their lawn. No kids ever visited. Their garage was the only one on the block that wasn't filled with junk and actually had room for a car.

He went down the sidewalk. Alberta and Cissy, who had nudged open the screen door, started to follow. "Stay!" shouted Everett. Why was he yelling at them? They hadn't done anything wrong. "Go back," he said more calmly, and they obeyed, turning to flop down together on the porch and looking at him over their paws.

He knocked on Curtis's door. There was no answer at first, so he rang the bell—two jabbing shrieks. Finally, Curtis came to the door. Tall, awkward, dressed in a long-sleeve flannel shirt even in spring, he seemed to flinch from the sight of Everett, and Everett had a pang of remorse at being here, how chronically bashful Curtis was around people. Arlene, as happens with couples, was the complete opposite: effusive, warm, spontaneous, always glad to see you. But here was a man who cowered inside, working on complicated circuitry or whatever it was he did. It brought back all the stressful memories of trying to talk with Curtis at the backyard barbecues, Curtis hunched over and listening intently, Everett allowing spaces in the conversation, but Curtis neither responding nor initiating anything of his own. It had unnerved Everett so much the last time that he'd begun babbling about his MS, and the more he talked, the more uncomfortable Curtis became until both men suddenly broke apart like a snapped wishbone to opposite sides of the yard, Everett with a spatula in his hands, Curtis simply rubbing his neck as though from whiplash, their wives watching them with curiosity. He hadn't spoken to Curtis since that evening last summer.

"I want to talk with you about my dogs," said Everett. Curtis looked past Everett, as if worried the dogs might actually be on his property. He was yet to open the storm door, forcing Everett to raise his voice. "Why didn't you come to us?" asked Everett. "Why couldn't you simply knock on our door and tell us to our faces that you had a problem?"

Curtis mumbled something.

"What?" said Everett through the glass.

"People are sensitive about these things."

Was this an explanation? Better to secretly report someone than to upset them in person? Or was he afraid of Everett? Is that what he was saying? It gratified him to know someone might be afraid of him in his condition.

"How about if I come in and we talk about it?"

Curtis shook his head. "I don't think we should talk here."

Everett was about to ask, why not? But he decided it wouldn't get him anywhere. Clearly, the man had peculiar ways Everett would never understand. What did Arlene see in him? Did Arlene know he had even complained?

"We can talk at your house," said Curtis. He stepped outside, pulled his door closed and stood with a bandy uncertainty next to Everett, waiting for him to move.

They walked in silence to Everett's house. Everett opened the door for Curtis who stepped carefully past Alberta and Cissy, thumping their tails. He followed Everett into the living room.

"Want something to drink?" asked Everett.

"To drink?"

"A beverage." He felt like a flight attendant. What was so difficult to understand? "Water, soda, lemonade?"

"I'll take a birch beer," said Curtis.

Everett stared at him. "We don't have birch beer."

"Water will do then."

Had he made a joke? Birch beer? Curtis hadn't cracked a smile. Everett walked across his new floor. He got Curtis a glass of water. When he came back, Curtis was peering at the fish tank. "Those goldfish shouldn't be in the same water with the tetras," he said. "They need different pH balances."

"I haven't had any trouble."

Curtis shrugged. He had a thin face and a crown of hair in tight gray curls. He blinked several times after he spoke, as if each sentence took enormous effort and temporarily exhausted for a few minutes his supply of communication, until at a timed interval, like a safe popping out a twenty-dollar bill, he could resume.

"I just wish you would have said something to us first," said Everett. Alberta and Cissy were looking in through the screen door.

"You need to control your dogs."

"But I do control them, Curtis. For God's sake, look at them now, what's the problem?"

"You need to control them," Curtis repeated. He twisted his long body around on the couch, then took a drink of the water Everett had put in front of him on a coaster. "Their barking," he said. "It's so . . ."

"What? Too loud?"

"No."

"What then?"

"Bark bark bark."

Everett remembered the computer printout. "What's that mean?"

"Monotonous. It goes all the time. Bark bark bark."

"When do you hear this 'bark bark bark'?"

"They do it when you leave. As soon as you pull out, they start."

"Really," said Everett. "And you can hear it? Two houses away when they're inside?"

"Yes," said Curtis. He took another sip of his water.

They sat in silence for a long minute. What could he possibly say? "Maybe you're just noticing it now because it's spring and our windows are open."

"Maybe," Curtis mumbled.

"What if I put them down the basement when I leave?"

"I'll still hear them."

Another minute passed. "What do you suggest I do then?" asked Everett.

"I don't know," said Curtis. "Control your dogs."

"You keep saying that, Curtis, but exactly how do you think that should be accomplished?"

"Give them more to do."

"Pardon?"

"Give them something to do while you're gone. Maybe they could chew on a rawhide bone."

"You think that would stop them?"

Curtis squirmed. After a moment, he said, "What's that noise?"

"What noise?"

"That sound. Hiss."

"Hiss? I don't hear it."

"Listen."

They both went silent. Everett sat motionless, straining to listen.

"You hear it now?" said Curtis. "Hissss."

"No, I'm afraid I don't."

Curtis got down on all fours. He began crawling: his large, bony body tracked slowly across the oval rug like a sea creature emerging onto land for the first time. "It's somewhere in here." He was up against the fireplace.

Everett got down next to him. They were both on all fours looking up the flue. "It's the pilot light," said Curtis.

"You hear the *pilot light*?"

"That's it," said Curtis, standing up, satisfied now. He turned and walked toward the door. He started to say something—control your dogs?—then thought better of it, and left.

After Curtis had gone, Everett felt a migraine coming on, his vision distorting. He drew the blinds and lay down on the bed in the dark. He tried to quiet his brain, soften the muscles in his face, picture his clean, unmarred, sunlit floor. He had Imitrex and painkillers and if that didn't work he could always get a shot of Demerol at the clinic.

Cissy and Alberta scratched at the front door. It was time for their late afternoon walk. He supposed they'd start whimpering soon if they didn't get it. Curtis would hear that too, with his super-sensitive hearing, like one of those big electronic ears that could pick up whispers from across a cornfield. Bark bark bark. Control your dogs.

The phone rang, then it rang again, then again. He finally forced himself to answer it.

It was Lauren. She wanted to know how he was. "I have a migraine," he said.

"Oh, Everett, I'm sorry. I shouldn't have called. Go back to bed."

"Okay," he said flatly.

"Can I tell you something?"

He nodded, then said, "Yes," remembering he was on the phone.

"I'm so excited. What we talked about."

He was going to tell her about Curtis, but why? What would Curtis have to say about a baby? A screaming child. But maybe that wouldn't bother him. Maybe that was okay because it wasn't monotonous. "I am too," Everett said.

"You still want to?"

"Yes, I do," said Everett.

"I'm coming home to take care of you," said Lauren.

"It's all right," he said. "I just need to lie down and relax."

"You're sure?" asked Lauren. "I really would be glad to."

"It's fine," said Everett. She was the most maternal person he knew who didn't actually have a child. It would be criminal to deprive her of one. "I can't believe it," he added.

"Can't believe what?"

"What we've decided."

She was silent, then said, "So you don't want to?"

"I do." What he couldn't believe, what he couldn't somehow manage to say with his head splitting, because he couldn't raise his voice enough, endure the inflection needed to express such an emotion, was that he and the child—this child he so much wanted too—were at opposite ends of the world, with so much ground to walk off in between; it was such a desperate, frightening wish. "I'll see you soon," he said.

"Love you," said Lauren.

He went back into his room and lay there in the dark. It wasn't long before he succumbed to taking two painkillers and closing his eyes for the twenty minutes it took for the pills to work. When he woke up, it was hours later and Lauren was beside him in her nightgown, curled up in sleep. Cissy and Alberta were there on the carpet, fast asleep too, both of them on their sides, their fur shiny. Alberta lifted her head from that position to look over her back at him. He went into the kitchen, across the new floor, stepping stiffly. His legs wobbly. It wasn't any better, after all.

He got some orange juice, then put the empty glass in the sink. He walked outside. The street was empty, the moon obscured by a ragged cloud. The roads were wet and the grass moist. He took off his sandals and stood in the grass, letting the wetness soak between his toes, the blades tickle his bare soles. It had rained hard while he was asleep and everything smelled fresh and fertile, sweet and loamy, a rich beguiling scent, and a taste of early spring and honeyed mornings from the crocuses pushing up. He could see Curtis's house, perfectly kept, quiet, motionless, dark.

Everett began to bark. Once, twice, three times. Bark bark bark. He stood there and barked, strong, potent blasts, until Curtis's light turned on, then off again, and didn't come back on.

BLOCKAGE

Patrick did his best. When Connie developed a migraine, he closed the blinds, set up a humidifier in their bedroom, kept the girls quiet downstairs—they'd been running in and out of the room to peek at Connie—and stopped their beagle from baying at the coyotes yipping in the foothills. They lived in Colorado, and the drier air out here had been particularly unkind to Connie's sinuses. Years of respiratory infections and rounds of increasingly less effective antibiotics had finally driven her to have surgery for her blocked nasal passages. The plan was for her to recuperate for a week at home and then take their long-planned, tenth-anniversary trip to the pricey resort on the outskirts of Sedona, a town known for its "healing" properties. "You'll be okay to travel," Dr. Kuhlman had told Connie two days after surgery when at his office he had extracted the endless trail of blood-soaked packing from her nose.

"Will you *please* get rid of that?" Connie begged him. "If I have to look at it a second more I'm going to vomit."

Dr. Kuhlman held up the bloody gauze with forceps like a dead python, admiring its absorption as only a clinician might, and then dumped it into a biohazard trashcan. Later, after Patrick drove her home and their daughters told Connie she looked like Vampire Mommy, and after she went upstairs and the migraine started, she would tell Patrick it was as though Kuhlman had been pulling her brains out her nose. It was right up there with childbirth as far as the most painful experience she'd ever gone through.

THOUGH on the day they were to travel Connie still had a mild headache, Dr. Kuhlman assured them this was normal and no reason to cancel the trip. The congestion from the swelling, dried blood, and mucous was causing blockage and bringing on the headache. He was confident once the swelling went down she'd be fine. They should go with his blessing.

They flew from Denver to Phoenix and drove the two hours up to Sedona where they were staying at a resort and spa described as a place where they could "detoxify, de-stress, and desist." Or just hang out, though not in so many words.

Their casita had a separate living room with a marble fireplace and not one but two couches. Patrick had gone all out, money be damned. The other casitas were scattered around the seventy-acre property, and they could walk the miles of trails in the adjacent forest where supposedly the energy vortexes would result in spiritual alignment. Earlier, on the drive up, Connie had said, "I want to get a massage once we get there. And you should get one too. You need it as much as me. You've been caretaking for a week now when you should've been on vacation." They'd made it through ten years of marriage, mostly in love but with some big changes, including Patrick's one-time plan of becoming a writer jettisoned for a career in dental sales. Probably little matched the disappointment of selling dental supplies after years of believing you were going to be an important writer. Well, perhaps having his ex-girlfriend, who coincidentally lived twenty-five miles away in Flagstaff and whom he'd called while Connie was taking a long bath in their suite, perhaps having his ex-girlfriend become a famous writer herself—perhaps this was more disappointing than selling amalgam separators and bonding agents.

Though he was happy for her. Quite happy, he told everyone. Luciana (she'd changed her name from the given "Lucy") deserved it. She was extremely talented. Never mind that she'd hit it big on her very first try, a novel that had been translated into twelve languages, sold to the movies (Brad Pitt's company had the rights, he was told); never mind that she'd been interviewed repeatedly and managed not to mention Patrick once, even though he'd read her manuscript three times, making copious suggestions and doing all the grunt work of submitting it to agents because she'd been daunted by the prospect of trying to publish a book.

"Are you nuts?" Connie asked him now. Having just gotten out of the tub, she was studying her bruised nose in the mirror, trying to decide how bad it looked without a bandage.

"I just thought since we were in the area I'd give her a call."

"It's our anniversary, Patrick."

He was picking up the selection of body products in their capacious bathroom: mint mouthwash, lavender soap, mango-scented shampoo, almond butter moisturizer—examining them like small toys from Santa. There was a Jacuzzi with gold-plated hardware and a shower with a showerhead the size of a mini pizza. He'd called Luciana on his cell phone, never expecting her to answer—she never did when they were living together, prefer-ring to let the answering machine get it—but she had, on the first ring. He'd been feeling aimless in the spacious suite while Connie was having a soak in the oversized tub. Luciana was packing to go to New York the day after tomorrow (for what he couldn't bear to ask—New York represented the literary Mecca of all he hadn't obtained), but she'd love to see him and Connie, too. How about dinner tomorrow?

"Do you want me to cancel?" he asked Connie. "I can call her back."

"Oh, that's great. And what would she think then? Connie. Connie the bitch."

"I'll just say we're going to be busier than I thought."

"Patrick, why didn't you check with me first?"

"It was a spur of the moment thing. I didn't really call to ask her to dinner. That was more her suggestion. I just felt like we were in the neighborhood. You know how it is. You call somebody, just because you're there."

"I don't. And I think you called her to punish yourself."

Patrick followed her out of the bathroom. "Well," he said, and lay down on the bed next to her, "I have no hidden agenda."

"I should hope not," said Connie. "I don't know why you want to torture yourself, anyway. You know she's just going to gloat." Connie had put her hand on his jeans and was lazily but confidently sliding it back and forth near his crotch. She would tease him, as if she had all the time in the world. Sex had been consistently satisfying with Connie. Luciana, on the other hand, might fling herself at him one moment, covering him with wet kisses, and the next lay there completely inert, as if she were strapped to a board and about to be sent through a buzz saw. Indeed her sexual mood swings had mystified him and eventually left him uncertain and hesitant—he wasn't sure whether he'd get the tigress or the ice queen—until he withdrew completely and they rarely had sex. When early in their marriage Connie had confessed to feeling threatened by Luciana, by her literary success, by her dark beauty, by her flash-bulb smile, by her smooth sun-drenched Mediterranean skin and full valentine lips, Patrick had told her that their worst moments of making love had been better than his best with Luciana. "What do you mean 'worst moments'?" Connie had asked.

"Theoretically. I don't remember a specific time."

"Do you find me attractive?"

"Of course I do," he'd said. "You know I do."

But Connie, though not unattractive, was not, well, exceptional looking. She had small features and wore her hair short, even though he had hinted around she should let it grow—it resembled too much the pixie cut of a child—and she dressed oddly sometimes, in wooly vests that were busily embroidered as if by a grandmother suffering a manic episode, and she still had the same pair of owlish glasses, replacing the lenses but not the frames, that she'd worn when he met her ten years ago, even though he'd hinted, too, how convenient Lasik would be. But such petty concerns didn't make up love, and anyway he was no special package, the pudgy waist and receding hairline, the bum knee that had him wearing a brace when he exercised. Sometimes he just wanted to come home, unsnap his trousers, and fall into bed—beached there on the shoreline of his predictable life. Indeed, catching sight of himself now in the full-length mirror, conveniently placed in front of their infinitely sinkable feather bed, he thought that at thirty-nine he looked exponentially older than when he last saw Luciana five years ago.

"Aren't you the minute man," said Connie, squeezing his hard cock through the cloth of his jeans. She'd let the resort's plush terrycloth robe fall open to her pale bare hips, and she smelled of exotic bath salts. The tender line from her neck to the rise of her breasts was a single brush stroke of bold, arousing simplicity. Nothing was wasted; nothing was excessive. Taking his hand, she licked his index finger and applied the tip of it, with the lightness of tapping awake a third eye, to the point of her sex.

THE massage therapist—Irene was her name—was telling Connie about the commune she'd belonged to in Massachusetts before coming to Sedona. Two women in the same commune both believed they'd been Mary Magdalene in past lives.

"Didn't that cause a problem?" Connie asked, wishing Irene would talk less and knead more.

"It sure did. Especially when there was a guy there who thought he'd been John the Baptist, and they were both fighting over him."

"Really," said Connie.

"Then we had this other woman who'd been told by a midwife that she was pregnant. It wasn't true, but the woman wouldn't stop believing it, even when the midwife admitted she'd made a mistake. It got to be a real problem. The woman was absolutely convinced she was having a baby. She even went out and bought a crib. Finally, I couldn't take it anymore—I felt sorry for her. It's one thing to think you're Mary Magdalene but another to be constantly living under the assumption you're having a child. So I told her in no uncertain terms she wasn't going to have a baby."

"What happened?" Connie asked, suddenly interested now.

"Well, the woman became very upset and she started telling everybody she was having a psychic baby."

"A psychic baby?"

"Yup."

"And did she have her psychic baby?"

"No. One day she announced that she'd given herself a psychic abortion."

"Oh."

"Am I using enough pressure?"

"Um, maybe a little more around my neck and shoulders." She'd been trying to nudge her shoulders back toward the tips of Irene's fingers so she would dig deeper. She really needed to have the tightness broken up because she didn't want to get another migraine. She'd made it through the plane ride, the part she worried about the most, and the drive up, and now she was ready to relax and give her body over to this woman to take out all the knots. Sex helped, and she'd come several times with Patrick—a little frisson of delight went through her as she remembered the rippling pleasure and pressed her pelvis into the table—but she could tell her neck and shoulders were still locked up from the surgery.

"Is this better?" Irene asked, digging into Connie's neck.

"Mmm," she said, though now it was a bit too hard. She tried to relax, just go with it; she was in Sedona after all. She should get in touch with her spiritual side, send out positive thoughts to the universe, stop identifying with her material self, including her sinuses, detach herself from her ego and all its desires. Though that would be a problem since secretly she was writing a novel. She felt terrible about it. She'd boot up her laptop as soon as she got the girls off to school and after Patrick left for work. She hadn't said a word to Patrick. The fact was they'd both agreed to give up writing. Oh, they never talked about it other than to say they were parents now, adults with real lives and responsibilities, and they didn't have time to pursue such pipe-dreams anymore. At some point the signs were there, or the luck wasn't, and you just had to accept your fate and get on with your life. At least that's what Patrick had said whenever he ran into someone who knew him from before and asked if he was still writing. As for her, well, she'd never even gotten as far as Patrick; she'd gone to a few writing conferences, and she'd tried her hand at some short stories and started a novel that didn't make it past page forty. But that was back then. Now it felt like cheating, worse than cheating. At least an affair could end and you could stop yourself and admit your guilt and promise never to do it again. But she couldn't stop writing. The words flowed and the scenes dropped in whole and the characters spoke convincingly and the tension was so good she could barely type fast enough; she flew to the novel in the middle of the night, crouching over her laptop in the basement and typing away, commanded by the voices of these characters she loved, watching them march across the page. She imagined telling Patrick and seeing his surprise then his hurt that she hadn't told him anything about it, then her explaining she wanted to wait to make sure she could really finish, which was true! But she knew she was hiding the real truth from him: she feared he'd be so jealous that his resentment would keep her from finishing. He wouldn't be able to help himself from feeling like it was a betrayal. And nothing was more important to her right now, not the children, not her marriage, not her temp job at the college library—it was horrible to admit to herself!—not protecting him from his own literary disappointments, nothing mattered in her life more than finishing this book. And worst of all, despite all the odds against it, she knew it was good and would be published.

A stabbing pain shot through the back of her head, just underneath where Irene had been deliberately pressing her thumbs at the base of her skull as if into a marshmallow.

"Did I hurt you, hon?"

"I'm okay," Connie said, lying. In fact she could feel a migraine coming on.

PATRICK had seen Connie sitting one day alone in an Adirondack chair on the rolling lawn and made his way over to her. He'd introduced himself, and she'd said, "I'm not very important, are you sure you want to be talking to me?" He'd found her delightfully blunt about the hierarchical rankings of the famous conference, and coincidentally, just at that moment, Luciana had breezed by in a whispery blue skirt, flanked by an entourage of newly acquired admirers who were crowding her as you might a star ducking into a premiere. She hadn't noticed him, or maybe she had and didn't want to be bothered or embarrassed by him. "That's my girlfriend," said Patrick.

"You don't sound very happy about it."

"No, I'm not."

"Would you like to talk?"

"I'd love to," he said.

"I've no clout here."

"You mentioned that."

"I just thought I'd remind you," she said. "Time is contacts."

"You're funny."

"You're sweet to say so."

He was charmed by her willful self-effacement and persuaded her, after many attempts, to show him her writing. He'd been impressed. It wasn't Luciana's sensuous, enveloping prose, nor the solid brick-laying edifice he toiled over, but it had wit and a fetching oddity that often resulted in genuine pathos, too. Her own assessment was that it was just dull. She told him she would never consider sending her work out. In fact, it had been a huge step for her even to come to a conference. Fortunately the big-name writer with whom she signed up for a private meeting had gotten sick and left for good. She was supposed to be assigned to someone else, but that person was yet to be determined. "Have you gone over to the office?" he asked.

She hadn't. So he escorted her over there and got her signed up with someone new, an elderly female writer of fading reputation who took a great deal of interest in her work and encouraged her to keep in touch. But Connie, being Connie, never followed up. "I'm not really a writer," she wrote Patrick in one of their e-mail exchanges when Luciana was traipsing around the country on her twenty-city book tour. "I'm not sure I am either," he wrote back. "How nice it would be just to think of myself as ordinary. Think how happy I could be!" It was the first time he'd seriously considered what life might be like without writing: No rejections, no defensively explaining when people asked if he'd published anything that he was a "long-distance" runner and that novels took time; no perusing authors' jacket photos to deduce how much younger they were than him; no reading over the day's work and swinging between megalomania and self-loathing; no more being jealous of the person you lived with who had struck it big and now had a movie deal and had you pretending to be ecstatic too . . . Connie was his only outlet for his real self, the person for whom he didn't have to pretend he would succeed one day. "Even if you became the most successful writer in the world," she wrote to him, "it wouldn't make one bit of difference to me. I'm not impressed by fame. You're more real to me than that."

And that was it; that was all she had to say. He told Luciana when she got back from her swing through the West Coast segment of her book tour that he was leaving her. She'd not been terribly disappointed. He didn't doubt that she'd had an affair or two along the way of her path strewn with roses.

Preparing to meet Luciana now in the resort lobby, he steeled himself for her undoubtedly dramatic entrance. Connie, meanwhile, had taken to bed to see if she could divert an on-coming headache before dinner. Luciana's website—admittedly he'd checked it out—had a message board where people could discuss aspects of her career, although at one book how much of a career could you have? The big subject presently was about the second novel—when would it be out? After ten years, the anticipation was killing her fans. Some speculated it was a sequel. Others thought it would be an entirely different book. *Someone like Luciana Gevani doesn't need to repeat herself,* one reader, assured of her own astuteness, had written.

Occasionally, Luciana would break into the message board herself and tweet an item or two about her daily existence, a trip she'd taken, or a word about her novel's putative progress, but he got no real sense of her personal life. As far as he knew she was still single and living with her two Persian cats. Patrick and she exchanged e-mails infrequently. What was there to say? They traveled in different circles—or circuits. She was on the literary circuit and he was on the dental one. He visited dentists with his tri-fold briefcase and waited patiently with his heavy samples on his lap to be admitted to the back office where a usually tolerant enough practitioner gave him fifteen minutes to make his pitch about the latest advances in composite veneers and invisible braces. Then he'd call home from some anonymous hotel room in Sterling, Colorado, or Farmington, New Mexico—his region was the whole Southwest—living to speak to his girls and Connie. They would put everything right, make the twelve-hour days all worth it, filling his ears with patter about baking cookies or giving Herm the diabetic hamster an insulin injection or buying a new tutu for Erin to replace her lost one or drawing a picture of him at school about which Sarah was giggling as she spoke, or both of them begging to know what he was going to bring them this time, and then Connie saying, "I miss you," and knowing that meant physically, emotionally, *temporally*—he shared a space in time with them, particular coordinates of belonging; he wasn't famous, but he wasn't alone and he was clearly needed and loved without reservation. And trusted. She had no reason to doubt that he would not look twice, well maybe not more than twice, at the blonde in the hotel bar, or put too much stock in the dental receptionist from Durango laughing extra hard at his jokes and leaning in close to him when she did. He'd learned to remember names of the staff—they were the key to his getting in the door—and their likes and dislikes and to bring them small gifts: chocolates, flowers, pen sets, sports teams' coffee mugs. And how to appear upbeat even when he was so weary he wanted to weep.

"Ciao, Patrick!" And there she was, coming through the lobby's high wooden double doors in a stretchy black-and-white-striped sweater dress with a feathery red boa and her hair in loose dark ringlets like a Spanish consort, her lips plump and pursed with greetings, her arms outstretched to give him a big hug. "Look at you!" she said, without specifying what that meant: You're just the same? Or you're so much older and chubbier? "Where is the lovely Miss Connie?"

"She'll be here soon. She's resting a bit before dinner."

Luciana raised her eyebrows. "Oh? Have you been tiring her out, my friend? I am joking. I am just joking!" This was new—this slight whiff of a foreigner's inflected and stilted English.

"I thought we could eat here," said Patrick. "Connie's still recovering from surgery, and I don't want her to have to take a long ride into town." He was trying to look off to the side, avoid Luciana's ample cleavage and high-heeled stance that cried out for a whip in her hand.

"Miss Connie had surgery?"

"Yes, I told you on the phone."

"I am so sorry! My goodness, I do not know this!"

"Luciana."

"What, my old friend?"

"Why are you speaking like this?"

She drew back in mock surprise. "How do you mean?"

"The 'I do not know this!' The 'my old friend.' You're American. You were born here."

"Sorry. I didn't know it was offending you." She smiled briefly for a bitter moment. "Sometimes I use a different voice for professional reasons."

"You mean to convince people you're Italian?"

"I think we should eat. I am *so* hungry. Oh, *so* sorry! I could eat a steer! Come on, pardner, let's chow down! Is *that* American enough for you?"

"Okay, okay," he said.

"I'll stop if you do."

"I never started anything."

Connie, Miss Connie, walked in, looking especially frail and colorless, a simple sleeveless A-line dress with a squared puritan front that made her breasts look flatter than they actually were. Her short hair, wet from a shower, was plastered to the sides of her head like earflaps.

Luciana captured her in a hug and said how sad she was to hear about the surgery, with a tone you might use to comfort a late-stage cancer patient.

"Sorry I'm late."

"Oh, don't say another word," Luciana told her. "I know how it is when you're recovering." She turned to Patrick, who stood under an Aztec sun god mask emanating metal rays that looked to him like pikes for severed heads. "Time to dine, no?"

CONNIE had tried on the three different outfits and finally decided on the plainest of them. No way could she compete with Luciana, so why even try? And sure enough, Luciana looked as if she'd just stepped off the fashion runway in Milan, wearing a sexy knit dress that fit her like a body glove. On Connie it would have looked like a grownup's costume. The massage had set off another headache that was getting worse, but she'd been determined to show up at dinner. She took Patrick's proffered arm on the way into the restaurant, as much to steady herself as to steady him—he looked unhappy about being here. Why had he called her? He and Luciana were like competitive siblings. She didn't know anybody who felt competitive with her. What was there to be threatened about? Just like tonight, in her dull dress, walking into the restaurant beside a flamboyant Luciana. She was going on about her most recent trip to France where she'd been given some award with the word "prix" in the title not once but twice—the prize for prize?—under the guise of telling them about the food over there, of course. And then, Connie wasn't sure why, but when Luciana asked her at the table, after telling a story about some Hollywood producer who was stalking her, what she'd been up to lately, she admitted, "Working on a novel." It just slipped out, and she tried not to look at Patrick, but she could see out of the corner of her eye that he was still, very, very still.

"Fantastico!" exclaimed Luciana. "What's it about?"

"Um, I'd rather not say."

"Would you like to send it to my agent?"

"Really?"

"Of course. And I'll write you a rave introduction."

"But you've never read any of my work."

"Does that matter? I know you're good. How could it be otherwise? Tell me the title and I'll jot it down."

"I don't have one yet—"

"Why not?" said Patrick. It was the first he'd spoken.

"What?"

"Why don't you have a title?"

"I just haven't thought of it yet."

"I'm sure you have," said Patrick.

"I've really just been fooling around," Connie said meekly.

"Doesn't sound like it."

"Oh," said Luciana, her eyes narrowing. And then again. "Oh! You haven't told him about this?"

"No."

"Well," said Luciana, looking sympathetically at Patrick. "It comes as a surprise then. But a happy surprise, right? So now we all know at once." Connie pushed her half-eaten steak aside. Her head was hurting too much to eat. "This deserves a toast," said Luciana. "Let us drink to your future success." She raised her wine glass, an expensive Bordeaux from a bottle she'd picked out without discussion of the wine menu. "You're going to have a baby novel!"

Patrick was poking methodically at his whipped sweet potatoes with the tines of his fork.

"I'm sorry," Connie said to him. "I wanted to—"

"It's all right," he said, dazed, though, she could see. "Will you let me read it at least?"

"Of course." She took his hand. He sounded so plaintive her heart was breaking. "Of course I will. Always."

"This is *very* touching," said Luciana, in a tone that could almost pass for sincerity. "To Connie's success!"

"I think we should drink to something else," said Connie.

"Oh? And what would that be?" asked Luciana.

"How about to our anniversary?" Connie tapped Patrick's hand, lifeless as a dead crab on the table. "Okay?" Her head was really splitting now. She could barely keep from seeing double. If this went on much longer, she would vomit.

"What do you think, Patrick? Shouldn't we drink to the success of your wife's novel?"

"I think we should drink to whatever she wants."

The waiter came by with the dessert menus.

"Well," said Luciana again, "my arm is certainly getting tired holding my glass aloft! I hope we can agree soon."

"Let's skip it," said Connie, squinting now. "I think . . . I think I might be getting sick."

IN the darkness, Patrick could barely see Luciana, but she had hold of his hand while informing him of a women's group that was giving her an award next month for her work in curtailing the sex slave industry. "You stopped sexual slavery?"

"I have supported so many brave women in their efforts to do so. They want to recognize me for my contribution."

"Which was what exactly?"

"You know, Patrick," she said, having slipped into that familiar New Jersey accent that she'd almost but not quite eradicated, "no one else but you always questions me like this. With other people, I make conversation. With you, it's always a cross-examination. Don't get me wrong, I love it, I really do! You keep me on point. But really, you should have been a fucking lawyer." She gave his hand a squeeze and drew him along.

They crunched ahead on the dark path, with the flashlights they'd borrowed from the front desk flickering off and on as the batteries waned. Connie had taken to bed and urged them to continue the night without her. Luciana, on this spring evening, with the sky clear and packed with stars, had persuaded Patrick to walk into the resort's adjoining woods, twittering and hooting with nighttime activity. They might see a fox or hear an owl or come across a black bear or encounter a javelina or step on a king snake and hopefully not a coral one, but probably they'd just pass by the two-hundred-year-old alligator juniper trees and make their way to a small church that she assured him was always open for worship. A church? What would he do in a church? Nominally Presbyterian, he was really a member of the order of religious boredom. "We are in the heart of darkness, no?" said Luciana.

Could he murder her? Could he get away with it?

"I sweat like the pig!" Luciana declared. She pulled down the top of her stretchy knit dress and wiggled on ahead of him— her rumba through the jungle. In the dark he could make out the bare silhouette of her naked shoulders. He shined his flashlight on her, the stretchy dress now rolled halfway down her back, the beads of perspiration and the tendrils of dark glistening hair at the nape of her neck. He could almost see her as the real person she'd once been before she'd become a caricature of herself. Generous, shy of her own beauty, more enamored of others than herself. Now she was no happier than him, and perhaps twice as lonely. He had Connie and the girls after all, and she had her art and far-flung adulation. Would he trade with her? Not for a moment.

That was a lie; that's what people always told themselves or had to believe to rationalize their regrets. You came to your senses about the really important things in life. The fact was . . . he could throw everything away out of some terrible self-destructive urge to be free of himself. That's what he'd always wanted from the writing, and that's what he saw in Connie's face tonight, transcendence. She had the glow and the certainty. That's all he had ever desired: the knowing. Not once in his three unpublished novels on even his best days had he achieved it. But he saw it in her, the proof, her deliverance. The migraines? They were just a symptom of the spirit of revelation about to crack her head open with delirious joy.

He called to Luciana. "So," he said, with great reluctance, "how's the novel coming along?"

She barked a laugh over her shoulder. "You don't want to know."

She was right. He didn't. He was only trying to be polite out of some obligatory deference that he presumed she expected. Though give her credit, rather than just being flippant, perhaps she was trying to spare him the details. "Where is this church exactly?"

"It's somewhere—"

Later, he would wonder about the church—when and how had it come into existence? In all the hubbub of the rescue and the ensuing charges by Luciana that the resort was at fault for not having adequate fencing, and the countercharges by the hotel that she was on private property without permission, Patrick had forgotten to ask. As far as he was concerned, it mattered that they'd been looking for some sort of holy sanctuary and not just traipsing off into the woods together while his wife Connie was back in the room with such a bad migraine that she had to call 911 and get herself taken to the ER. And it was here, in the emergency room of the Sedona Medical Center that Connie was being examined, unaware of any further mishaps other than her own miserable condition. She had tried to tough it out in her hotel room. She'd forced herself to breathe through the pain. When it became unbearable, she'd cried out helplessly for Patrick. But hours after he left her, he was still not back, and when she could stand it no longer, much to her mortification, she called the front desk and asked if a doctor was available. She explained that she'd just had sinus surgery and was in so much pain that she believed she was going to have a seizure. The desk clerk had an ambulance at her casita within fifteen minutes. The ER doctor asked her on a scale of one to ten, with ten being the highest, how bad her pain was and Connie said ten thousand. He ran an IV and gave her a shot of Demerol, reluctantly, because he didn't want her to drift off to sleep without observing and interviewing her further. She confessed the head pain had persisted to a lesser or stronger degree for days. His conclusion: she was nearing status migrainosus, a prolonged condition that if untreated could lead to stroke. Stroke! She was on vacation! Dr. Kuhlman had told her to go! It was her wedding anniversary! She started to sob and begged the nurse to try her husband's cell phone again.

But Patrick, beneath the now cloudy two a.m. sky, with only the aid of his flashlight, his cell phone dead, was presently trying to make his way down the unstable wall of the excavated pit that was to be the site of the resort's greatly expanded wellness center. His dark wish for Luciana's demise had come true: she'd disappeared mid-sentence over the side, and his panicked shouts to her below had been met with a harsh and ominous silence. The beam of his flashlight diffused blindly into the bottom of the pit in search of her body. Carefully, he tested a wall of the pit, but the red earth crumbled beneath his feet.

A thin noise filtered up to him, a whimper or a cry or just a faithless moan for help. "I'm hurt." But it sounded like I'm hoit. No mistaking the inflection this time—it was Lucy, the girl from New Jersey, without her guard or accent up.

"I'm going for help!" he called to her. No good would come of his trying to reach her and getting trapped below too. He stumbled through the woods thinking of Connie back in their casita, and how he wished he'd never called Luciana, and why, why, he wondered, had Connie told him about her novel in front of Luciana? Was it to humiliate him further? No, that wasn't Connie. Maybe she'd simply wanted to hold her own with Luciana. He would apologize for his smallness. He'd be happy for her, help her, as he had once helped Luciana: he was—he hated to admit it—a better editor than a writer. His greatest fear was not that Connie would become the successful writer he had never been but that she would turn into a monster of raging self-importance and forget about him. Like Luciana. Whom he had to save!

Connie, meanwhile, felt the first wave of relief from the Demerol, the throbbing block of pain on the left side of her head breaking up like an iceberg calving. The ER doctor explained that the migraine had probably been triggered by the combination of sinus surgery and—his phrase for the massage—inopportune manipulation. Irene, the massage therapist, had claimed many people believed Sedona was the center of the planet for electromagnetic field activity. Such vortexes contained ten different dimensions: three of space, one of time, and "six others you can't even imagine." Linear energy fields were in these vortexes, and if Connie opened herself to them she could be healed of almost any affliction, even the deepest psychic wounds. "Do you have trauma in your life?" Irene had asked, and when Connie said, no, she had been spared the usual ones of divorce, incest, alcoholism, rape, war, or murder, Irene had held her hands an inch above her forehead and declared, "But I'm feeling some blockage here that you haven't dealt with, I'm afraid."

The nurse and doctor, satisfied she would not have a stroke, had left her alone and told her to rest. They'd work on getting in touch with her husband. Wherever he was. Patrick felt distant to her, off in some faraway land, while she lay in this cool dark room on the padded examination table, telling herself she had to call her mother back home in Denver and check on the girls. But they would all be sleeping now, awaiting daybreak when Sarah would be sure to trip over the bottoms of her pajamas that belonged to her older sister. Connie's mother would be up at six a.m. and have a pot of coffee going by six-thirty. Her father, dead three years, was either in the vortex with Connie stroking her hair and healing her poor gouged sinuses or he was nothing more than an atomized memory in the mind of a dutiful daughter. She'd always been good, except for those moments when she was awash in the glow of her laptop typing her heart out and no one could know her.

LOST. He'd wandered off the path on his way back to the hotel for help and had twisted his ankle crossing a stream. Patrick had no idea which direction to head. He swept his flashlight around trying to determine where he was in relation to the hotel. Nothing. Just the ponderosa pine forest dense as cell bars. He considered weeping: he had last done so when his first daughter, Erin, was born. After cutting the cord, he'd excused himself for a moment and stood outside the birthing room. A cry of gratitude had rented from somewhere deep in his soul. The nurse—bless her for the twenty-four hour shift she'd put into Connie's forty-two hour labor—had rubbed his back gently and said he'd be amazed by how many fathers lost it afterward. It was a good thing, she said, a lovely newness.

Now he leaned his forehead against the rough bark of a vanilla-smelling pine and thought of Luciana swallowed up in a pit, cursing him in her fake Italian, and of Connie needing him.

He saw off to his right in a small clearing the outline of a building the shape and size of a gate house, perhaps large enough for two people to squeeze into—or just one with a heavy burden. He shook his dying flashlight. The light flickered brightly enough for him to see an arched and slightly crooked door with a wooden cross nailed to it. Limping across the forest floor, he pushed open the surprisingly heavy door and looked inside for anyone or anything that might be waiting for him.

THE THEORY OF EVERYTHING

M Y SON is fearful. Not scared. Scared is all right. I was scared during the war, but fearful is something else. He can't get out of bed some days. He stays in his condo with the blinds closed. After his wife Cheryl left him, I went over there one morning and found him walking around in a daze without his pants on, just a t-shirt. The kids were there. This is why he can't take care of them.

Even when Cheryl was around we'd come over and the house would be a mess, dirty dishes, not even in the sink but still on the table, clothes on the stairs, the kids—Abby two, Jeremy six then—plopped in front of the TV. And always fighting, the parents, not the kids. Over money. Rex asking where it went what he gave her, and she telling him he's a lazy son of a bitch and got no right to accuse her. He's not lazy, he's got this disease, so I want to take up for him, but you should see how she lights into me. "Mind your own business!" she shouts at me. "I'm trying to do the best job I can and all I get is criticism." Then she turns to Rex. "I married you, not your whole fucking family!"

All this happens in front of the kids. "Please," I say, "the children."

"Fuck this," Cheryl says and goes into the bedroom and slams the door.

Rex stands there with his shoulders slumped, his belly bigger each time I see him. He's always struggled with his weight. Comfort food he takes to a whole new level. He's got a handsome face, his mother's green eyes, thick curly black hair, but he can't take care of himself, and always that shameful look. "I'll talk to her, Dad," he says. "She gets upset when she thinks everybody's blaming her. It's not her fault."

I look around the house. At this time, they're living in one of my rental places that I let them stay in for half the going rate. Is it too much to ask that they don't keep it like a pigsty? I go over to where Jeremy's watching cartoons. "How you doing, buddy boy?" I ask.

"Fine," he says, and keeps staring at the TV.

"You want to maybe go to the batting cages after school today?" They got a slow pitch one that he likes.

"Okay," he says.

In the high chair Abby pokes at her Cheerios with her finger. I can smell her dirty diaper from here. "Maybe you should get some help," I say.

"We're fine, Dad. We're just under a lot of stress right now. Cheryl wants to go back to school and get her nursing degree, and she's frustrated trying to do everything." This woman wants to be a nurse? "We don't need to see anyone."

"See anyone? I'm talking about a maid. Somebody to sweep up, make a nice place for the kids—"

"Shhh," Rex says, "she'll hear you."

"She should hear me," I say. Something smashes, like glass breaking, in the bedroom. I look at Jeremy, who doesn't budge. You'd think the little boy was deaf.

"You better go," Rex tells me. "I'm in a difficult position here. She doesn't need to get any more upset."

"Fine," I say, and that's the last time I see the woman. This is more than four years ago. She walks out the door with the money that I leave for the kids' new clothes for school. Up her arm. Jeremy, he'll remember her. Abby won't know a thing. Better off she's got no memories.

Since then, Louise and I take care of the kids full time.

I STOP over at one of my houses. It's near the beach on Dakota Avenue right beside San Lorenzo Park, a very nice neighborhood, a two-bedroom home that three girls share who go to the university here in Santa Cruz. I don't allow more than three in a place. These girls, I know their families. The parents gave me their home numbers and said if I should have any trouble call them right away. But so far so good. Now I understand a window is broken— somebody threw a rock through it. They want it repaired; I said I'd come over and take a look. "Did you call the police?" I asked them. They said they didn't realize it was broken until this morning, and so here I am.

Two of the girls are at home, one with blonde hair and wearing flip flops and a flashy green jogging suit, the other with the low-cut jeans and the belly exposed like they all do now and golden tan. I'm not a man immune to the charms of young women. Believe me, I still look. The cleavage, this bare midriff business, but I keep my eyes on the girls' faces when they tell me they woke up this morning and the window was broken. It's a big window that looks out on the front yard. It will cost me a pretty penny to fix it.

"So you didn't hear anything?" I ask.

"No way," says Shannon—she's the one with the shiny green jogging suit. "We came out and we're like *what happened?*"

"You were sleeping," I say.

"Yeah," Angela, the other one, says. "We had the fan on."

"So maybe we should call the police," I tell them.

I see them glance at each other. "I'm sure it's okay," Shannon says. "It was probably, you know, a one-time thing."

"You think so," I say.

"Oh, yeah," Angela says. She's got a big smile that could light up a tunnel. They're nice girls, but I know they're lying to me.

"You could be in danger," I tell them. "What if this person comes back and makes more trouble? We should let your parents know about this."

Shannon fingers her necklace. Why she's wearing a fancy pearl necklace with a jogging suit and flip flops I don't know. But I got some idea. I bet if I search in the garage I'd find a recycling bucket full of beer bottles. "I have to ask," I say, "where's the rock?"

Angela looks at Shannon who says quickly, "We put it back."

"And you cleaned up the glass?"

They nod their heads. I look at the window. Most of the glass is on the outside of the window. I checked before I came in. "So did anyone have to go to the hospital?"

They both look at me.

"I'll tell you what," I say. "I'll make you a deal. You pay half, I pay half. I won't ask for details. You had a party maybe. It got a little wild. Maybe there was a fight. Somebody got pushed against the window or just backed up too hard. I don't know. You're lucky no one got seriously hurt. You promise me you won't have a party again, and I don't call your parents. Plus I help you out with the cost. You've been here almost a year, with no problem. We got a deal?"

Angela, the one with the bare stomach, crosses her arms over her belly, as if to hide herself, shame on both their faces. They nod, and I tell them I'll have the glass company here by the afternoon. It's too big to glaze myself. They tell me they're sorry, they were afraid if they told me the truth, I'd evict them. I'm the nicest man they've ever known, they say. Young people say such things to old people. I'm eighty-two, I should know. They think we're like children who surprise them with how smart we are

200

sometimes. Then they fall all over themselves heaping praise on us just for having a brain that still works.

AFTER school gets out, I take the kids to their swim lessons. We go to the municipal pool at the Simpkins Center. They've got four pools, including a big warm water pool they keep at eighty-six degrees. Abby, she took to the water right away. She raced through the different levels—seahorse, barnacle, guppy, gold-fish . . . now she's up to a sea otter. This would be a good thing, except her brother who is four years older and eleven is at the same level. He should be at least a sea lion. All his friends, they're already barracudas. So I said, enough with the fishies, let's just learn to swim, and we got a private instructor who teaches both of them. Dana. She's a college student, full of "awesomes" and high fives.

I sit on the bench and watch where Jeremy can't see me. He stands on the edge of the pool, and Dana tries to teach him how to dive. He's got to do a standing dive to pass his test and be allowed to swim in the deep water here with friends. She shows him how to bend at the waist and point toward the water.

"Hey, Jer," Dana coaxes, "just aim and fall in."

"I can't," he tells her.

"Sure you can!"

"I can't."

"You can't or you won't?"

"Is there a difference?" he asks.

"Of course there is, sweetie," says Dana. At which Abby, sitting nearby on the edge of the pool, stands up and offers to show them. "Let's just concentrate on your brother," Dana tells her. "Maybe you want to go down the slide a few times."

"Can I?" Abby says.

"Absolutely." She goes off, happy as can be. When she's around older females it's like she's auditioning to be their daughters. It breaks my heart.

Dana says, "Should I give you a little push?"

"No!"

So he stands there, looking down at the water like a man on a cliff.

Amazingly, he does it. Okay, it's not the best dive, more a roll into the water, but still it counts. Dana high-fives him. Jeremy doesn't crack a smile, but on the way home he tells me he's glad that's over with. He won't have to do it again. "Of course you'll do it again. You did terrific!" I tell him.

"I looked ridiculous," he says, staring out his window. Abby is in back playing with a purple-sequined wrist purse Louise bought her the other day.

"You did not," I say. "You tried, that's what counts. And you went in."

"I half did it."

"You'll do the other half next time." We stop at a light on Ocean Street. I look back at Abby. She's dangling the little purple purse on her arm and inspecting it in the light from the window.

"There's Daddy," she says. She rolls down the window. "Daddy!"

I see him now. Rex is coming out of the bank. I pull into a handicap space and wait for him to walk over.

"Hey everybody!" he says. He's got a suit and tie on, his curly black hair nicely cut and combed, and a royal blue dress shirt with gold cufflinks. I haven't seen him wear a suit in years. When he dresses up like this he's an attractive guy. You'd stop and think here's a man who's somebody's handsome husband.

He works putting up drywall, a job he's had almost three years, a record. I don't know what he's doing here in the afternoon.

"Daddy!" Abby says and reaches through the window for him. She's a small child, and he pulls her out, grabbing her under the arms and spinning her around. If you didn't know better, you'd think he was just getting off work and thrilled to see his kids at the end of a long day.

Abby hugs his neck, and he boosts her onto his back, then he taps at Jeremy for him to roll down his window. "What's happening, pal?" he says and bumps knuckles with Jeremy, who lets his wet hair be ruffled. "Looks like you've all been hitting the surf."

"Tell your father what you did," I say.

"What'd I do?" Jeremy says.

"The dive."

He shrugs.

"He dove into the pool."

"You did?" says Rex. He acts puzzled. And why shouldn't he? He's got no idea that his son practically has a phobia. "That's great. From the high dive?"

Jeremy stares at him like he's crazy. "From the side. And I wouldn't even call it a dive. I *interacted* with the pool," he says. This is the way he speaks. Half the time I don't get what he means.

Abby, still on Rex's back, stretches her neck around to him and shouts in his face, "I'm a sea otter!"

"Wow," Rex says.

"Daddy, I want to go with you," says Abby. "Take me to your house."

"Hey, pumpkin, can't do it today. But soon. You want to come over and cook spaghetti with me again?"

"Yeah! Now!"

"Soon, I promise."

He puts Abby down beside the car and opens the door for her. She gets in reluctantly. By now, she knows there's no use begging.

"Dad," Rex says to me. "There's something I want to talk with you about." All smiles. "It's exciting. Really exciting."

I look at the bank. I look at Rex in his suit. I know it's got something to do with money. "I have to get the kids home," I say.

"We'll talk tomorrow then, all right? I'll call you." He puts his hand on Jeremy's shoulder. "I'm going to be at your soccer game Saturday. Okay, tiger?"

"Don't bother," Jeremy says. "I hardly do anything except stand there and let them kick the ball by me. I might as well be an obelisk."

"Great, then," says Rex. "Wow, I can't believe I ran into you guys. You're all so——" He steps back and pumps his fist in the air. "Unreal!"

Two days later I get a call from Rex, who says he needs to meet me for lunch. I tell him I've got a busy day. I have to pick up the tile for a bathroom I'm redoing in one of my places. "What's it about?"

"I'd rather tell you in person, Dad."

"I'm in person," I say. "As in person as I got time for today."

"I'm sorry."

At least once every time we talk he says he's sorry. It doesn't do any good. He doesn't change, and what am I going to do? He can't take care of himself, simple as that. You have to be in the situation to understand. I sat with him during his worst spells, I got him into the bathroom after he soiled himself, I made him take his medication, I stayed all night in a chair and watched him that he doesn't slash his wrists again. And how's he going to take care of the children when he's like this? When you got a child's welfare on the line you don't make ultimatums, because you're making them to somebody who doesn't react like a sensible person. From the outside it looks like we're hurting more than helping—we make it possible for him not to take responsibility. I've heard it all before. Coddling, spoiling, "enabling," whatever term you want to use. But throw the children in there and all the tough love goes out the window, in my opinion.

When I think of dying, this is the worst part. I don't know what I believe. If an angel shows up and says, "Mr. Lettler, please step this way for your heavenly reward," fine, I'll be the first on the bus. If there's nothing afterward, I know from nothing. Either way, I don't place bets. But if you ask me what I'm ready to do now, I'll tell you. I'll make a deal with anyone, good or evil. It doesn't matter what happens to me afterward. Just let me live until the kids don't need me anymore.

"Dad, just listen. Can you hear me out?"

"I can do that," I say, and for the next ten minutes he tells me about this coffeehouse he wants to buy in Watsonville. The owner is selling. Rex says it's on a side street but business is booming. In Watsonville, the market isn't saturated like it is in Santa Cruz. And farmland there is being converted into residential property every day—upscale homes—and retirees are moving in too. He's got all the figures on the business. It hasn't turned a profit yet but he knows he can make it happen if he takes over. The bank's willing to give him a start-up loan. Only one catch. I got to be a co-signer. The collateral? My three rental houses.

That's my income, beside my pension from the aerospace company.

But I know better than to say anything on the phone. "You get all the figures together and we'll talk."

"So you're interested?"

"I'll hear you out. That's all I can promise."

"Dad, thanks, thanks. We can drive out there tomorrow and see the place. When do you want to go?"

"Since when do you have all this time on your hands?" There's a big pause. My question has already been answered. "You're not working, are you?"

"It's not what you think. I didn't get fired. I'm just taking some time off. Preston told me I can come back anytime. I needed to stop for a while because my back was killing me. Last week I pulled something and I couldn't even straighten up. And I'm taking Advil like candy. That's not right. I have to find something else."

"So go back to school, study for a career."

"I'm forty-one, Dad. I don't have time to be a freshman again. Just let me show you the place. It's sweet, I'm telling you. You'll fall in love with it."

I can't give him money, and I'm not signing away my security so he can open the billionth coffeehouse in California and then go out of business. He'll scream at me that I never support him, that I've got no confidence in him, that I'm the reason he's screwed up, that I never give him the chance to help himself, that I want to keep him "infantilized" (this he got from years of therapy), that he's going to take back the kids. Can you imagine? He's going to take back the kids. That's what he threatens me with. But it's what scares me, too. "We'll talk about it tomorrow," I say, just so I can think.

IN the afternoon the following day, I've got an hour before I pick the kids up from school. Jeremy has soccer practice and Abby a sewing class that she's in with her grandmother. Louise doesn't drive much anymore, so I have to take her places, to the doctor, shopping, to her hairdresser. Sometimes we call Lift Line and they come for her. The sewing class is something Abby and she are doing together, even though Louise could make a whole dress from scratch if she wanted. But she says it's an activity to do with Abby that doesn't require too much exertion, and anyway, it's a mother-daughter class, so she needs to go.

The blinds are drawn at Rex's apartment. The porch light is still on at two in the afternoon. My heart starts beating fast. I'm always afraid of what I might find.

I knock, I hear shuffling, then the door opens. He's washed and shaved, dressed and in a clean knit shirt and navy slacks. Nothing's wrong. He's not curled up on the floor with his hands tucked between his knees as I've found him other times.

"Dad?"

"I thought I'd stop over before I pick up the kids."

"Um, maybe I should . . ." He steps outside and closes the door behind him. "I'm a little busy right now."

I get what he means. I'm not naïve about such things. "You've got company, no problem." I apologize for not calling first and start to leave when the blind is pushed aside and I see Cheryl.

"What's she doing here?"

"Now just take it easy," he says. "Everything's fine."

"Everything's fine? How long has she been here?"

"Dad, I know what you're thinking, but we've been talking—"

"Who's been talking? You and her?"

"Things have changed. Cheryl has a job in San Jose and she's been living by herself and staying clean. She wanted to see if she could reach the one-year mark before she even contacted us again. It's her anniversary today—"

My head's exploding with questions. "Anniversary? She got remarried?"

"Her anniversary of staying clean and sober, so I made arrangements for her to come here last night."

I feel my knees go weak, and I sit down on the white plastic chair on the small balcony. "She's gone four years and she just shows up and everything's fine?"

"Listen, Dad, you're not an uninvolved party here. I know that. And I know I can never repay you for all you've done. I can't change what I did, but I can change. Cheryl wants to be part of that."

"My God," is all I can say. I feel my age suddenly. "Why doesn't she come out here?"

"This isn't the best time. She's doing great. Maybe a little shaken up about coming here and trying to prepare herself to see the kids. But she's taken responsibility, Dad, that's the main thing. And she did it on her own. She's not asking for anybody's forgiveness. Believe me, she'll be the last to ever forgive herself. But we want to try again."

I can't even show him my face, which is hot with fury.

"That's why I need to talk with you," Rex says. "I know we can make a go of the business."

"What business?"

"The coffeehouse. We've got a lot of it figured out. Cheryl's been working as a hostess in a restaurant. She knows about keeping the books, about how to manage a business. It's still a work in progress, but everything's falling into line. Just let me explain it all to you, okay? Not now. But tomorrow. I've got to go up to San Jose and talk to someone about a new roaster for the place. But after I come back?"

"Look," I say, and forget what I'm going to say.

"You all right?"

"I have to pick up the kids now."

"Actually, we were thinking about doing that this afternoon. A surprise."

"No!" I say. I stand up and tell him to his face. "No more surprises today. You don't just show up and introduce her to a daughter who has no memory of her! Are you nuts?"

"Calm down, all right? We weren't going to do it that way."

"I don't care how you're going to do it. Not today. I'm picking them up like always."

"WHAT should we do?" I say to Louise that evening. Jeremy and Abby I've told nothing. Jeremy complained of a sore knee after soccer practice. He said, "This could be as serious as Osgood-Schlatter disease, which tends to primarily affect boys my age, or as minor as a sprain. I suspect the swelling will respond to a combination of ice and anti-inflammatory therapy, but the prognosis isn't good for me to play in Saturday's game." This is his way of explaining he's looking for an excuse not to play.

I tell Louise that I've heard of grandparents going to court over such matters. "We have no official custody but we could make a case, a good case."

"I'm not so sure we can," Louise says.

"You want to just hand them over to her?"

"Keep your voice down. The children." She's got a gray shawl around her shoulders and her lips are blistered from the cold she's had. The kids bring home all the stuff that's going around. "We need to speak with Marvin," she says. Marvin's our lawyer, who's helped us in the past. He's got a young associate in his office who knows the ins and outs of family law.

"And what if Marvin tells us that they're the parents and that's who gets them? Are you prepared for that? Are you willing to list in affidavits all the bad things she's done and talk about your son's problems in front of a judge?"

I can see by the way she twists her mouth she isn't. She's always felt it was her fault what problems Rex has. She was forty-two when she had him, and it wasn't so common back then to have a child that late. We tried for years with no success. He was our miracle baby. Somewhere he's still a miracle in her mind.

She pulls the shawl tighter around her shoulders.

"You should go to bed," I say.

"And you," she tells me. "You hardly touched your dinner."

"I'm fine." Inside my stomach turns over as if I'm on the Cyclone at the Santa Cruz boardwalk, a ride Abby makes me go on with her.

"We find out what they have in mind," Louise says. I say nothing. "When we know the facts then we can discuss it with Marvin."

"Marvin's got nothing in his pocket to help us. We should have severed her legal ties when we had the chance."

"We never had the chance."

"When she abandoned her children, we had the chance. We waited, like fools."

Louise gets up from the table and pours a little cream over sliced pears for me. "Eat," she says. "It will do your stomach good." She sits down next to me and puts her hand on my neck and rubs with her thumb and forefinger. Her fingers feel tiny back there, but they still got strength in them. "We do this together," she says to me. "You understand that, right?"

I carve a crescent of sweetness from my pears and eat. I can promise nothing.

WE talk to Marvin. He says the law is on the parents' side. "There are precedents for grandparents' having custody but the case has to be clearly that a child's welfare is endangered by remaining with the parents. It's a high bar. It might be easier to have a child yourself." Louise snorts at this. "The truth is," Marvin says, "if she's clean and sober, and willing to assume her parental responsibilities at this time, it's going to carry a lot more weight than anything that's happened in the past, particularly if you haven't carefully documented it. And if they want to, they can even contest visitation rights by the grandparents. It's a question of how much to push before they push back. You can gamble, but they could win and be vindictive. I've seen it happen too many times."

I leave discouraged. Louise and I don't speak for a while in the car, then she says, "We have to accept the inevitable. He didn't divorce her. She never gave up custody. We stepped in and now we have to step aside."

"So that's it? Just like that? Since when are you so blasé?"

"I'm realistic," she says.

"I am, too. That's why it's not going to happen."

"What's not going to happen?"

"I'm prepared for a fight," I say.

"You're prepared to take the children away from their father and mother for good?"

"She comes back from God knows where, supposedly all cleaned up and motherly, and wants them back, and our son says, great, terrific, we're a family again, come home, children, and you say we're taking them away? What about them taking away from us!"

"You heard what Marvin told us."

"I don't care what Marvin told us. And you're always too ready to do whatever your son asks."

Louise puts her hand on my arm. We're at a stoplight on Mission Street and a boy not much older than Jeremy, a Hispanic kid, crosses in front of us with a surfboard on his head. "It will come to this eventually," Louise says in a quiet voice.

I remember a piece of a conversation I heard at the pancake house when Louise and I took the kids out for brunch one weekend. A young man was saying to a woman, maybe his wife, "I'm talking about thirty years down the road." I imagined he was speaking about their future, what his business might be, or what he pictured for their kids one day. Maybe a second home somewhere they all could meet for vacations. I thought to myself I can't even say, *I'm talking about five years down the road.* This is what Louise means in her soft voice when she talks about "eventually."

WHAT did I expect? Maybe somebody in a nice pair of slacks, a tasteful blouse, a trim-cut blazer, and a little makeup to freshen the face, like the moms at Jeremy's soccer games. Cheryl was always a pretty girl. But this Cheryl is thin and all sharp bones, her cheeks more sunken, her eye shadow too blue, and rings on four of her fingers, including a big silver one with a black stone. She wears snug jeans with embroidered pockets and a leather vest over a tight white sweater blouse.

Cheryl bends down and extends her arms for Abby who shies away. On the way here we told the kids, "Your mother is in town and wants to see you." Jeremy nodded. Maybe he knew this day was coming. He remembers her, of course, but he never speaks about her. Abby said, "I knew she'd come back. I knew she would." She became so excited that she made us go back so she could wear her Annie Oakley costume that she got for Halloween in three weeks.

Abby, a finger twisted tightly around her hair, finally goes over to her mother.

We all stand there a minute while Cheryl makes a big scene of hugging her. Cheryl's on her knees in the sand. We decided it was best to meet at Seabright Beach and have a cookout in one of the fire rings. A neutral place.

Louise gives Jeremy a little push to go over too. I feel like he's being shoved toward a stranger, but I keep my mouth shut. Now the tears come. Cheryl is crying, hugging Abby and reaching out her other arm for Jeremy, who keeps his body sideways but lets her put an arm around his waist. She turns her face from one to the other like she's been on a long trip and planned all along to come back. I look away.

"Let's eat," Rex says. He's got his hand on Cheryl's shoulder this whole time.

"Wait a sec," says Cheryl, and she jumps up and runs over to where they put down their stuff. She comes back with a present for each of them. Abby, who's in her Annie Oakley outfit—never mind that her brother told her not to wear it because it looked stupid—gets a stuffed orangutan with a baby orangutan wrapped around its neck. Jeremy, who doesn't rip open his present like his sister but instead neatly peels off the tape, has some kind of board.

"It's a skim board," Cheryl tells him. "You throw it out along the shore and jump on for a ride."

"I know what it is," Jeremy says, staring at it. He's folding the wrapping paper back up in a perfect square.

"Oh, honey," Cheryl says. She's got a husky smoker's voice. "Do you already have one? Rex said no. Right? You said he didn't have one."

"That's what I thought," Rex says.

"Do you have one? You're not disappointed are you?"

"It's fine," Jeremy says flatly. "I don't have one."

"But you like it right, honey?" Cheryl asks.

Jeremy looks at me.

"He's not so big on water sports," I explain.

"Oh," says Cheryl. Her face is about to collapse.

"It's fine," Jeremy says again.

"Fine?" Rex says. "It's a little more than fine, son. This is a top of the line model."

Jeremy turns it over in his hands. "I'm most appreciative," he says, "of your generosity." This is the way he talks when he doesn't want to talk anymore. He makes a little house of such language and shuts the door from the inside.

"Anybody hungry?" Louise asks.

While Rex starts a fire in the pit, Cheryl takes Abby by the hand and walks along the beach. Couples, groups of teenagers, other families come down to watch the sun set. It's already too cold to go in the water but surfers go out with their boards and kids slap their bare feet along the water's edge on this Saturday evening.

"So what do you think?" I ask Louise. Jeremy is next to his father who's fussing with the fire. Cheryl walks with Abby down the beach, telling her something. Her arms fly out, she jumps up, she squats down and gives Abby another hug. Then Abby shows her how she can do a cartwheel and a handstand.

"I think," Louise says, "that Abby's vote is yes."

"You notice she hasn't said a word to us. She went right to work on the kids."

"She's their mother. What do you expect? She doesn't have to win our approval."

"We're fools."

Later in the evening, Abby will get on the skim board and zip along. Jeremy won't have anything to do with it. Cheryl will show Abby her blueberry-colored nails and tell her that they can get manicures. Jeremy she's going to take to the music store. She says she wants to buy him an iPod. Does he download music? What are his favorite bands? Does he play an instrument? She wants her kids to play instruments. What's his best subject in school? She hardly gives him a chance to answer, and when he does, he says, "The sun is supposed to set at 6:02. It's a minute and a half late. The tides must be disappointed." Rex chews a burnt marshmallow and says, "You kids!"

I watch the waves break on shore. My heart gets pulled out to sea like it's in a rip current.

THE kids spend the next week at the apartment with their parents. At first, Abby, when we pick her up for the sewing class with Louise, is all smiles and glee. She tells us Cheryl takes her shopping. They go out for fudge sundaes and to the movies. They carve pumpkins and bake the seeds. They cut out pictures from *American Girl* magazine and put them on Abby's side of the bedroom she shares with her brother. But then, the following week, she doesn't say so much. "Tell me what you're up to, snookums," I say. I'm trying not to make judgments. I keep busy on my houses, read a biography of Eisenhower, catch up on my sleep. My arthritis lets up a bit. I'm thinking I can make the adjustment. They're trying hard to be good parents. In fact, Rex doesn't even call for my help with the kids.

"Can you get me a new leotard?" Abby asks. "Mine is ripped."

"You can get one at gymnastics," I say. They have a little store there that sells all the accessories the girls need.

"Can you buy it?" Abby asks.

"Yes," Louise says.

"Did you ask your parents?" I say.

"Cheryl says she can't afford it."

"We'll get it," Louise says.

"I thought she had all this money saved," I say, referring to Cheryl. That's what she had told us.

"Never mind," Louise says.

"You got anything else you want to tell us?"

"Shush," Louise says.

"Don't shush me," I say. "Maybe she wants to talk. Abby?"

"What?"

"You got anything else to say?"

"I'm tired," she says.

Two days later, when Jeremy comes over to the house, I find out things aren't going so well. Rex and Cheryl are fighting again. We're sitting on the hood of my Chrysler Imperial. I've had the car for eleven years and I should trade it in for one with better gas mileage, but I bought it the day Jeremy was born. He has his soccer uniform on now. I've had to pick him up from his game because Rex and Cheryl drove out to look at the coffeehouse. I went with them once and was not impressed, a rundown building with too many flies inside. Every day Rex calls and asks if I've made up my mind. I tell him no, I haven't decided, and in the meantime he should think about going back to work for Preston. Why don't I tell him the truth? That I'm never going to sign. Because he's got the kids as leverage. He could hold them hostage from us if I don't cooperate, and in the meantime I can only hope he loses interest or the place gets sold to somebody else.

Jeremy and I are sharing a package of black licorice. It's his favorite candy. I eat one piece because of my dentures, but he chews away. Between bites, he tells me about physics and sub-atomic worlds, that we exist in multiverses. He thinks we have many parallel lives that we're undergoing at the same time. "In one universe I've scored five soccer goals. In another I'm just an energy force. Another has no cause and effect and I'm able to jump off a building and land safely on my feet. That one is very dreamlike. But in this one I'm sitting on a white car believing in time."

"You don't believe in time?" I ask.

"For the moment, I do." He gives me a sly smile. I get the joke and punch him in the arm like I imagine kids still do. At this "moment in time" I ache over how much I love him.

"She's drinking," he says out of nowhere. He's got a long sad face. He takes my index finger and wraps his own fingers around it. "One day, Grandpa, I'll be able to merge into other universes. I shall call myself The Permeator and solve TOE."

"What's this TOE?"

"The theory of everything, Grandpa," he says, as if I should know. "I expect that won't be soon enough, though." Tears start down his cheeks. I know what he means: I'll be dead by then.

WHAT I do next I'm not proud of. I call Cheryl when I know Rex isn't at home. She agrees to meet me at Lighthouse Point, and I wait for her on a bench. I can see her approaching across the grassy park behind the bluffs. It's the day before Halloween, and Abby has asked if we could take her out in our neighborhood, where she knows more people (and can get better candy, she believes).

"What's so important?" Cheryl says, getting right to the point. I've only seen her a couple of times since that first night at Seabright. She wears a baseball cap with her hair in a ponytail threaded through the back. From one shoulder to the other she keeps shifting her suede handbag.

"I wanted to talk," I say.

"So let's talk. I'm here." She's wearing open toed white sandals and I see her nails don't have that pearly polish they did the first night. Now they're chipped and dull, and I wonder if she ever took Abby for the manicure she promised. "If you came here to give me a lecture, you can save your breath. I'm not in the best frame—"

"I don't want to lecture. I want to make an offer."

"What offer?"

I gesture toward the bench for her to sit down. It's eleven a.m. and people are coming to eat their lunch. She sits carefully, not taking her eyes off me. I see an unhappy woman, a tormented person, a scared little girl inside her, but I got to do what I think best.

I reach in my sport coat and take out money from my inside pocket and hold it in my lap, then cover my hands over top like I'm putting a damp cloth over warm dough.

"What's this?" Cheryl asks.

In the park, there's a bunch of people around my age doing Tai Chi. They've got loose white clothes on and look like ghosts. The waves crash below, seagulls above caw, and here I sit with ten thousand dollars in my lap.

"You can get a new start," I say.

"Are you trying to buy me off?"

"I'm giving you options."

"Oh, my God. You think I'm going to take this money and leave the kids? You must really think I'm scum."

"Not everybody should be a parent."

"You arrogant old man. Who the hell do you think you are?"

I expect ugly names, but she hasn't walked off yet. "You let us take care of the children. Maybe you live nearby. Maybe you live, say, in Watsonville and run a coffeehouse. I don't know. Maybe you want to go away and think about whether you're up to being a mother with full responsibility right now." I don't say maybe you shoot the money up your arm and drink it away. "Maybe we have an agreement about this, and then nobody makes a big legal scene."

Cheryl's mouth twists in an unpretty way, like she could spit on me, which would not be a surprise or undeserved.

"You've always hated me," she says.

"I don't hate anyone. I'm a practical man."

"I've never been a whore. No matter what happened I've never gotten that low. You want to know something? This is lower than that."

I look at my fingers. They got dirt wedged in them from crawling around under one of my houses to fix a pipe.

"Rex would think you're despicable. You'd be lucky if he ever speaks to you again. You'll be lucky if I ever do. Shit, you think you can hustle me!"

"I'm making you an offer. What you do with it is your decision."

"I should tell you to shove that money up your ass."

When I hear this word, this simple word "should," because everything when you think about it comes down to the difference between should and did, I know what will happen. I stand up and leave the money on the bench. I count to myself, one, two, three seconds, and I know if I make it to ten, she won't run after me and throw the money in my face. When I get to nine, I keep walking. I'm afraid to turn around, just like in the Bible because I've done a terrible thing that could turn me into a pillar of salt. But I don't look behind me. I don't look ahead. I just keep going.

acknowledgments

I wish to thank the publications where these stories previously appeared in slightly different form: "Bless Everybody," *Ploughshares*; "Absolute Zero," *Kenyon Review*; "Galisteo Street," *Prairie Schooner*; "Natural Causes," *American Literary Review*; "Indie," *TriQuarterly*; "Seeing Miles," *Florida Review*; "Opposite Ends of the World," *Bellevue Literary Review*; "Blockage" and "The Theory of Everything," *Crazyhorse*; "Stranger" and "The Last Communist," *North American Review*.

I'm grateful to my readers, and to my colleagues and friends at Colorado State University and in the Warren Wilson MFA Program, and especially and lastingly to my family, Emily, Zach, and Elena.

The Autumn House
Fiction Series

*Winners of the Autumn House Fiction Prize

design and production

Cover and text design by Chiquita Babb

Cover photo: iStockphoto

Author photo: Stephanie G'Schwind

Text set in Monotype Joanna, font designed by Eric Gill in 1930–31 based on the work of Robert Granjon

Printed by McNaughton & Gunn on 55# Glatfelter Natural Antique